A Navajo Saga

By Kay and Russ Bennett

The Naylor Company
Book Publishers of the Southwest
San Antonio, Texas

Fic
Ben

Dedicated to
our daughters, Rosalie and Alyce,
and
our grandchildren

Preface

IN THE YEAR 1846, THE UNITED STATES SEIZED the Mexican state of New Mexico, which covered an unknown area including the present states of New Mexico, Arizona, Colorado, Utah and Nevada. This area was populated largely by Indian tribes which were called Navajo, Apache, Acoma, Zuñi, Hopi, Ute, Taos, Jemez, Zia, Tewa, San Felipe and Santo Domingo. Only a portion of the Rio Grande Valley was occupied by the Mexican and Spanish ranchers.

The Mexican governor, Armijo, was supposed to rule this vast area from the capital city of Santa Fe, but, of necessity, confined his rule to the towns and pueblos along the Rio Grande. He was not interested in the unexplored territory to the west, as his friends at that time were not interested in moving westward. He was primarily interested in keeping the Indians from raiding the homes of Mexican and Spanish people, and in protecting the pueblos, from which his people drew much of the help they needed to cultivate the fields and tend the sheep.

For perhaps four hundred years, the Spanish-speaking people had been raiding Indian villages and the homes of such nomad tribes as the Navajos to obtain slaves. The Navajos had also conducted raids against the Spanish-speaking people and the Indian pueblos to obtain slaves, sheep, and horses to better their own economy. As Armijo had no army available to march against the raiding Indian tribes, he tried to stop the raids by presenting gifts to the headmen, or Indians claiming to be headmen, that he chanced to meet in Santa Fe. However, his gifts of silver and clothing accomplished nothing.

When the Americans seized New Mexico, Armijo and many of his people fled south to the area now known as El Paso, and the United States appointed Charles Bent, of Taos, as the new governor. Mr. Bent was soon murdered by the Mexicans and the Taos Indians who had met and decided they preferred a Mexican governor. Following this murder, a military governor, Colonel Washington, was appointed to rule the territory, and Mr. Calhoun was appointed agent to help him establish peaceful relations with the Indian tribes. Thus started the American occupation of the Navajo Nation, which is now in its 120th year and which, now under a federal bureau instead of the army, is likely to last for many hundreds of years to come. Fortunately, thousands, perhaps even a million, Navajos escaped from bureaucratic control. The offspring of Navajo slaves throughout the Southwest who speak Spanish or English are considered to be Spanish Americans or English Americans, and are therefore not in need of the guardianship provided by the United States government.

On the other hand, thousands of the descendents of the Spanish people who were slaves of the Navajos and preferred to stay with the Navajos, now live in Navajoland and help to swell the number of Indians being helped by the Bureau of Indian Affairs.

Actually, there are few pure-blooded Indians or Spanish people in the Southwest, just as there are few pure-blooded people in any country in this world. There is little difference between the people with Indian blood who are wards and those who are non-wards of the United States, except that the former are told they are not capable of self-government, and the latter share in governing the states in which they live.

One wonders why there has never been a Bureau of African Affairs, or Asiatic Affairs, to help the people who have come from these areas and who are different because of the color of their skin. Of course in the case of the American Negro, this oversight is now being corrected and, under a variety of bureaus, they will soon become wards of our benevolent government.

An understanding of the Navajo people comes through an understanding of the religion by which they live. Their religion is simple and yet so powerful it has sustained them through years of warfare against superior odds and against the forces of nature in their barren land.

Christians have a Bible which was written to govern their thoughts and actions. The Bible is compiled from the legends of many tribes: Jewish, Buddhist, Hindu, Egyptian, and many others from the Middle East and Europe which through enslavement and intermarriage added their stories of creation, how to ward off dangers, how to invoke supernatural help, and stories of what life may be like in the next world. In its present form, the Christian belief is in a Holy Trinity, three manifestations of God as a creating spirit, a preserving spirit called Christ, and a destroying spirit called the Holy Ghost. The Preserver appeared in the form of a man, and the story of his life among mankind is recorded in the Bible for all Christians to read and follow. The Virgin Mary might be considered as another manifestation of God, the Preserver. She has appeared in many forms and in many places in recent years.

Christians believe that God is everywhere at all times, but they do not say that He is contained in any particular rock, plant, or animal. To laymen, God is all around them in the air. To invoke His help they pray for Him to deliver them from evil. They go to a selected place called the House of God and are taught the legends of creation and are told of the adventures and the teachings of Christ by which they should pattern their own lives.

They sing songs which they hope are pleasing to God. In a few Christian homes God's presence is recognized at all times. He is thanked for the food that is eaten and for the protection He extends to the members of the family.

The Hindus have absorbed and added the legends of the many tribes of the Middle East and the Far East to their books which tell of creation, how life can be preserved in this world, and what may be expected in their next life. They believe in a Holy Trinity, three manifestations of God as a Creator, Preserver, and Destroyer, but picture Him appearing in many forms as men and animals to represent the dangerous and the desirable things in life to be prayed for.

The Navajos have no written book of legends by which to pattern their way of life, but they have many legends passed down by word of mouth. These legends are a mixture of stories originating in the far north, or perhaps as far away as Mongolia, stories of the Pacific Ocean tribes and stories of the Pueblo and Mexican people whom they enslaved and with whom they intermarried. Many of the legends they tell today must have originated about the year 1700, when the great merger of Navajo and Pueblo people occurred following the Pueblo people's revolt against Spanish rule. By 1700, there were many Navajo clans scattered over the area from the Rio Grande to the San Francisco Mountains. The Nanasht'ezhi formed by Zuñi refugees; the Kinlichine, formed by Mexican slaves; the Naakiidine, also formed by Mexican slaves; the Dibezhiini, formed by San Felipe refugees; and the Miidiisgizhni, formed by Jemez refugees, were some of the newer clans. The older clans, which were also a mixture of Navajo and Pueblo people, included the Kiya'a'anii (Tall House Clan), To'di'chiini (Bitter Water Clan), Tabahii (Water Edge Clan), Ah'shii (Salt Clan), T'o'a'hani (Near Water Clan), Hash'clishnii (Mud Clan), T'o'a'heglinii (Joining Waters Clan), and many, many more. The religions practiced by these clans are basically the same.

The Navajo believes in a God who manifests Himself in many forms. He is the Creator, the Preserver and the Destroyer of all things within, on, and above this earth. He appears as the earth itself and all there is thereon. He is the grain of sand as well as the sand dune, the small rock as well as the mountain, the blade of grass as well as the meadow, and the tree as well as the forest. He is the wind, rain, thunder, lightning, sun, clouds, and the rainbow. He is everywhere and is all things. He manifests Himself in countless forms, some of which are beneficial to the people and some of which could destroy them. The Navajos believe that everything in this world was created solely for the Navajo people. They believe that God is concerned only with their tribe. When God manifests Himself as the Destroyer and causes sickness, death, destruction of food, or destruction of their property, they realize they are not following the pattern of life given to them as explained in their legends, and they hasten to perform rituals to invoke the help of God, the Preserver. They go to a selected place and reenact the legends of creation. They believe these ceremonials drive away evil and replace the void left with the good, provided the ceremony is performed correctly and in a manner pleasing to God. All of the unfavorable manifestations of God must be asked to move away, and must be replaced by the manifestations mentioned in the legends as being favorable to the creation and preservation of the people.

The Navajo legends of creation, which are the basis of the Navajo religion, are stories of the experiences of supernatural beings, or manifestations of God, who prepared the world for the people and, finally, created the Navajo people to live thereon. The legends tell of a process of evolution which began in the first world, far below the surface of the earth. The superhuman animal life from the first world passed through three more worlds, each a little larger, until the fifth world, which is the surface of the earth, was reached. The legends tell of the sixth world containing the sun, moon, and stars, which were created to light the earth and to provide a place for supernatural beings to live. A seventh world was also created above the sixth world as a home for God.

Navajo rituals and chants, used to gain the favor of God and his help in overcoming sickness and misfortune, are patterned after legends which tell how evil creatures were overcome and how the world was put in order, so people could live on the surface of the earth in safety. Legends contain a great deal of detail because they have been added to and greatly expanded by the legends brought to the Navajos by so many other tribes. The legends tell of the many harmful monsters which had to be destroyed to make the land safe; fire, which had to be controlled so it could be used for cooking and to provide warmth; animals, which had to be controlled so they could be used to provide food and clothing for the people; and materials, which had to be created for the use of the people. Finally, the people had to be taught how to use what was provided for them. Legends tell of how supernatural beings, called "Yeis," came to the Navajo people and taught them, by example, how to perform the rituals and the words to use in the chants which are used today.

1

IT WAS IN THE SPRING OF 1846 THAT A COUNCIL was held at Red Lake by a headman of the Kinlichine (Red House Clan) of the Dine'.

"We are strong," spoke the man with the gray squirrel hat, "but there are many wolves and coyotes who run at our flanks and decrease our numbers. The Utes cross the River San Juan from the north to raid our herds and steal our women and children, then disappear into the mountains. When we try to follow them many of our men are killed. Our neighboring clans will not join us to invade the Ute country, and we cannot destroy these enemies without their help. To the east are our good friends of the

1

Kiya'a'anii, but their clan is scattered and small in numbers. It is said that they are protected by the gods and to harm them may bring bad luck. It is said that they are descendents from the Changing Woman, favorite wife of the Sun God, and the God of the Waters, and that her sons will avenge the Kiya'a'anii if any one harms them. The Miidiisgizhni will not help as they are only interested in acquiring more sheep for their families.

"To the far east at the foot of the sacred mountain, Soo dzilth, are the Dine'Anaii led by the evil Crooked Foot. He and his people have joined the Mexicans and lead them into our land to steal our women and children. When we are stronger, we will kill all the Dine'Anaii and their Mexican friends and we will move to the Rio Grande where there is always plenty of water and grass for our sheep and horses. When we are strong, we will drive the Comanche and Kiowa from the Rio Grande, and they will be afraid to attack us. We are the Dine' and we will go where we will and take what is ours, and no one shall stop us. But now we are surrounded by our enemies and no other clan will help us. We must grow larger. We must have many children. We must become a large and powerful clan and lead all the Dine' against our enemies.

"Now, I have called you together to plan a raid on the villages of our enemies on the Rio Grande to obtain some of their women so more children will be born to our clan. It is said that the blood of the Dine' is strong and that the children of our slaves will be as strong as their fathers. We must have many children and grow quickly. We must ask the gods to help us. We must meet the Morning God with a gift of yellow corn meal; we must give corn pollen to the God of the Sun at noon; and we must give white corn meal to the God of the Evening. Now, I plan to take twenty of our strongest men with me and twenty-five good horses. I think we should leave in a few days as the snow is melting and the people along the Rio Grande will be driving their sheep away from the villages. We can go through the black rock country where there is plenty of

2

water and where we can find deer and rabbits. We must avoid the land of the Zuñi as they are our enemy and will warn the Mexicans that we are coming. We must surprise the Mexicans and return to our land as quickly as possible. What do you think of my plan?"

As they listened to the speech of Gray Hat, the men sat and rolled cheroots of mountain tobacco and corn husks. They smoked in silence as they listened to their leader standing so straight and strong by the fire.

"Our leader is right," said Red Horse. "I will go with him. The last Mexican raiding party surprised us and took many of our women. Since the raid, some of our men have been without wives. If our clan is to grow, every man should have two wives. On our last raid we went only as far as the Acoma Pueblo and took only two small girls who were herding sheep away from the village. This time I think we should go to the Mexican villages first. If we do not capture enough women there we can raid the pueblos on our way back. We must have horses for the women and there are many horses to be had along the big river."

One by one the other men at the council rose and agreed to join Gray Hat. Each man had some suggestion to offer. Some of the men thought it would be better to raid the closer pueblos instead of travelling all the way to the Rio Grande, but in the end it was decided to follow the plan of their leader.

While the men were discussing the raid, the women were busy butchering sheep and preparing cornbread. They listened closely to what the men said but offered no comment, as this was the men's business. As was customary at any gathering, after the business had been taken care of, the people ate, then formed groups to play a stick game which was one of their favorite forms of gambling. They bounced black and white sticks on a rock and bet on how they would fall. Slave women brought food from the fires and saw that eveyone was well fed.

3

2

THE FOLLOWING DAY PREPARATIONS FOR THE raid were started. All of the medicine men of the clan assembled to perform the rituals required for this important undertaking. In turn, they asked for the help of the gods of the bears, the winds, the snakes, and the thunders in making the raid successful. Several small sweat houses of branches covered with clay were built in a canyon near the lake. Men and boys built fires and heated rocks, then carried them on forked sticks into the sweat houses. The raiders undressed and entered. Some men shouted that the raiders were taking a sweat bath so all the women and children would be kept away. The men sat in the sweat houses for more than an hour singing sacred songs. They drank, from gourds, a medicine prepared by the medicine men from a health plant which would make them strong so they would be able to subdue any enemy they encountered.

When the sweat bath ritual was over the men washed their heads with yucca roots and took their places behind the medicine man who was in charge of this part of the ceremony. Following his instructions they gave corn pollen

4

to the gods of the East, South, West and North to invoke the protection of the great gods living in the four directions. Without the help of many gods it would be futile to start out on such a dangerous mission.

The men chose horses to be taken and with the help of their sons, prepared a large supply of arrows for their bows and resharpened their already sharp knives. The women repaired water jugs by plastering them with pitch from the piñon trees so they would not leak and saw that their men had a good blanket to carry with them.

The women made plans to scatter their families and sheep throughout the small valleys of the Tunicha Mountains where they would be hidden from any Mexican or Ute raiding parties passing through the Red Lake Valley. It was still cold in the mountains and the snow lay deep in some of the valleys but it would soon melt and they would be safer in the mountains.

The ceremonials lasted four days and all went well. More corn pollen and sacred cedar twigs were given to each man to take on the journey. Everyone assembled in the Canyon Bonito at a spring sacred to the God of the Waters. The men were dressed in short buckskin pants, leggings and moccasins, and carried small pouches in which to keep the medicine given them by the medicine man. They wore vests of heavy leather which would protect them from partially spent arrows and bullets. All carried bows made of wood reinforced by the sinews of a deer, a plentiful supply of arrows and a sharp-pointed wood lance about five feet long.

The medicine man stood facing the spring and the members of the raiding party advanced and stood in a circle around him. In a husky tone so low he could hardly be heard, he started to sing. As he sang he dropped small bits of shell and turquoise into the spring as an offering to the God of the Waters. He sang on and on as the men stood quietly listening and waited for the prayer to be finished.

Some of the women stood a short distance away holding the horses on which their men were to ride away. They

5

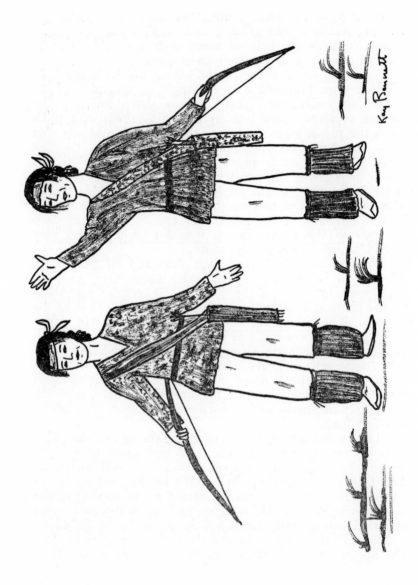

Kay Bennett

knew the mission was a dangerous one and tears welled in their eyes as they watched their men, for they might never see them again.

When the medicine man finished, each man advanced and sprinkled a little corn pollen on the water. This completed the ceremony and the men broke the silence with a loud shout, mounted their horses, made them rear and then, with bows held high over their heads, raced out of the canyon. The women stood, seemingly afraid to move, until the last rider had vanished and only a huge cloud of dust remained.

After the party had travelled about a mile at full gallop, they settled down to a slow trot which would place many miles behind them by the time the sun had set. The party headed for Bear Springs, which was another place the Dine' held sacred and from which they would obtain water for good luck. Two of the men, Little Man and Black Horse, were sent ahead to keep a sharp lookout for anyone that might be herding sheep or passing through the valley of the Puerco. Black Horse circled and went to Bear Springs alone. He found a small group of the Dine' watering their sheep and, as he watered his horse and filled his water jug, he asked the sheepherders if they had seen anyone passing by. They told him they had seen no one. Meanwhile, the main party was led by Gray Hat and Red Horse along the mountain range south of the spring.

"It is not likely that we will be discovered here in the mountains as grass and water are still plentiful in the lower valleys," said Gray Hat, "but we must take no chances."

"You are right," replied Red Horse. "We will wait for our scouts. There is always danger along the Zuñi trail. I think we should avoid Inscription Rock as it is a favorite camping place for many people."

When the scouts returned, they reported no movement of whites or Indians along the Zuñi trail, and the raiding party quickly crossed and entered the black lava country where it was not likely that they would be discovered. As they left the hills a black bear crossed their path. "It is a good omen," said Gray Hat. "Our raid will be successful."

7

3

AFTER THE MEN HAD LEFT RED LAKE, THE clan separated and each family group drove their sheep into the Tunicha Mountains. It was lonely without the men. Mother Red Lake, older wife of Gray Hat, took charge as they packed all their possessions on the horses and started the sheep moving up the mountains. As soon as she saw that the march was underway, Mother Red Lake went on ahead with the pack horses to look for a place to camp, leaving Gray Hat's younger wife, Nazbah, to follow her with the sheep and the horse travois which carried the skins to cover their shelters, sheep skins for their bedding and the poles for her loom. As she rode along she thought of Gray Hat and the many years they had made this same move to the mountains together. Tears came to her eyes as she thought that she might never see him again.

Snow still lay in the higher mountain valleys, but there was plenty of grass for the herds in the foothills and enough cedar and piñon to shield them from the view of any raiding parties travelling through the valley. Mother Red Lake selected a spot on a high mesa just below Bear Mountain and sent her son, Kee, back to tell Nazbah and the others. Most of the lambs were now a month old and able to keep up with the older animals, but some had to be carried on horseback by the children. At the chosen grazing grounds the boys cut cedar branches and helped the women build shelters against the rock outcroppings.

Mother Red Lake decided to split the herd into ten groups, about one hundred sheep in each group, and to keep them separated in the nearby valleys around the mesa. These smaller groups would not be so easily seen or heard should some hunter be riding through the area. She warned the boys that all strangers, Navajo or other, must be killed if they discovered the herds because, if they were allowed to escape, they would return with raiding parties. The older girls were told to keep the sheep hidden and not to let them join the other groups while the boys kept watch. Some of the boys took the horses to a small valley near the main camp and hobbled them so they would not wander back to Red Lake Valley. This disposition of the family and herds was good. They were spread out over an area about five miles long halfway up the slope of the mountain.

Mother Red Lake kept all of her unmarried children at the main camp. Her two sons, Kee, who was sixteen year of age, and Chiquito, thirteen, would keep her camp supplied with meat. Her daughters, Hesbah, fourteen, and Shebah, twelve, would watch the sheep and help her take care of the others.

The family also included a Mexican slave girl called María. She had been obtained in a raid five years before and now at the age of fourteen was a trusted member of the family. She usually accompanied Hesbah when the sheep were taken out to graze. Now the girls carefully unloaded the two grindstones and placed them in the shelter. Several bundles of shelled corn were placed in the shelter with the stones. The family would live on corn saved from last summer's harvest, small animals killed by the boys with their arrows and throwing sticks, and an occasional

9

sheep. There were many wild plants which would supplement the meat and corn diet. Some plants were already sending up tender shoots which could be boiled and eaten as greens or eaten raw and soon there would be wild onions, mountain celery and wild carrots. Later there would be the sweet fruit of the yucca, wild strawberries, wild raspberries and the fruit of the cactus. As soon as the snow melted in the high valleys they would plant small fields of corn and melons as they did every year.

Everything was in order when Nazbah arrived with the small children and relatives. She had left the sheep at places Kee had shown her under the care of relatives and slaves and warned them not to let the animals out of sight. Nazbah was a quiet young woman, the daughter of one of Mother Red Lake's sisters. She had married at an early age but her husband had become ill and died shortly after the marriage. Mother Red Lake had then agreed to accept her as Gray Hat's second wife in her household. Nazbah called Mother Red Lake Mother, and her aunt soon came to think of her as one of her own children. Nazbah looked around the camp site and said, "Mother, I will set up your loom. Would you like to have it on the bare spot in front of that brown rock where you will be protected from the wind?"

"Very well, my daughter," responded Mother Red Lake, "We will stay here for a week or two and I will be able to do some weaving. Hosea will help you with the poles."

Hosea, an old and wise man from the Hopi Pueblo, was an important member of the family group. His Navajo wife had died twenty years ago, and after her death he had decided he would stay with the Navajo people. He was an expert basket maker and a welcome addition to the clan. He was also an experienced story teller and had added many of the Hopi legends to the oft repeated legends of the Red House Clan. The children gathered around him to hear his stories as his busy fingers wove baskets for the family or for trading with less fortunate family groups. Now he rose and went to help Nazbah raise the well-worn

11

poles of the loom and to brace and tie them firmly with buckskin thongs.

When they were settled at their first camp, Mother Red Lake said, "Hesbah, you and María are responsible for the sheep. See that they are kept well hidden and that they are not allowed to wander beyond the fringe of trees into the valley. You must hide if you see any strangers and contact the boys as soon as it is safe for you to move. Come back as soon as you can and tell me what you have seen." The family had been grazing their sheep in this area for many years and the girls knew every path and landmark in the area. They walked quietly from one herd to another and asked the sheepherders if they had seen anyone. They repeated Mother Red Lake's warning then returned to report to their mother that all was well.

All was quiet in the Tunicha Mountains; the weather became warmer and the families moved further up the slopes into the higher valleys. Gray Hat's family moved toward Chuska Peak where on a high mesa they knew there was plenty of grass and water for the sheep. They avoided the large meadows near Washington Pass, as the trail that led through the pass was a favorite route for soldiers and raiding parties passing through the Tunicha Mountain Range.

A month passed and the clan began talking of the return of the raiding party. What would the captured women be like and what stories would they bring with them of life along the big river? All of the captives would, of course, know how to farm, herd sheep and cook, but what other skills would they bring to help make life better for the clan? "I wonder if my father will bring back any girls my age?" asked Shebah.

"I hope he will bring back a fine horse for me," said Chiquito.

"Your father did not make the long trip to get horses and girls for children to play with," scolded Mother Red Lake. "He will bring back some women to help herd the

12

sheep and to gather wood for the fire. Look at our wood-pile. There is not enough wood left to cook another meal. Shoo, both of you, get busy and bring me some more dead oak branches."

4

WHILE THE CLAN FOLLOWED MUCH THE SAME routine as they did every year, moving the herds up into the valleys of the Tunicha Mountains, the raiding party continued on its way toward the Rio Grande.

By early April, they were within ten miles of the valley. They had seen no one along the way, as they had kept to the rough country and away from the valleys and plains which were used at this time of year as grazing grounds. They had seen no sign of their "cousins," the Apaches, who sometimes hunted in this rough country or sent raiding parties through it to capture sheep from the Pueblo and Mexican herds.

"We must camp here in the rocks," said Gray Hat. "Little Man and Black Horse will go to the river and look for a village or ranch that will be easy to attack." The two scouts rode to within a few miles of the river, tied their horses in a grove of trees and proceeded on foot to the top of a hill from where they could overlook the valley. They avoided the trails leading to the villages of Alamillo

13

and Socorro and found themselves near a large ranch in an open area near the river. The main ranch house of the owner stood by itself on a slight rise near the river. It was surrounded by a log fence. The farm hands and other workers were quartered in small two-room adobe houses built in a straight line about five hundred yards from the main house and less than a mile from where Black Horse and Little Man lay watching. There were no sheep in the corrals as the herds had been taken to grazing grounds away from the ranch houses. In one of the corrals they saw twenty horses. As the sun began to set, a few men rode in and turned their horses into the corral.

"We will stay here tonight and see what the Mexicans do in the morning," said Black Horse. At daybreak, they saw the doors open and some of the people walking around. "We will go now," said Black Horse. "This looks like a good ranch to raid. You run about five miles down the river, and I will go up the river and see if more ranches are nearby."

"Very well," said Little Man, "I will meet you where we left our horses at noon time."

The sun was high overhead when they returned to their horses. Black Horse had seen a smaller ranch about six miles to the north but thought the first ranch would be the best to raid. Little Man had seen a sheep camp, but there were only two women at the camp to cook for the sheepherders. The two men returned to Gray Hat's camp to report what they had seen. As they sat leaning against the small cedars eating more of the cold rabbit meat, Black Horse said, "We found a large ranch where there are about thirty women and children and only a few men. The men and boys have taken the sheep to camps in the hills. All of the people left at the ranch live in a long house with many doors and behind their house is a corral in which there are twenty horses. We saw a few dogs but this can not be helped as everyone has dogs to protect their homes and their horses. The people wake before the sun rises so we must attack early."

14

"You have done well," said Gray Hat. "We will send two of our men to the horse corral. They will rope and take some of the best horses to our meeting place in the mountains. They will drive the rest of the horses away from the corral so they will not be used to follow us. The rest of us will lead our horses as close as possible to the house and when the first dog barks, we will ride in as quickly as possible and break down the doors. We must get the women on our horses and take them to the mountains. We will meet here after the raid and follow the same trail west that we came on. We will attack just before daybreak tomorrow." All the men agreed, and two men skilled in roping horses were detailed to break into the horse corral. The other men gave the ropers enough rope with which to lead six horses.

After their plans were made, everyone laid down and slept. They rose two hours before sunrise. A fog hung over the valley, and the men were damp and cold as they sat silently munching cold meat. It was still dark as they led their horses toward the ranch house. Even at this early hour lights were appearing in some of the rooms as the people rose to eat and start another day.

The two men chosen to get the horses circled the ranch house and went in first. A thin streak of hazy light appeared over the hills east of the river as they mounted and started for the corral. A dog barked. The head horseman headed for the corral, and the rest of the raiding party jumped on their horses and in a few minutes were at the house.

Most of the people were just preparing breakfast when the raiders arrived. The Mexican men who grabbed their guns and stepped outside to see who was coming were killed by lances and arrows. Only half a dozen shots were fired and in such haste that none found its target. The Navajos dismounted and entered the rooms where they were met by frightened women and children holding sticks and pans. Many of the women and children offered no resistance but simply cowered in the corners, some quietly and others screaming. The raiders quickly knocked down the women

15

and boys who tried to resist, picked up the women and older girls too terrified to move, tied their hands and threw them across the backs of their horses. The raid had taken scarcely ten minutes and lights were beginning to appear in the main house as the raiding party galloped away. With them went twelve women captives half unconscious, bouncing up and down on the horses.

A few miles away from the ranch house they were met by the two men who had raided the horse corral, leading six stolen horses. The party stopped long enough to transfer some of the women onto the backs of the ranch horses, then proceeded on to their previous camp where they stopped to rearrange their loads and decide what to do next. Gray Hat had spoken of raiding the small ranch that Black Horse had seen, but now he said, "I think we should return quickly to the Tunicha Mountains. We will not stop to rest until we reach the safety of the black rock country. Now let us put as much distance as possible between us and the Rio Grande before nightfall." The captives were put on the spare horses with their hands tied around the horses' necks. Most of the women were crying softly with their faces half hidden in the horses' manes as they started off again.

It was not two hours before the first of the prisoners fell and hung from her horse's neck. She was tied across the horse's back, and the party moved on. Other women fainted and Gray Hat finally stopped to allow the prisoners to dismount and rest. Water was given to them, and he asked the women in Navajo if they would try to escape if they were untied. None of the women appeared to understand Navajo, but they begged with gestures not to be tied. One of the women tried to escape into the trees and another picked up a branch and attacked her escort. Both were quickly caught and tied. They resumed the march with the women's hands tied in front of them so they would be able to hold on to the horses' manes and make faster progress.

By nightfall the party was twenty miles from the ranch, and Gray Hat ordered everyone to dismount and walk. They led the horses five miles farther before stopping to

16

rest. The captives were told to sit down with their backs to the small trees and were tied securely. The men gave their prisoners water and a little cold meat. The women accepted the water as their mouths were very dry, put a little on their tear-inflamed eyes, but refused the meat.

"Very well," said Gray Hat, "we have scarcely enough food for ourselves. When we get to the black rock country, we will stop and hunt. Until then we will all be hungry. I think that the next time the women are offered food they will accept it."

The exhausted women sat in silence, staring into the darkness. Their thoughts were of families at the ranch. They strained their ears listening for sounds of a rescue party but all was silent except for an occasional rustle of some small animal. One by one they drifted into an uneasy sleep.

5

MOTHER RED LAKE HAD SLOWLY MOVED HER family group to the mesa on the west side of the Chuska Mountain where they would remain until the snow fell in the fall, forcing them to return to Red Lake Valley. The family built a corral of oak branches for the sheep and planted corn and squash in a small valley fed by a mountain spring. After this was done, she settled down in front

17

of her loom to weave blankets for her family. Hesbah and Shebah sat with her, carding and spinning the black wool for their mother. Nazbah supervised the work in the garden and the cooking. The servants hoed the rows of corn and dug small ditches to divert the water from the spring so it would cover the field. They brought in the wood and the water and helped the children herd sheep.

One day Hosea brought a partially finished basket over to the loom, and as they worked, he told them of the days when he was a young man. He told them again of the time he had accompanied a group of men from his village on the high mesa on a trip to the Colorado River, a river larger than the Rio Grande.

"We went to the river," he said, "to trade with a group of white men who called themselves Mormons. The Mormons lived on the other side of the river but they built a raft for us to cross on. We visited their store in which there were many coats and hats, bridles for the horses, bright-colored blankets and beautiful necklaces made from stones and shells all colors of the rainbow. There were many knives with handles made from the horns of animals and of dark polished wood. There were iron cooking pots and ribbons and thin woven cloth of every color: bright red, blue, and yellow. The Mormons welcomed us and gave us brown bread which they baked in a mud brick oven, and they roasted a sheep for us to eat. We traded baskets and our woven belts to them for knives and cooking pots. They said many of the Ute and Paiute Indians come to their store to trade and that we should come again soon with more baskets and belts."

The women listened closely in silence, except to say, "Yes, yes, go on," when he paused to think of what he would say next. Hosea spoke of the great Colorado River which at one place flowed through a canyon much deeper than the Canyon de Chelly. It was so deep that a man standing on the edge could hardly see the bottom.

"I wish I could go to that store and see all of those beautiful things," said Hesbah. "I would like to have some

of that cloth of every color of the rainbow." The girls asked Hosea more about the things he had seen in the store and said they would like to have everything. As always, they were interested in hearing of faraway places.

Most of the women who lived in the clans along the Tunicha Mountains had travelled as far as the Canyon de Chelly, but only the men made long trips. The men travelled as far as the Rio Grande in the east, to the San Francisco Mountains in the west, and more than five hundred miles to the south. There was little reason to make such long trips into Mexico except to satisfy the strong curiosity which is such a dominant trait of the Navajo people. Only the trips to the east were profitable, as they usually resulted in the capture of sheep, horses, and women to add to the wealth of the families.

6

GRAY HAT'S PARTY FOLLOWED THE GALLINAS Mountain Range to the Continental Divide, a distance of about seventy miles in two days. They had started before sunrise and travelled after the sun had set, leading the horses in single file over the rough mountain trails when it was too dark for the animals to see. Gray Hat told two of his men to stay about a mile behind the main party and to look back from every high point to see if they were being followed, but all was quiet. The prisoners' hopes of escape faded as their captors led them through the mountains. The women were not experienced woodsmen who could find their way back through such a rugged country. They were all tired and hungry. Finally Gray Hat said, "We will camp here for a day as we must have food for ourselves and our captives. Our horses are tired and must be fed and allowed to rest before we continue on. Tie the prisoners to the trees so they will not try to escape as we have no time to look for them."

Red Horse said, "Yes, we must rest. I will take the horses to the small valley we just passed where there is plenty of grass and water. We will hobble the horses and let them graze. Black Horse can take some of the men hunting tomorrow."

"No," said Gray Hat, "I will lead the hunt as we must hunt for deer. Our party is too large to provide smaller animals for. We must kill a deer so everyone can be fed."

The night before the hunt, Gray Hat sat for more than an hour in a secluded place chanting the prayers necessary before hunting the deer. In his chant he explained to the gods that it was necessary to kill the deer because his people were hungry and he asked that the gods help him. In the morning, about an hour before daybreak, Gray Hat led four of the men toward a spring where there were many signs of animals coming to drink. Just before they reached the spring, he again prayed for help and for forgiveness.

Near the spring, Gray Hat stationed his men on the downwind side of a plainly marked trail by which deer were accustomed to come to drink. They did not have long to wait. As the first light of day appeared over the mountains in the east, a fat buck followed by two does appeared. The men held their breaths and became as motionless as the rocks and bushes behind which they had crouched. The buck stopped and looked around but saw nothing, then nervously approached the water. Arrows flew from the men's bows and at that short distance, no one missed his mark. The three animals fell and were quickly dispatched

21

by the knives of the hunters. Gray Hat made sure the windpipes had been cut thoroughly, then standing erect beside the carcasses, again apologized for having taken the lives of the animals. Finally he removed the horns of the buck and placed them on a rock. He sprinkled corn pollen on the horns, then told the men to take the carcasses away from the spring. When they had gone a short distance, the deer were split open and the tips of the hearts removed. Gray Hat dug a small hole and placed the tips of the hearts in the hole as he chanted a prayer to Mother Earth to whom he was returning a gift of some of the food she had created.

At the camp small fires were lighted and small strips of meat were soon roasted and passed around. The half-starved prisoners scarcely took time to chew the strips of venison that were handed to them.

Soon there were many hawks, attracted by the smell of the meat, circling overhead and Gray Hat became worried. "The hawks will show anyone who has followed us where we are," he said. "We must fill our water jugs and leave this place quickly."

With food in their stomachs and the horses once more fed and rested, they trotted along the trail, in better spirits, to the safety of the rough lava country. Once in the fields of lava they left the trail they had been following and picked their way through the sharp-edged black rocks until they found a pool of water. Here they stopped, set up camp, and cooked the rest of the deer meat. The horses were hobbled and some of the men left with them to watch and see that they did not cut their legs on the sharp rocks as they searched for the small clumps of grass. The party was in an area which the Spaniards had named the Mal País (bad lands) and which the Mexicans and Indians avoided, as the sharp-edged black lava could cut the leg of an unwary man or animal like a knife. The only animals which thrived in this area were the field mice and their enemy, the rattlesnake. As the men sat around the small fires, Gray Hat said, "My sons, some of you have

22

brought knives and guns from the ranch. We cannot take anything that belonged to our enemies as the spirits of their dead owners will follow us to recover them. I have noticed that already some of you do not look well. We will hide everything that belonged to our enemy in the rocks where they will be hard to find and cover them with charcoal so the spirits of the dead will not be able to use them against us."

When this was done, the party resumed its way through the Mal País. It was now late in April and pleasantly warm during the day but still cold at night. In June, shimmering heat waves would rise from this black wasteland and the temperature would climb to over one hundred degrees. The party continued northward through the Mal País for another day.

They were approaching the Zuñi Pueblo trail and must again take precautions against discovery. Gray Hat sent Little Man and Black Horse ahead to scout the area they would pass through as there might be soldiers or raiders on the trail. When the scouts returned, the party moved on crossing the trail at dusk and entered the Zuñi Mountains. If all went well they would be with their families in about four more days.

Twelve days had elapsed since the raid and, except for the one-day halt in the Gallinas Mountains and a half day in the Mal País, the party had travelled at a steady pace. Everyone was tired and hungry as they pushed slowly ahead. The horses were getting thin and weak, and the men dismounted frequently to lead them where the trail was rough. All plans of a raid on the Zuñi sheep herds were abandoned, and the men thought only of the time they would rejoin their families where they could rest and be well fed. The captives were also praying for the trip to end. As they plodded along, tears came often to their eyes, but somehow they kept moving. Each step seemed more difficult than the preceding one, but the fear of being left behind to die in this unfriendly country was stronger than their weariness. They knew nothing of the more well-travelled

23

trails to Albuquerque and believed that if they escaped
or were left behind, they would have to find their way
back through the wild mountain country and the rough
lava beds through which they had come. It was better to
stay with the party than to face certain death in such a
country. Besides, they had not been too badly treated
except for the first two days when they had been tied over
the backs of the horses. Since those days, they had been
allowed to ride as much as possible and had been given as
much food as their captors. None of them had been beaten
or tortured. The Navajos considered the women a valua-
ble asset to be kept in good condition and to be brought
safely to their families. They had travelled a long way and
risked their lives to capture the women and had no wish
to harm them.

In time these captured women might become heads of
families, but first they would be distributed among the families of their captors. Some of them would become second
wives but, unlike a Navajo second wife, they would become the servants of the first wife. The children of these
servants would be considered the children of the Navajo
wife and would be treated the same as her own children.
In the Navajo society, servants owned nothing. They could
be sold by the first wife if their work or behavior was
not satisfactory. Some of the captives would be taken by the
mothers or sisters of the unmarried men to be kept as their
servants but would not be given the status of a Navajo wife.
The children she bore her master would be considered the
children of his mother or sister rather than her children.
All Navajo women have a great love for children and the
birth of any baby, especially a male child, is an event for
rejoicing. During this time, a great many babies died at
birth and when one was born live and well, the women
came for miles to hold and to kiss the tiny face. The children of these captured women would be as well loved and
as well taken care of as any of the other Navajo children.

During the long ride, the men had watched the behavior of their prisoners and, in their minds, had selected

24

the one each wanted as his share of the raid. Did she walk freely or did she limp along the trail? Was she strong, or did she have to be carried on a horse because she tired easily? All the men preferred the young girls rather than the older ones who were in their late twenties or thirties. They did not discuss the distribution of the women among themselves . This was a matter to be decided upon at a meeting of the clan after they were safely in the Tunichas.

7

THE FAMILIES IN THE TUNICHA MOUNTAINS were worried. Although Gray Hat had told them the trip might take two moons, no one expected the men to be gone that long. Had all of the men been killed or captured? No one spoke of his fears, as to speak of trouble would bring trouble. They must only speak of the success of the mission in order to insure the safe return of the men to them.

The corn was just beginning to make its appearance in the small fields. The lambs were growing larger every day and all was quiet. No strangers were reported near their camps or in the valleys below by the scouts. There was plenty of grass in the mountain valleys, and the children became less cautious as they sat with their backs against the warm rocks, half asleep as they watched the grazing sheep. What could happen to them in this remote mountain country? The boys shouted to one another as they hunted rabbits and the fat prairie dogs for their families to eat. Even the women became accustomed to living without the protection of the men and rode the mountain trails alone to visit their neighbors or to gather greens to add to the family stew.

One day Mother Red Lake said, "Kee, we must shear some of the sheep as my supply of wool is nearly gone, and there are many more blankets needed. Go to my sister's camp and ask her to lend us her oldest son to help us. Tell him to bring a large knife to cut the wool."

Hesbah, who was sitting nearby skinning a rabbit, asked, "Can I go with him, Mother? I have not seen my cousins for a long time."

"Yes, my daughter," replied Mother Red Lake, "you may go, but do as your brother says. Always stay behind him so you will be able to hide if you see any strangers."

The camp they were going to was about three miles north and within easy walking distance. Kee took his bow and some arrows as well as his hunting knife, as there was always a possibility of finding some small game along the trails. The children had not gone far when Hesbah called to Kee that she saw a patch of wild carrots and celery. She picked up a stick and started digging. Kee dug around the plants with his knife so they would be easy to pull out. "I will take these to my aunt," said Hesbah, as she put some of the vegetables in her blanket. "We can stop and gather some more for Mother on our way back."

The children were met with smiles and greetings. They were given fresh wild tea and corn bread to eat. After they finished, the aunt cleared away the dishes and said to Hesbah, "It is good to see you, my daughter, and how is my sister?"

"She is weaving, my little mother," replied the girl, "and I have been carding the wool and spinning it for her, but now we have no more wool."

26

"Yes," said Kee. "Mother has sent us to ask if you will let your son come and help us shear some sheep."

"Of course I will," answered his aunt. "I will come myself as I, too, have been busy and will also need some more wool in a few more days. We will have a nice visit."

While they were talking and eating, one of the boys, who had been scouting the area, rode up. He spoke quietly but his eyes shone as he greeted them. "Yah tah hay, my mother," he said. "I bring good news. The men are returning and will be here in a few hours. They are coming up the mountain trail now. I must go and tell all the women to be at Gray Hat's camp tomorrow morning." He rode away to tell the good news to the other families scattered throughout the mountains.

"We will go now to my sister," said the aunt. "She will need help preparing food for so many people. I will bring some cornmeal which my girls ground yesterday. Your mother has plenty of lambs. I wonder how many women the men have brought back with them?" As she talked, she loaded food and cooking utensils in a blanket and placed it on a horse.

When this was done, she quickly brushed her hair, put on her newest blanket dress and necklace of blue and red shells. As they hastened toward Gray Hat's camp, she never once stopped talking. As she talked, her feelings of worry and fear that had been with her ever since the men had left, slowly disappeared. When they arrived at the camp, she clasped her sister and tears streamed down their faces. They had been greatly worried, but now the worry had ended. Their men were coming home.

8

IN SINGLE FILE THE MEN AND THEIR PRISONERS
rode slowly into the camp. Some of the children had run
down the trail to meet them and ran about them, pointing
and chattering. At the clearing, Gray Hat told his men
to dismount and to have the prisoners line up at one side.
As they stood in line, one of the young women spoke in
Navajo, "It is good to be back in the mountains among
my own people."

Gray Hat looked at her in surprise and asked, "Why
did you not tell us before that you are a Navajo?"

"You did not ask me," she retorted.

"Very well," he said, "since you also speak Spanish, you
can help us with the prisoners. Tell the women to sit
down and my wife will feed them. Tell them they will stay
here tonight." The girl spoke to her companions and they
sat down in a sullen line staring at the ground in front
of them. The men sat at the opposite side of the clearing
and their relatives brought them roasted lamb and corn
bread. After the men had been served, Mother Red Lake

told some of the slave women to take food to the prisoners.

Mother Red Lake went to the Navajo-speaking girl and asked, "What is your clan?"

The girl replied, "I am of the Bitter Water Clan. My mother and I were taken by Crooked Foot four years ago when we were out with our sheep. He sold us to Don Pablo, lord of the ranch your men raided. My mother was in the main house when the raid took place."

"Very well," said Mother Red Lake, "you will stay with me. We will see what you can do."

Most of the women of the clan had come to Gray Hat's camp as soon as they heard that the men had returned. They had all taken time, however, to put on their best blanket dresses held together at the waist with bright red Hopi belts. As each woman arrived, she went first to shake hands with Mother Red Lake, then with the other women. No one looked at the prisoners until the usual greetings had been exchanged and a cup of tea had been drunk. After these amenities had been exchanged, the women went in pairs to look at the prisoners. With their shoulders thrown back they walked proudly along the line of prisoners and with expressionless faces remarked how this one was too fat or that one too thin and made other disparaging remarks as they compared the women with various animals. The haggard, ragged, and dirty captives did look more like animals than human beings in comparison with the clean, well-dressed and comely Navajo women, who believed anyone not a Navajo to be inferior and of very little value. As the women sat and talked, the tired men gathered their blankets around their shoulders and went to sleep. Finally, everyone, except a few men appointed to stand guard, was sound asleep.

The following morning, Gray Hat took charge of the meeting. Mother Red Lake had kept María to act as interpreter and told her the prisoner from the Bitter Water Clan would also help. She sent Hesbah and Shebah to look after the sheep.

29

"We have brought back twelve women to give to the families of the twenty men who took part in the raid," said Gray Hat. "Two of the men who went with me have no wives, so we will first let the mothers of these men choose the women they want in their households. We will let the mother of Black Horse choose first. María, tell the prisoners to stand up so we can see them better." When the prisoners were lined up, Black Horse's mother walked the length of the line and back again. She had made up her mind the night before which captive she would choose, but did not want the one she chose to think she was in any way superior to the others, so she pretended to find the choice difficult.

"None of these women are of any value," she said, "but if I must choose one, then I will take this woman. Perhaps I can teach her to be of some help to me." As she walked back to her place, María took the woman chosen and told her to sit in back of Black Horse's mother. The mother of the other wifeless raider chose the captive she wanted. The other women, in order of their husbands' positions in the clan, were told to select the prisoner they wanted in their household.

Finally, when all the prisoners were disposed of, Gray Hat said, "Every family that has received a prisoner will bring ten sheep to my camp, and I will divide the sheep among the families of the men who did not receive a woman. On our next raid, the families of these men will be given first choice of the prisoners we bring back."

This decision made by Gray Hat was accepted with little argument. The distribution of the captives was not final. The women would be traded by their new owners to other families and it would be several weeks before they would become a permanent part of any family and find their places in the clan. In time, each prisoner would contribute her help in the struggle for food, clothing, and shelter in which all of the members of the family were engaged.

30

9

THE RAID WAS OVER AND THE SPOILS DIVIDED
among the raiders. Now a ceremony must be performed
which was of even greater importance than the raid to
insure the well-being of the clan. The raiders must be
purified or else they would become sick and die, or at
least lose their minds. Evil spirits of the enemy which
may have followed them back to the mountains must be
forced to leave before they could do any damage. Three
sweat houses were built, and after the men had taken
emetics to remove evil from inside their bodies, they stripped and stepped inside. For several hours they sat in the
sweat houses rubbing the loose skin and dirt from their
bodies and singing sacred songs. Blue Cloud, the oldest
and most respected medicine man of the Red House Clan,
had been asked to come and take charge of the ceremony
the night before. Women and boys hastened to build a
ceremonial shelter of cedar branches for him to use.

He arrived in midmorning wearing white buckskin
trousers. His chest and back were painted with white clay,
and over his shoulders he carried a black and white striped

blanket and his buckskin medicine bag. He went at once to the ceremonial shelter and placed his bag inside, then sat down just outside the doorway. Gray Hat went to sit down beside him and Mother Red Lake came to welcome the old man and to bring him food.

After the medicine man had eaten, Gray Hat asked him what was to be done. "We must perform the Enemy-Way Ceremonial," said Blue Cloud. "Which of the other clans will you ask for help?"

"There is a group of Kiya' a' anii people on the east slope of the Tunicha Mountains just below Bear Mountain," said Gray Hat. "We will ask Peace Speaker, headman of the group to take our sacred ceremonial stick and help us with the ceremony. We will give him four horses and six sheep." Blue Cloud sent his brother, who assisted him in the rituals, to speak to Peace Speaker. The Kiya' a' anii headman agreed to help and the Red House Clan was happy, as its neighbors were believed to have special protection from the gods and would make the invocation of the gods more likely to succeed during the ceremony.

The first day of the ceremonial, Blue Cloud brought a smooth cedar stick about three feet long and some cedar branches and plants to be used in the making of the ceremonial stick. He also brought a small, black, round-bottomed jug from which to make the ceremonial drum. He placed them on a blanket and told the men of the raiding party, who were now considered to be his patients, to sit in a half-circle facing him. A small fire was built just east of the blanket, and Blue Cloud and his assistant sat down to prepare the sacred stick.

As they worked, they sang the sacred songs of the Enemy-Way Ritual. Everyone was very quiet as the medicine men chanted in a tone so low they could hardly be heard. As they concentrated on this first part of the ceremony, they sought spiritually to place themselves in the company of the gods whose adventures during the original overthrowing of earthly evils they were about to imitate. The stick now being prepared would become the same

32

jeweled arrow of the sun that had been used to overcome the evils which the gods had destroyed when they were making the earth safe for the people. While his assistant held the stick upright with one end in a basket, the medicine man took cedar branches and other sacred plants and tied them so they flared out at the top of the stick. Next, he tied four eagle feathers with buckskin evenly spaced around the head. Just below the head he tied a long red woven belt, letting the ends hang down almost to the basket, and on the side opposite the belt he tied two more eagle feathers. He finished the stick by tying strings of red and blue yarn from just below the belt knot to within a few inches of the foot of the stick.

He then laid the stick on the basket with the head pointing to the north. This done, he again gave his attention to his patients, who had silently sat watching him prepare the stick and listening to him as he chanted the ancient legends. "My sons," he said, "we are engaged in a very important ceremony which will drive away the spirits of your enemies which seek to kill you. You must do exactly as I tell you for the next four days. Now we are ready to take this sacred stick to the camp of our Kiya' a' anii friends. Gray Hat will carry the stick holding it upright at all times. The rest of you must stay close to him within the protection of this holy arrow of the sun.

While the stick was being made, the slaves were cooking and dying wool in red and blue dyes. The girls were busy carding and spinning wool for the ceremonial. Those women and girls who would accompany the men to the camp of the Kiya' a' anii were busy making themselves beautiful. They washed their hair in yucca suds and brushed their hair until it shone, then tied it up with new yarn. They put on their best blanket dresses with bright red belts around their waists and put strings of colored shell around their necks. Everyone carried a patterned blanket to impress the neighbors.

It was only ten miles to the Kiya' a' anii camp so the party ate and delayed their departure so as to arrive just before sunset. There were about sixty in the party, including the patients. Blue Cloud's brother distributed red and blue yarn which had been kept near the stick in order that it might acquire some of the magical protective qualities and the women and girls tied the yarn to the shoulders of their dresses.

When all was ready, Blue Cloud told the men to mount their horses. He handed the stick to Gray Hat and cautioned him again to hold it always in a vertical position and to be careful not to drop it. "You must not let your horse race," he said. "Hold him to a slow gallop." Gray Hat turned his horse and moved away slowly holding the stick erect. The patients followed him in single file as the path was narrow. They were followed by other men and then the women and girls of marriageable age riding sidesaddle. Excitement filled the air, and soon the column was moving at a gallop and the women and girls were laughing and shouting to one another. This was a great occasion, an occasion to be long remembered as it was seldom that two clans met, and although the purpose of the gathering was a serious one, still it relieved the monotony of their daily life. As they moved along through the pine trees and the cedars, the men sang the sacred songs of the Enemy-Way to the accompaniment of the little drum.

They followed a small mountain stream down the east slope of the Tunicha Mountains until they reached a meadow. Here the men grouped around their leader and the women and girls bunched together behind the men. Suddenly they were shy, as they had never met these strangers of this neighbor clan. As they approached the hogan of Peace Speaker they saw a large crowd of the Kiya' a' anii waiting for the stick to arrive. Gray Hat galloped up to the hogan, dismounted and entered. Peace Speaker and two medicine men were sitting at the west side and some women of his family were sitting on the north side. Gray Hat advanced and solemnly handed the stick to Peace Speaker who took it and laid it on a basket with its head pointing to the north. The medicine men began their chant

34

and, as they sang, one of them removed the wool yarn and handed it to the women.

Gray Hat remained in the hogan until the medicine men had finished, then stepped outside. His appearance was a signal for everyone to dismount and lead their horses to a brush corral which had been prepared for them. When the horses had been taken care of they returned and sat in a great circle, the men in front of Peace Speaker's hogan and the women on the other side where the Kiya' a' anii women had built cooking fires and were roasting sheep and preparing piles of corn bread for their guests. The corn bread was placed on blankets and carried to the men, along with jugs of hot mountain tea, which they passed back and forth as they ate. As night fell, the men of the Red House Clan formed a group at one side of the head-man's hogan, and the men of the Kiya' a' anii Clan formed a group at the other side and, to the beating of the small jug drum, began to chant. "It is good to hear the men sing," Mother Red Lake said to Hesbah.

The singing continued for more than an hour. Then the young men built a large fire which lit up the entire circle. Peace Speaker's daughter, Desbah, came out of the hogan, holding the sacred stick high and walked to the center. She located Gray Hat, took his arm and gently led him to the center of the area. The tempo of the songs now grew faster as Desbah danced slowly around Gray Hat keeping time with the singing and the beat of the ceremonial drum. As she danced, the mothers sent their daughters to choose dancing partners. Those from the Kiya' a' anii Clan danced with the men from the Red House Clan, and those who had come from the Red House Clan chose partners from the young men of the Kiya' a' anii Clan. It was customary for the girl to "ask" the man to dance simply by taking hold of his arm or garment and giving a gentle tug. Upon the completion of the dance, which lasted with each song, every man who was asked to dance was required to give his partner a gift of turquoise, white shell, or a piece of colored yarn.

35

Kay Bennett

For an hour or more, everyone relaxed and enjoyed themselves. The women watched their daughters pick out partners, and hopefully, prospective sons-in-law, and hummed in time with the singing. Finally, the women and girls tired, found an appropriate spot, sat down, wrapped themselves in their blankets and slept while the men continued the sacred songs of the ceremonial until dawn.

At daybreak, the women went to the stream to wash their faces and to bring water for tea. Jugs of water were taken by slave women to the men so they could refresh themselves. There were not enough pots in camp to prepare a stew for such a crowd so more lamb was roasted and more corn bread prepared. After they had finished eating, everyone formed a circle around the hogan to wait for the "give away."

One of the older women of the Kiya' a' anii Clan stood up and said jokingly in a loud voice, "Let us see how quick our in-laws are." She and some of the other women removed branches from the doorway of the hogan and a small goat was pushed out. He stood and looked at the crowd, then turned to go back but was stopped by another goat. Soon a stream of baby goats came bouncing out of the hogan. The women and girls of the Red House Clan ran here and there trying to catch the elusive animals while the men and the women of the Kiya' a' anii Clan stood in a circle so the fast little goats would not get away. Finally, they were all caught and both participants and spectators were weak with laughter as they sat down to regain their breath.

After the "give away," the Red House Clan left to return to their camp in the mountains to prepare to receive the Kiya' a' anii. Blue Cloud's brother stayed behind to represent the Red House Clan and to lead the Kiya' a' anii to a place in the mountains where they would spend the night. Everyone raced home, the men to sleep for a few hours and the women to prepare food for the next day. The women would take turns sleeping.

While the Red House Clan prepared for the next day,

37

those of the Kiya' a' anii Clan who would accompany the stick made ready to move to the temporary night camp. They rounded up their best horses; the men put on their best buckskin trousers and the women, their best blanket dresses. All Navajo women dressed in the same style of blanket dress but each clan incorporated a slightly different design in its blanket weaving. Stripes, either horizontal or vertical, of colored yarn when possible, were woven into the blankets of the Red House Clan, whereas the Kiya' a' anii women usually preferred a zigzag design. All of the women experimented with vegetable dyes, but they preferred the vermillion and indigo dyes which could be obtained from the Santa Fe Trading Post or from the Mormon's store. Occasionally their men went as far as Santa Fe, and the women sent blankets to trade for the red and blue dyes they admired.

Shortly after noon they were ready. The medicine man told Desbah to mount her horse, and when she had done so, he handed her the sacred stick warning her to be careful not to drop it and always to hold it erect. The guide mounted his horse and trotted a little way down the trail, being careful to follow the same path along which Gray Hat had ridden when he brought the stick to his friend. The guide was followed by Peace Speaker, then Desbah and her mother, then by Blue Cloud's brother with the drum and a group of about twenty men. A crowd of about forty women and girls followed the men. As they rode they sang the sacred ceremonial songs, keeping time with the beat of the small drum.

The place selected for the night camp was in the high mountains, at the foot of a bluff from the base of which flowed a clear spring. Peace Speaker dismounted near the spring and after placing a blanket on the ground took the sacred stick from his daughter and placed it on the blanket with its head pointing to the north. Then he sat down in front of the stick while his wife broiled a piece of lamb and prepared a bowl of cornmeal mush for him to eat. The other women quickly prepared food for the men.

38

At sunset the Red House Clan arrived at the night camp. The women had brought some of their children with them to watch the ceremony. Mother Red Lake brought Hesbah, Shebah and the little Bitter Water Clan girl whom they now called Joni because she was always happy and smiling. The men of both clans formed in groups and started singing. It was late that night before the huge bonfire was built for the dancing. Desbah started the dancing as she had done the previous night, but this time she chose Red Horse to dance with. She was followed by the unmarried girls of all ages who chose their partners and led them to the circle. After the women danced, they walked back to Gray Hat's camp and continued making preparations for receiving their neighbors in the morning.

Just at sunrise, the beating of the ceremonial drum was heard, and the men of the Red House Clan, who had just returned to Gray Hat's camp a few hours before, were awakened. They hastened to arm themselves with knives and bows and arrows then mounted their horses and raced around with wild yells. The sound of the drum and the singing became louder and soon the Kiya' a' anii Clan could be seen moving up the trail. The men of the Red House Clan raced to meet them. They rode around the Kiya' a' anii group as though they were attacking and bent on the group's destruction. Then the two groups of men joined and raced back to the ceremonial shelter, yelling loudly. They circled around the shelter, then raced back to where Peace Speaker and Desbah, with the sacred stick, sat waiting.

They repeated this warlike maneuver four times, then the Kiya' a' anii group rode to where a pile of cedar branches had been made ready for them and proceeded to build their camp. They built a circular enclosure about thirty feet in diameter. Peace Speaker, the drummer, and Desbah sat on their horses until the enclosure was completed and a fire built at the center. When this was done, Peace Speaker dismounted and, taking the sacred stick from his daughter, placed it on a blanket with its head pointing to the north. The men from his clan started singing while they waited for the food to arrive. They did not have long to wait. Women and children of the Red House Clan arrived with roast lamb, corn bread and cornmeal mush, and jugs of hot tea.

When they had finished eating it was time for the Red House Clan "give away." Again, young lambs and goats were let loose, giving the women of the Red House Clan a chance to laugh at their neighbors as the women raced about after the elusive creatures. Even the new slave women laughed as they watched the fun. While they were resting, small bundles of dyed yarn were passed among them. Gray Hat walked about among his guests, thanking them for their help.

It was almost noon when the patients were assembled again to sit in a group facing the medicine man. Blue Cloud told them to remove their clothes and to blacken themselves with charcoal. A mound of blackening from the ashes of sacred plants, cedar wood, and sheep tallow had been prepared, and now Gray Hat walked to the medicine man who took a handful of the blackening and made a line across the headman's face, one on his chest and one down his back, then gave him a handful of the blackening to complete the blackening of the rest of his body.

The other patients followed Gray Hat and when the medicine man had given them each some of the blackening, they helped each other until they were all black from head to foot. As evil spirits cannot touch anything covered with black ashes, there was no chance of any spirits that might be hovering near entering the bodies. When the blackening was completed, the medicine men continued their chants. A bowl of medicine which had been prepared was passed around for the men to drink. Thus fortified, the patients were led a short distance away from the crowd to a place where Blue Cloud had laid a scalp taken by one of the men from a Mexican he had killed during the raid. They stood around it while the drummer beat the drum. The drumming exorcised the evil spirits into the ground. As the drum beat, the men approached the scalp. Blue

40

Cloud threw ashes on it, and the patients beat it into the ground with their cedar sticks. This ritual was repeated four times before they returned to the ceremonial shelter, where the crowd joined them as everyone stood on the south side facing the sun. Everyone joined in chanting a prayer to the God of the Sun. They threw corn pollen as a gift to the god and, cupping their outstretched hands, brought them to their mouths as they drank in the sun's rays. As they chanted, they thanked the God of the Sun for his help in the raid and his help in chasing away the evil spirits and prayed that he would give them good health in the future.

When the mass prayer was finished, everyone returned to his campfire while the patients put on their clothes. Blue Cloud tied a scarf around the head of each of his patients and fastened an eagle feather to the scarf. He said, "You must not wash the ashes from your bodies or remove this sash and feather from your heads for four days. You must sleep apart from your families and think only of the stories you have heard me tell you during this ceremonial. You must concentrate on these stories and thereby erase all memory of the raid from your minds. You must not hunt or handle your weapons during these four days. It is best that you sit quietly, helping to herd the sheep and thinking of what I have told you until you are completely cured."

At sunset Blue Cloud led the men of both clans to the ceremonial shelter. They sang the ceremonial songs as they walked and then formed a group at the shelter to chant the evening prayer. From the shelter they went to Peace Speaker's enclosure to chant more prayers and ceremonial songs until it was time for the girls to dance. After the dance, the medicine men of both clans led all the men in singing until dawn.

In the morning, the Red House Clan sang the four sacred morning songs for their friends to conclude the ceremonial. Peace Speaker and his people mounted their horses and started for home. Desbah still carried the stick erect as she followed her father down the mountain trail. When they were nearly home, Peace Speaker halted the column. "We must put the stick away here," he said. He placed his blanket on the ground and, taking the stick from his daughter, placed it on the blanket. Everyone dismounted and stood quietly while Peace Speaker removed his pouch of corn pollen and told his daughter to pass it around.

As the pouch was passed, each person took some, placed a little in his mouth, a little on top of his head and tossed a little as a gift toward the sun. Then Peace Speaker and a medicine man knelt and sang very softly as they removed the cedar branches, the sacred plants, the feathers and the red sash from the stick. When the stick was bare, Peace Speaker put corn pollen on it and placed it under a rock. He wrapped the things he had taken from the stick in his blanket to take to his home. When this final ritual was completed, the group mounted their horses and quietly went to their own homes.

10

THE KINLICHINE CLAN SOON SEPARATED AND went about their routine lives of herding sheep, farming, hunting, gathering wild plants for food, gathering medicinal herbs; and, of course, corn pollen was replenished once a year at harvest time. The women spent long hours at their looms as there were many people to be clothed that winter. They wove black blanket dresses for the slave women with wide red borders to identify them when they were in the fields. The captive women seldom saw one another and soon gave up any plans they might have had to escape. Of course, some of them continued to hope that they might be discovered by raiding parties from the Rio Grande and returned to their people. The naturally friendly Navajo children soon made friends with the captives and helped them learn a little of the Navajo language which was the main barrier between the women and their masters. Few Navajos, even though they understood a little Spanish, would speak the language of their traditional enemy except when they visited the trading post at Santa Fe.

The new servants had plenty to do and little time to feel sorry for themselves. They weeded the patches of corn and melons, helped harvest the crops, ground the corn, fetched the water, cooked the food, and helped gather the firewood. At least one member of the family always worked alongside them, and as they worked together, performing the chores necessary for survival, they learned to respect each other and even to develop feelings of friendship. The captives who were not pregnant at the time of their capture were soon carrying the babies of their masters and the clan looked forward to a sizeable increase in numbers in the spring.

The months passed and everyone was busy gathering food for the winter. No crops had been planted in Red Lake Valley, as there had been no one to protect the fields while the men were gone. The families would have to subsist on what they were able to harvest from their mountain farms and what they could gather in the forest. Men, women, and children looked for and gathered acorns, piñons, berries and plants to eat while they conserved their small supply of corn. The women scraped the hair from sheepskins and softened the hides by rubbing them with sheep brains in order to make more bags in which to store grass seeds and the dry seeds of other plants which they

43

Kay Bennett

would add to stews during the winter months. When the crops were harvested, they shelled the corn and dried slices of the melons to take to the valley. Everyone worked from morning to night, but the supply of food was small compared to that which they had been accustomed to storing away in previous years. Sheep and wild game would provide them with meat, but there would be a shortage of corn and other foods. Some of the men talked of raiding the Zuñi and Hopi fields.

At a meeting Gray Hat spoke against raiding the Pueblos. He said, "All of the crops of the Pueblos have been harvested, and we do not have enough men to attack the villages. I think it is better that we trade with them. We will take blankets to trade for corn with the Hopi. I will take ten men with me so we will not be attacked, and we will take Hosea to speak to his people for us." The women renewed their efforts to produce more blankets. When one tired of weaving her daughter took her place at the loom so that no time would be lost. By late October, enough blankets had been woven and the men started for Hopi country.

Snow fell early in November, but word of raiding parties in the valley kept the families in the mountains. In mid-November Little Man and other scouts brought word of a large raiding party in Red Lake Valley. The scouts followed the party and watched them from well hidden vantage points as the Mexicans rode through the valley, crossed the Tunicha Mountains at Washington Pass and then turned southward along the eastern slopes of the mountains looking for Navajos who should be returning to their winter grazing grounds. They found no one, as the Kiya' a' anii scouts had seen the raiders in the Washington Pass area and carried word to other members of their clan. Families who had already moved into the Chuska Valley hastily moved their herds and supplies back into the snow-covered mountains before they were discovered. Finding no Navajos along the Tunichas, the raiders turned eastward where their quarry would have less cover and be easier to pursue.

45

When the raiders were gone, Gray Hat's group moved into the Red Lake Valley and reoccupied the hogans they had left in the spring. They quickly repaired the old shelters and corrals and resumed their normal lives of sheep herding, hunting, and weaving. The new servants took over some of the duties of the younger girls whose mothers now put them to work at looms set up alongside their own.

Gray Hat returned with corn from a Hopi village and said they had been well treated. It seemed that the winter would not be as bad as the family had feared. He arrived just in time for a meeting with the leader of a small group of the Kiya' a' anii. Black Weeds, who was called Manuelito by the Americans, had become the leader of a group of his wife's people who lived on the east side of the Tunicha Mountains just south of Washington Pass. The recent raids had angered him and he had tried to persuade his father-in-law, the great peace chief, Narbona, to attack the raiders; but the old man had said it was better to hide than to fight. Now he felt that he must go to the other clans and try to enlist their help. "Next time the raiders come to our valleys, will you help my people destroy them?" he said to Gray Hat.

"Yes," replied Gray Hat, "we will send word to you next time we see a raiding party, and we will join forces against them. We must stop these raids before we lose more of our women and children. I think all of the clans should join together to fight any strangers who invade our land. I have spoken of this before to some headmen of the Kinlichine, but they are like Narbona. They think they can hide and that the raiders will pass by. They think only of their own families and will not help their own clan brothers. Some of the poorer men even join the raiders and guide them against their own people when the raiders promise them gifts."

"I know," said Black Weeds. "We work against one another and are becoming easy prey for those who would destroy us. My father-in-law speaks only of peace and thinks only of his large herds. My clan, the Bitahni, will fight the

46

raiders. We lived in the Ute hunting grounds for many years and learned to band together to fight the Ute and the Comanche. Twelve years ago, after the big meteors came down on our land, we joined with the men of the nearby clans and defeated a thousand Mexicans and their Indian friends who came to make war on us at Washington Pass. There were not many of them that escaped our arrows. Later the Bitahni attacked and destroyed the Hopi pueblo known as Oraibi. I will ask the headmen of all our clans to help us again to kill our enemies.

"We cannot ask the Americans to help us. When I went to the American council meeting at Bear Springs last fall, with other headmen who wished to help the Americans destroy their Mexican enemies, we were told that the Americans did not wish our help. The American leaders told us that we must stop fighting with the Mexicans or the American soldiers would join the Mexicans against us. There are not many Americans and they are not familiar with our country. I do not believe they would be of much help to us or to the Mexicans, whichever side they fight on."

The two men talked and planned. The following day Gray Hat called his group together and told them of his plans. All the men volunteered to join any war party Manuelito would lead; however, no more raiding parties were reported in the Tunichas that winter. The next raid was in the fall of 1848.

11

SHEBAH HAD TAKEN THE SHEEP ABOUT A MILE
from the hogan to a sunny spot where the snow had melted.
She could see the smoke rising through the smoke hole of
her mother's hogan and her mother sitting on the sunny
side, busy at her loom. Her father had joined a group of
headmen several days before to make the long trip to Santa
Fe to speak to the headmen of the Americans and to find
out what their intentions were. Would they send more
soldiers to ride through the land of the Navajos, and for
what purpose? Would the Americans take any action to
stop the Mexicans who continued to raid Navajo families
and to steal the women and children?

As she sat with her back against a warm rock, Shebah
dozed, wakened and dozed again. Suddenly a cold rough
hand was clamped over her mouth. For an instant she froze!
Then she opened her eyes to see a wild-eyed, swarthy face
close to hers. She instinctively bit hard and struggled to get
away. The man jerked his hand back and hit her alongside
her head with his other hand. She lost consciousness and

48

the man and his companion dragged her behind a nearby hill where they joined two more men holding the horses. One of them threw Shebah across a horse, mounted behind her, and the four men disappeared quickly into the hills.

Mother Red Lake continued her weaving. Looking up occasionally, she could see the sheep grazing peacefully. Now she noticed that clouds which had been forming all afternoon in the west were being blown more swiftly toward the valley. Hesbah, María, and Joni came with bundles of firewood which they gathered in the hills, Mother Red Lake sent María to help Shebah bring in the sheep before it started snowing. María walked down the trail to the herd and called to Shebah, but there was no answer. She circled around the herd and started them toward the lake; still Shebah did not appear. "She should not leave the sheep alone," María said to herself. "Mother will be angry." She climbed a small hill and looked around. She was puzzled and began to get worried. She thought, perhaps, Shebah might have been climbing among the rocks and fallen and hurt herself. María quickly returned to the sheep and started throwing rocks at them to start them moving. As they neared the corral, the other girls came to help her.

"Where is Shebah?" they asked.

"I don't know," answered María. "I called her, but she did not answer. I thought she would join me when she saw the sheep heading for the corral. We must all go back and look for her."

Mother Red Lake and the girls returned to where the sheep had been grazing and started walking in circles through the small hills. The girls climbed the rock bluff bank and looked in crevices where Shebah might have fallen. As Mother Red Lake walked around the small gray hill, her sharp eyes noticed where the raiders' horses had been held. "Someone has been here, and it was not one of our men!" she thought. She followed the footprints of the two men to where Shebah had been sitting and read the signs of the struggle. She called to the girls and said, "Hesbah,

50

get your pony quickly and ride as fast as you can. Tell the men your sister has been carried away. Hurry now, as it looks like she was taken about an hour ago. I should never have let Kee take our sheep dog when he went hunting. If the dog had been with her I would have been able to hear him bark. Hurry now and get the men. They must follow the raiders and get Shebah back before dark."

With this, Hesbah ran off. Mother Red Lake and the two girls were all crying as they returned to the hogan. Mother Red Lake sat down at her loom, but she could scarcely see as she kept wiping the tears from her eyes. The two girls picked up the wood they had brought from the hills and stacked it near the hogan.

It was dusk before Hesbah and a half-dozen men galloped up to the hogan. They shouted to Mother Red Lake and continued on to where the trail of the raiders started. The trail led over the rocky bluff and they followed at a slow walk. They travelled about two miles before the light faded, making it difficult to see the trail of the horses. A strong wind was blowing, driving a light snow which threatened to become heavier.

"I think they are heading south and will follow the trail to Albuquerque," said one of the men. "We will ride fast and catch them."

The party rode about ten miles down the trail and made a camp on a high bluff overlooking the valley of the Rio Puerco through which the well-travelled trail to Albuquerque passed. They looked for signs of a campfire and rode slowly down the trail listening for the sounds of horses, but all was quiet. Snow and wind blanketed the smoke of any fire the raiders might build at their campsite.

The following day the men covered a great many miles, but in the wrong direction. They finally returned to Mother Red Lake to report their failure. She listened without comment while she continued with her weaving. After they had gone she sat quietly at her loom, her usually busy hands now folded in her lap. Tears blurred her eyes as she thought of her daughter, whom she might never see again. After a while she rose, straightened her skirt and went to walk with María among the sheep. The calmly grazing sheep soothed and comforted her and helped to bring her shattered world back together again.

Gray Hat returned a few weeks later from his fruitless visit to Santa Fe. The governor had promised the Navajo headmen that the American army would stop the Mexican raids against the Navajo people. He had told them that the New Mexicans and the Navajos must stop all raids and that if they did not stop, they would be hunted down and killed by the American soldiers. To show his good will, the governor had given each headman a pair of black trousers with silver ornaments and a black, wide-brimmed hat.

Gray Hat was very angry when he heard of the loss of his daughter. "The Americans will change nothing," he said. "We must continue our fight with the Mexicans until they are all destroyed, or they and their American friends will destroy us. I will have another talk with Manuelito and plan what is to be done."

12

THE RAIDERS WERE NOT THE USUAL MEXICANS from the Rio Grande settlements which their Navajo pursuers had supposed them to be. They were part of a large group of sixty men recruited from the vicinity of Chihuahua, the capital city, to obtain Indian slaves for the rich ranchers and Mexican officials. Slave trade was very profitable, and it was hoped that this raid would net the backers at least twenty thousand dollars.

The four men who had captured Shebah headed southwest and crossed the Albuquerque Trail about ten miles west of where their pursuers were looking for them. They crossed the valley of the Rio Puerco that night and continued south to the Little Colorado River. Other small raiding parties joined them along the way to the rendezvous at the river. The raids had been successful, and the leaders planned to start for home. Hopis had been taken from their fields surrounding the high mesas; Navajos had been captured near the mouth of the Canyon de Chelly and along the Little Colorado River; and Zuñis had been surprised in their fields outside the pueblo. Fifty live sheep were taken from the Zuñi herds to be killed, as needed, to feed the party. As group after group joined the main party, the prisoners' hopes of escape faded. The party had no fear of attack by pursuers or by any small Apache hunting party as no one would attack sixty men armed with rifles. The problem now was to find enough food to sustain the raiders and their prisoners on the four hundred mile journey which lay ahead.

Shebah sat looking sullenly at the ground in front of her in the group of about one hundred other captives comprised of men, women and children. Their hands were tied behind their backs and their feet tightly tied with leather thongs. Most of the women and children cried softly. She let her eyes wander occasionally to the strange men, dressed so differently from her people, as they went about their camp chores, speaking to each other in a language she did not understand. Most of the Mexicans wore loose fitting black trousers and loosely woven black wool jackets. On their heads they wore wide-brimmed hats held by leather straps which they tied under their chins. Many had bewhiskered

53

faces and bushy mustaches. Others were smooth-skinned like the Indian people. They carried coarsely woven blankets tied behind the saddles, and lassos of woven horsehair were tied to every saddle. A leather pouch held their prized muzzle-loading rifles, and a lance of wood tipped with a steel knife blade was strapped to their backs.

When all the raiders had assembled, their leaders started the party moving southward along the west side of the Continental Divide. The high, pine-covered Sierra Escudilla Mountain Range at the headwaters of the Little Colorado River was the major obstacle to be surmounted. Snow lay deep and their progress would be very slow. They would avoid the rough Mogollon Mountains as it would not be possible to pass through them at this time of year.

For three days they plodded southward, making camp in open areas where the sheep could find patches of grass not covered by snow to regain their strength. Some of the men hunted deer, which were plentiful in the lower valleys. When they were rested they started southward again. Finally they crossed the Gila River into Mexico. As they descended from the high mountain country into the land of the giant saguaro cactus, the prisoners stared in amazement at these people-like plants which seemed to be standing in groups or trying to climb to the tops of the hills to look around. They soon learned to avoid the chola cactus with its sharp needles which seemed to leap from the plants to embed themselves in any unwary horse or human.

They passed by small ranches located on small streams which flowed from the mountains only to be lost in the prairie before reaching the Rio Grande. The ranch owners had built dams to impond the water for their livestock and canals to lead the water to their fields. The party stopped at these ponds to water their horses and to fill their canteens. Many of the ranchers rode over to greet the party and to bargain for the prisoners, but few were sold as the party leaders knew their captives would bring higher prices farther south. Most of the field hands working on the border ranches

54

were Pima and Papago Indians, but a few of the more northern tribes were represented as the ranchers preferred sheepherders from the Zuñi and Navajo tribes. They used their own Mexican cowboys to patrol the range and to take care of the cattle.

About fifty miles from Chihuahua, they stopped near the large ranch of Don Pedro. The Don owned more than one hundred thousand acres of good farming and grazing land granted to his family long ago by the Spanish king. He also owned silver mines in the nearby mountains. His family had managed to maintain good relations with those in power after the overthrow of Spain and the establishment of the Mexican Republic and had many influential friends in both Chihuahua and in Mexico City. One of his sons was a government official in Guadalajara, where he protected the interests of his father and father-in-law. One daughter was married to a rich merchant in Mexico City and his other daughter was the wife of a large rancher near Guadalajara. His oldest son, Juan, and wife, Isabella, stayed at the ranch to help Don Pedro. The Don's wife had died ten years before, but even during her life she had spent as little time with her husband as possible, as she preferred the social life of Mexico City and Spain.

Although Don Pedro was in his early fifties and gray streaks were appearing in his coal black hair, he was still as active as a young man. His slim, neat figure on his great, black stallion was a common sight as he rode constantly over the ranch, stopping to discuss ranch problems with his overseers. He prided himself on his immaculate appearance and demanded that his servants keep his stock of white shirts and black trousers spotless. One of the house boys spent most of his time polishing his master's boots and silver ornamented saddles.

The Mexican raiding party camped near a pond a few miles from the ranch, and Don Pedro, accompanied by two of his overseers, rode over to look at the captives. The Don was in need of sheepherders, as favorable weather had increased the size of his herds. He chose six of the Zuñi captives, four men and two women. He asked the leader of the party if he had brought any of the famous Navajo weavers.

"All Navajo women are weavers, my patron," answered the leader, "and all Hopi men are equally skilled at the loom."

"If they do not have the skill now, they can learn," replied Don Pedro. "Weaving is in their blood. I will take that young husky girl over there," pointing to Shebah, "and that man who sits so patiently plaiting a few strands of grass," a Hopi man about thirty years of age. Two men of the raiding party led the captives he had chosen over to where Don Pedro sat straight and proud, looking down on the tired and dirty assembly. "What is the price you are asking for these Indians I have chosen?" he asked the leader.

The leader lined up the captives and said, "This one is worth four hundred dollars and this one three hundred and fifty dollars." As he walked along the line, he set a price for each of the captives which the Don had selected.

When he had finished, Don Pedro turned to his overseers and asked if they were satisfied with the prisoners. They both pointed out defects and reminded the Don that the prices he had paid for servants in previous years had been lower. Finally a price of twenty-five hundred dollars for the eight prisoners was agreed upon, and one of the overseers was sent back to the corral near the main house for horses to transport the new servants to the ranch houses. Shebah and the two Zuñi women were turned over to a Mexican woman who locked them in a room of one of the long, adobe servants' quarters. The men were taken to a bunk house where they could be watched until such time as they could be trusted not to attempt to escape.

Don Pedro had more than one hundred servants and employees on the ranch and at the mines. Most of them were content to stay and work at the jobs assigned to them. The work was not too hard; they were well fed, provided

56

with sufficient clothing, and sheltered in adobe buildings which were superior to the homes from which they had come. It was true that they were slaves in that they were not permitted to leave the ranch, but in exchange for their freedom, Don Pedro supplied them with the necessities of life and provided security for them and their families, from cradle to grave, provided they did as they were told. Although the servants were content, they were not always happy. At times they thought of their own people and of the land of their birth so far away and longed to return even though it meant a return to a harder life.

13

SHEBAH WAS FRIGHTENED AND VERY UNHAPPY. There was no one she could talk to. She had been put in a small room along with the two Zuñi women captives in one of the adobe buildings that housed some of the field workers. The room was empty except for a pile of sheepskins in one corner. The prisoners sat at the far side looking at the barred door. In a short while the door opened and a Mexican girl brought them enchiladas wrapped around some ground meat and an earthen water jug. She talked to the prisoners as she entered, but they could not understand anything the girl said. Finally she placed the basket of food and the water jug in the center of the room and left. When she had gone, Shebah and the Zuñi women ate. The frightened Zuñis talked in low tones for a while, then the older one rose and tried to open the weathered pine door but it was barred from the outside. She looked at the small high window so narrow that a person would have had difficulty squeezing through even if it had not had wooden bars set across the opening. She looked at the pile of sheepskins, selected two, laid them in one corner, then lay down on them and closed her eyes. Shebah and the other Zuñi woman sat with their backs against the wall, watching. Finally they rose and went to get sheepskins from the pile. They made themselves comfortable and slipped into an uneasy sleep.

In the morning the Zuñi women were taken to join other men and women of their tribe. A pretty young Mexican woman in a long tan skirt and white blouse came to get Shebah. She spoke kindly as she took the Navajo girl by the arm, but Shebah quickly jerked away and stepped back. The Mexican woman continued speaking softly and motioned for Shebah to follow her. She led the frightened girl to the walled courtyard of the main house. Against one wall of the courtyard Shebah saw two Navajo women sitting at their looms weaving blankets. Her guide led her to where the middle-aged Navajos were weaving and spoke to them in Spanish. They answered her, then one of them turned to Shebah and said, in Navajo, "This woman, María, wants you to stay with us. She will have another loom brought so you can weave blankets. Sit here now by me, and I will tell you what you are to do." Shebah sat down and María left them.

The Navajos were eager to hear about their people, but as neither of them were of the Red House Clan, Shebah could tell them nothing about their families. She told them of how she had been captured and of the long trip south. Shebah had spoken to no one for over a month, and now her words tumbled out as she told her story to her tribeswomen. They welcomed her and encouraged her to keep talking. It was good to have another Navajo to talk with.

"We will teach you how to speak Spanish," they said. "Life here is much easier if you understand what these people are saying."

As they sat and talked, Shebah looked around at the courtyard. All around the walls there were bright-colored flowers of purple, red, and yellow. Some of the flowering vines tumbled over the adobe walls. Roofs shaded the flagstone verandas on two sides from which doors opened into the homes of Don Pedro and his son, Juan. On the side of the courtyard, where the women were weaving, four doors opened through the adobe walls into the family warehouse rooms and servant quarters. Strings of bright red peppers hung from the wall near the warehouse door. The courtyard was neat and clean as the packed earth and flagstones were swept daily by the house servants. In one corner there was a well from which the family obtained water for household purposes.

Shebah became calmer as she sat in the pleasant courtyard, talking in her own tongue to the Navajo women, but she was startled every time a door opened. The house servants made frequent trips to the warehouse and to the well in order to see what kind of new Navajo slave Don Pedro had bought. Soon two men came with smooth poles for Shebah's loom. They spoke to the Navajo weavers and the women showed them how to set up the loom alongside the ones they worked at. María brought another servant carrying a basket of various colored balls of wool for Shebah to use.

"What shall I weave?" asked Shebah.

The women said, "Don Pedro likes the blankets we weave. Make yours the same size as ours. What design does your clan use?" Shebah drew a sketch on the ground of a striped blanket while the women watched.

"I will make this stripe red, this one blue, this one tan and this one black," she said. "Does this family have enough red and blue yarn?"

"Don Pedro has yarn of all colors," replied the women. "He has enough yarn to make a thousand blankets."

At noon, María came with a house servant, bringing the weavers enchiladas and goat milk. As they ate, Shebah asked, "Why do you not run away from this ranch and return to your people? You are not tied and no one watches you."

"We are watched," replied one of the women. "We would not go far if we did leave the courtyard. If we did manage to escape we would soon be killed or captured by the Mexicans or the Apaches. There is no way for us to travel alone back to our people. They are too far away. Five years ago, when we were brought to this place, we made many plans to escape. Since then we have heard of the men running away, but they are always brought back. It is best that we stay here. We are well treated, we have good clothing, we are well fed, and our room is warm and dry. Besides we each have a child born here at the ranch. María keeps them with the other children while we weave, but you will see them tonight. Since they were born, we have not been so lonesome for our people. If our families were here with us, we would be happy. Maybe some day we will take our children and return to our country."

María returned in midafternon with a blanket dress over her arm. She spoke to the Navajo women, asking, "What is this girl called?"

One of them turned to Shebah and asked, "What is your name?" The girl hesitated as she tried to think of a name to tell them, but she could not seem to think and finally admitted that her mother called her "Shebah."

"Very well," said María, "have Shebah wash her entire body as I have taught you to do, with soap, and put on this clean dress. Her hair must be washed and brushed. Tell her she must keep herself clean as you do."

The Navajo women took Shebah to their room which was bare except for a large pile of sheepskins in one corner,

60

a few loosely woven blankets hanging from wooden wall pegs and two large earthen water jugs which stood near the doorway. One of the women picked up a jug and told Shebah to bring the other one. They went to the well and she showed Shebah how to drop the wooden bucket into the well and how to turn the windlass to wind up the rope that brought the bucket of water to the top. They filled their jugs and took them to their room. "Wet your hands then take this soap and make a lather to wash yourself as I do," explained the woman. "It will wash off the dirt and the dry skin just like yucca root. I will go to the warehouse and get some yucca root for you to wash your hair."

While she was gone, Shebah washed, and the other Navajo woman poured water over her, then gave her a blanket to keep her warm until she was dry. Shebah washed her hair, then went outside to sit in the sun. She brushed her hair until it shone, and as she brushed, she began to feel better. She even hummed a little tune.

Just before sunset, the children came running to their mothers who gathered them in their arms and spoke to them as though they had been gone a long time. The children chattered in Spanish until they noticed Shebah; then they became shy and tried to hide behind their mothers. The mothers explained in Navajo that Shebah had come to live with them and told them to make her welcome. They built a small fire outside and brewed some wild tea until dark. Then they went inside and were soon asleep.

The next morning they were up early. The women washed their children's faces and brushed their hair. When María came to get the children, she looked at Shebah and said, "Now that you are clean, I see that you are a very pretty girl." The two Navajo women looked at each other but said nothing. María turned to the children and said, "Come on with me, and I will get you something good to eat for your breakfast." The children ran to her, and she took them into the house to eat with the other children.

Shebah and her two companions went to their looms and started working. Shebah asked, "What did María say to me when she came for the children?"

The older woman replied, "María said you looked better now that you are clean."

14

ALTHOUGH THE RANCHERS AND GOVERNMENT officials were worried and met to discuss the possibility of an invasion of their country by the Americans, life went on as usual at Don Pedro's ranch. The servants rose at the usual hour and worked at their usual tasks.

The days and months passed, and Shebah gradually adjusted to her new life. She learned to recognize the people who came and went through the courtyard. There was Don Pedro, the master, who mounted his great black horse about an hour after sunrise and returned from his tour of the ranch just as the shadows stretched halfway across the court-yard. Some days he stopped to look at the work of the weavers.

There was María, a pleasant young woman, who saw that everyone was fed and who watched the progress of the weaving and, occasionally, suggested patterns to be followed. María was the efficient head housekeeper who saw that the house was kept clean, the clothes washed and the food prepared. She directed the work of the eight house servants who came and went in the courtyard. They swept the courtyard daily as soon as the Don had left; once a week they hung the master's clothes and his snowy white sheets and pillow cases in the courtyard to dry, and in the evening they sprinkled the yard and watered the plants that grew along the walls.

There was Don Juan, the son of the master, who spent most of his time at the mine but returned to his father's house occasionally to discuss mine operations and shipments of silver. Don Juan's wife, Doña Isabella, divided her time between her house at the mine and her rooms at the south side of the courtyard. She was seldom seen in the courtyard before late afternoon. She usually appeared in immaculate riding clothes, spoke kindly to any servant who happened to be in the courtyard, then mounted and rode away on her sorrel mare. It was her custom to ride slowly through the servants' quarters where the women bowed and gave her a friendly greeting, then to ride on until she was out of sight in the hills. Once out of sight she tied her hat tightly under her chin and let the mare race until both of them were exhausted. With nerves once more calmed, she would ride slowly back to the ranch house, bathe and dress for dinner.

When she was dressed she would have a rocking chair brought out on the flagstone and would sit, pretending to read, while she waited to see if Don Pedro would ask her to have dinner with him. She disliked her father-in-law but was polite to him and considered it her duty to have dinner with him if he so desired. When her husband was at the ranch, they ate in Don Pedro's dining room so the two men could discuss the affairs of the ranch and any news that may have been brought by riders from their friends and relatives in the cities.

At Christmas time Don Pedro always arranged a fiesta to be held for all his people. Indians and Mexicans alike looked forward to this fiesta, which broke the monotony of

64

their everyday lives, and to the gifts which were passed out by the Don.

As the women sat and wove, her two friends explained to Shebah what had happened at previous fiestas. "The fiesta will be just outside the gates of the courtyard," one of them said. "There will be many fires to roast the sheep and beef. There will be baskets of enchiladas, tacos, and brown sugar candy, and there will be barrels of red wine on stands along the courtyard wall. Everyone may have all they can eat and drink."

On Christmas morning everyone appeared at the small chapel and the Mexicans went inside to worship. Soon Don Pedro appeared to speak to all his people and to hand out gifts, bright-colored necklaces for the women, beaded hatbands for the men, and small toys for the children. Homemade gifts were exchanged by the women and children. Many of the Mexican men had brought their guitars and sat around playing and singing. As the day wore on, the fiesta became lively. Barrels of wine were opened and the tempo of the music became faster. The men started dancing and a circle was formed around them. Everyone clapped and shouted as they urged the dancers to greater endeavors. Many of the women had brought their clicking castanets to keep time with the music and they were soon twirling and stamping as each one tried to outdo the other. The crowd applauded constantly, pausing only to get a bite to eat or another drink of wine. Soon the Indians were following the lead of the Mexicans making up their own steps as they stamped about the fires.

When the dancing was well underway, Don Pedro entered the circle to show the people his skill in dancing, and he was soon joined by his son. Both men were excellent dancers and drew loud applause from the crowd. As the night wore on most of the celebrators either staggered away or were carried to their beds, and only a few of the more hardy cowboys lasted until the wine barrels were empty.

Doña Isabella sat at a table on the roof of the ranch

65

house where she could watch the dancing and, incidentally, the behavior of her husband and father-in-law. Don Juan joined her occasionally, but the more she drank wine to relieve her bitter feelings, the more acid in tone her criticisms became. Don Juan was angered by her unladylike behavior, so he decided to stay below and enjoy himself. He drank a great deal and joined his father in the fast dancing with the women.

Doña Isabella's servants tried to comfort her as they always did. They felt very sorry for her because she was kind to them, but she was very lonely and very bored with life at the ranch. Her only pleasure seemed to be when she raced across the prairie on her sorrel mare. Now she sat watching the crowd, but her thoughts were of her son whom she had sent away to school in Mexico City. She decided she would go to the capital in the spring to see him and her relatives. She motioned one of her servants to prepare her bed, then rose and retired to her room.

15

THE YEARS OF 1848, 1849, AND 1850 SAW NO changes in the American, New Mexican, and Navajo relations. Raids by Navajos and New Mexicans continued; threats and promises were made by Governor Washington

and his successor, Governor Monroe. The rapidly changing army officers and men brought new ideas of how to deal with the Indians. Some of them realized that the real trouble was due to the New Mexican desire to expand westward into Navajo country. Others were anxious to fight the Indians in order to gain promotions and to further their army careers. Occasionally, small groups of soldiers were sent to ride along the well-worn trails passing through Navajo country. However, as these soldiers never encountered any Navajo or New Mexican raiding parties, they had little effect on the continuing warfare between the two races.

In 1849, Colonel Washington led an expedition into Navajoland to meet with Narbona. The great chief and a group of his people met the Colonel's American and New Mexican troops near Washington Pass. While the headman was talking to Colonel Washington, a New Mexican guide claimed he recognized a horse ridden by one of the Navajos to be one that had been stolen from him, and demanded that it be returned. The Navajo refused and the New Mexican, under the protection of the soldiers, boldly tried to take the horse by force. When the Navajo resisted, the soldiers opened fire killing Narbona and several of his men.

The other Navajos fled into the mountains, and some of them brought word to Manuelito of the murder of his father-in-law. Manuelito set off at once to avenge Narbona but arrived too late. He led his angry band to the Rio Grande, attacked a village north of Santa Fe, killed a few New Mexicans and drove off several hundred head of sheep. Narbona was dead and could no longer speak of keeping the friendship of the Americans. Manuelito could now speak to his wife's people, without opposition, of banding together to fight their enemies.

In 1851, another new commander, Colonel Edwin Sumner, was sent to reorganize the army in New Mexico. He decided to construct a fort in the heart of the Navajo country at the junction of Bonito and Black Creeks and to name it Fort Defiance. There was good grazing and water for the horses in this beautiful valley, and trails from it led in every direction making the Tunichas and the Canyon de Chelly areas easy to reach by scouting parties. The soldiers laid out a parade ground covering about twelve acres, and around it they built a quadrangle of rock and adobe buildings to serve as offices, barracks, and storehouses.

The Navajos watched with great interest as the construction progressed, and they returned to their homes with new ideas to be incorporated into their hogans and corrals. Rock walled hogans began to appear here and there replacing the cedar and goat skinned tent-like hogans commonly used. (However, it was not until the Navajos obtained axes and saws that any great change was made in the style of dwellings.) It was not until another twenty years had passed and the railroads started crossing Navajoland that the Navajos adopted notched logs, similar to the hewn ties used to construct barracks for the railroad workers, to construct the log hogans in use today.

The plowing and cultivation of the garrison garden was of equal interest to the Navajos, who had no gardening implements other than pointed sticks. The fort commander noted their interest and sought their friendship by giving them a few hoes and spades, which they put to good use in their own fields. This small gesture of friendship brought peace to the area around the fort for several years.

The new fort effectively stopped raiding in the nearby area lying west of the Tunicha Mountains, but had no effect on the eastern portion of Navajoland. In the east, raids by both Navajos and New Mexicans continued as the latter continued pushing westward from the Rio Grande, grazing their herds on larger and larger areas of the lands claimed by the Navajos.

Under the protection of Fort Defiance, the Red House Clan prospered. Gray Hat's family farmed and raised their sheep without fear of attack. Favorable weather and the use of the new farm implements increased their crops to such an extent that they had a surplus of corn and melons to

69

trade at the fort. Navajo men and women began drifting into Fort Defiance to trade sheep, wool, and blankets for tools, clothing, and silver ornaments.

At Gray Hat's camp, the main subject of conversation as the family sat around the fire eating became what was happening in the Canyon Bonito. The women and children listened to the stories told by the men and boys and became more and more interested in seeing what the white men were doing. One morning as the family was eating, Gray Hat announced that he was going to the new fort. Hesbah said, "I would like to see the fort you have been telling us so much about, my father. Will you take me with you? I will give you a blanket I finished yesterday to trade for one of those iron pots like you brought for my mother. I will need it to take to my new home next week when I am married."

Gray Hat and his wife laughed. "I think our daughter will be a good wife," he said. "She is already planning what she will cook for her man even before the wedding."

"Yes," said Mother Red Lake, "we must see that our daughter has everything she will need. I would not want our Kiya' a' anii in-laws to think that their son is marrying the daughter of a poor family. I, also, would like to go to the fort. The boys will go with us and we can stay in the hills and watch when you go into the American camp. I will give you a blanket to trade for an axe which my daughter will also need to take with her to her new home. It is very easy for a woman to keep a supply of wood for her fire if she has a fine axe like the one the Americans gave you. We can bring in larger pieces of wood than we did in the old days when we had to break the tree branches with a rock."

"Very well," said Gray Hat, "but if we have so much business to attend to at the fort, I think we should wait until tomorrow. We will plan to start early in the morning so we can return before it becomes dark."

The next morning everyone was up before the sun ap-

70

peared. As they packed the horses Mother Red Lake asked Joni, "Would you like to go with us, my daughter?"

Joni replied, "No, my mother, I do not like to go near the soldiers. Those who came to Don Pablo's ranch were very rough men. They threatened us with their great knives and their guns. You must be careful that they do not see you or they will take you into the fort and we will never see you again. I will stay here and look after the sheep."

Mother Red Lake spoke to her husband of what Joni had said. "The girl is crazy," replied Gray Hat. "The soldiers are our friends and will not harm us. They have given me many gifts to take to our home. You and Hesbah can stay with the horses a short distance from the fort, but you do not have to hide from the soldiers."

They arrived at the fort shortly before noon and tied the horses about five hundred yards away from the entrance. Mother Red Lake built a small fire and set a jar of water to boil for tea. Gray Hat took the rugs to be traded and walked slowly toward the fort. The two women and the boys stared at the fort. They could see soldiers walking about between the buildings.

It was not long before everyone in the fort knew that two Navajo women were camped outside. Four of the soldiers started walking toward the little party but turned away when an officer shouted for them to leave the women alone. A small detachment of mounted men rode out of the fort and passed close by to look before starting out on their scouting mission. Mother Red Lake and Hesbah were very nervous and wished that Gray Hat would hurry so they could leave.

After several hours had passed, Mother Red Lake sent Chiquito to see what had happened to her husband. Chiquito found his father in the building the army used as a trading post with several other Navajos looking at the guns and knives. The boy stood just inside the doorway looking at everything in the room. He noticed that his father still had the three blankets they had brought to trade hung over

71

one shoulder. Gray Hat looked directly at the boy but did not speak or motion to Chiquito to join him.

After one more glance around the room, Chiquito slipped out of the door and went to tell his mother that Gray Hat had not yet traded the blankets. Mother Red Lake sighed and settled herself more comfortably to wait. She and the children were not bored. This was an exciting adventure. They made Chiquito repeat what he had seen inside the building and the boy added something new each time he told the story. They watched the soldiers and, as none came near, lost a little of the fear they had first felt. They talked of the soldiers' nice clothes and of the well-built stone and adobe houses the Americans had built.

Finally Gray Hat returned with all the articles they had come for, wrapped in his blanket. The boys ran to help him and carried the bundle back to their mother. She did not examine the contents as she did not want the soldiers to think that she did not trust the judgment of her husband. She told the boys to pack everything on the horses. Then, with Gray Hat in the lead, they left the fort and headed home.

16

THE YEARS OF 1847 THROUGH 1851 BROUGHT little change to the lives of the people at the ranch of Don Pedro. Twice during this period slave traders had stopped near the ranch, but no new slaves had been purchased. Many of the slaves' children were now old enough to help with the chores, and the older men they replaced were sent to help at the mines.

At sixteen Shebah was a beautiful young woman. She tried to copy María as much as possible. She had learned to braid her long black hair and to tie it up in rolls like her Mexican friend. The designs of her blankets had become more imaginative and the geometric figures now covered them from top to bottom. Even Don Pedro stopped more often to observe her work and to compliment her on her skill. María had taken an instant liking to the young Navajo girl, and with her help, as well as the help of her two weaving companions, Shebah had learned to speak the Spanish language. Occasionally, with the Don's permission, María took Shebah on short rides around the ranch. On one occasion they rode as far as one of the sheep camps to watch some servants shearing the sheep. As they approached two Navajo men, one of them spoke to the other in a tone loud enough for Shebah to hear. "If you were a woman like that one who sits so grandly on her horse watching us work," he said, "you would not have to shear the sheep."

His companion spat on the ground in the direction of the girl, then spoke directly to her. "Do not come to watch us as though we are your slaves," he said. "You seem to forget that you are also a slave and no better than we are. Go back to the bed of your master. You are a disgrace to our people."

Shebah blushed, but said nothing as she turned her horse and rode a little distance away. She felt very lonely, as though she had been rejected by all of her tribe, and decided she would remain in the safety of the courtyard where she would not be subject to any insulting remarks. María, sensing that something was wrong, asked, "What did those men say to you? They are your people but they did not seem friendly." Shebah replied, "Oh, they just said they had many sheep to shear and that I should be

helping them." No more was said, but on future rides Shebah was careful not to go close to the servants who worked
in the fields.

It was well known by all the servants that Don Pedro
had fathered many of the children at the ranch, but they
could only resent and say nothing. The Don explained to
his son that only by siring the children of the servant women could he ever improve the quality of his servants.

When Don Juan tried to explain his father's actions to
Doña Isabella she laughed and asked him sarcastically what
he thought of his half-brothers and sisters. "You know my
father does not consider the children the same as his legiti-
mate offspring," he said. "He does not even think of them
as his children. He is only concerned with developing a
smarter group of servants."

The Doña always became angry when her husband de-
fended his father. "And I suppose you are following your
father's example," she said. "How many of the children I
see when I ride around the ranch belong to you? Never mind
answering. You and your father may do as you like. I have
made up my mind to leave the ranch so I will not interfere."

17

IN 1853, CAPTAIN HENRY DODGE WAS APPOINTED
Indian Agent and, unlike previous agents, this brave man
decided to live in Navajoland and get acquainted with the

Navajo people. He built a stone house at Sheepsprings near the east end of the historic invasion trail which ascends the Tunicha Mountains and passes over the range at Washington Pass. His predecessors had preferred to live in the comparative comfort of Santa Fe or Jemez where they would not be bothered by the Indians they were paid to represent. The previous agents had been well entertained at the homes of wealthy ranchers with good food and tales of the savage raids which the Navajos had made on their homes and their herds. The agents had closed their eyes to the sight of the hundreds of Navajo slaves working on the ranches of their hospitable hosts. As it had long been the hope of all the ranchers along the Rio Grande that some day they might take over the lands of the Navajos, they spared no effort in their attempt to enlist the aid of the Americans in their war against the Indians.

The Navajos made Captain Dodge welcome to their land. It was not long until he was accepted as a friend by the tribe. He travelled constantly with his interpreter to the camps of the headmen. As he became better known, many of the young men rode with him. They told stories of what "Red Sleeves" had done or said at the homes he visited, of what gifts had been exchanged and of what games had been played to honor the Captain. Finally the Captain moved to Fort Defiance where he believed he could promote better relations between the army and the Navajos. He continued his visits to the people from his new headquarters.

In Red Lake Valley Gray Hat planned a rabbit hunt in honor of "Red Sleeves." He sent word to his clansmen along the Tunicha Mountains and westward to the Canyon de Chelly. It was September and most of the families were still in the mountains harvesting the crops from their small mountain farms and getting ready to move down to their winter homes in the valley. A few families had already returned to harvest crops they had planted in the low valleys. The Navajos had not planted the seed corn which had been given them as they feared the gods would not approve

75

of any corn other than the varicolored kind that they had given the people. The yellow corn might bring bad luck, and besides, the pollen from the alien corn would not be acceptable to the gods, so the cornmeal could not be used in any ceremonials. The seed corn had been eaten and nothing had been said.

As word of the rabbit hunt reached the families in the mountains, they started moving back to the valley, leaving only a few members and some slaves to finish the harvest. The sheep and horses were driven down to the winter corrals, and the best horses were chosen to be used in the hunt.

Captain Dodge waited at Fort Defiance until his Navajo friends brought word that the people were assembling at Gray Hat's camp. He and his young admirers arrived at the camp in a cloud of dust, yelling as loudly as possible to make their arrival noticed and to gain the attention of their audience. Kee held the Captain's horse while he dismounted, then led it away with the other horses to a brush corral which had been built a short distance from their camp. He admired the well-tanned leather saddle and the polished silver ornaments and remarked to one of the men that "Red Sleeves" must have bought the saddle from the Spanish. "I will have one like it some day," he said.

When Kee returned to the fire, the Captain was already seated and was drinking a cup of tea while he conversed with Gray Hat. Mother Red Lake had put some lamb ribs on the fire as soon as the Captain had arrived, and now she told Hesbah to take them to the men. She placed a basket of hot corn bread between them, then went back to her cooking. Soon medicine men and other headmen arrived to shake hands with Gray Hat and his important guest. They then sat down in a circle to take part in the talk and to be fed.

When he had eaten, Captain Dodge talked of some of his plans to help the Navajo people. He talked slowly and quietly in the manner of his Navajo friends in order to

77

gain their confidence. He told them of the blacksmith, George Carter, who would teach them to make bits for their horses, spades and hoes for their farms and knives. "George Carter will teach you how to make many useful things from iron," said the Captain, "and you may keep all the things you make. I think every family should send one young man to Fort Defiance to learn how to make the things his family needs."

He also told his attentive audience of Juan Anea, the silversmith, who would teach them how to make the beautiful ornaments they so greatly admired and for which, for many years, they had gone to Santa Fe to trade their blankets. Captain Dodge spoke with great enthusiasm, and his interpreter translated and added his own observations to the Captain's remarks.

In the evening the crowd gathered to take part or to sit and watch the men as they formed a large circle and sang songs of the old days. The women hummed or sang very softly as they sat and watched. After a while Gray Hat went to the center of the circle and held up his hands. "Let us show Red Sleeves how we dance the circle dance," he shouted. Many of the women and their daughters rose and formed a circle inside the men's circle. One of the men started beating a small drum, and the men started singing. Then the women added their voices. As they sang, the men's circle moved in one direction and the women moved in the opposite direction. Mother Red Lake pulled her husband to one side and said, "I think we should ask our guest to dance." Gray Hat went to the Captain, who was sitting by the fire watching the dancing with apparent pleasure, and took him by the arm. The Captain looked startled; then, realizing what his host wanted, he rose and walked to the circle. Gray Hat made a place for both of them and they danced with the men. Captain Dodge added his voice to the singing as he tried to follow the tune without the words. Finally the dance ended and the crowd dispersed to return to their camps.

The following morning everyone was up at sunrise. The

78

women and children and the men who were not riding climbed the small bluffs and hills on each side of the valley from which they could watch the riders. Gray Hat took Captain Dodge to a vantage point from which he could watch the rabbit hunt from start to finish. The men who would ride in the hunt led their bareback horses to the starting point and formed a line across the valley. They had removed all their clothing except their short buckskin breeches and head bands and carried only a smooth, curved stick about four feet long to throw at the rabbits. At a signal from the starter they yelled as loudly as possible and raced up the valley, each rider trying to outdistance the others.

Rabbits jumped up here and there from the high grass, and the sticks flew at them. In the excitement of this mass hunt, the men who ordinarily threw with great accuracy seemed to have lost their skill and many rabbits escaped only to be hit by the stick of the next rider. Some rabbits ran for the hills but were turned back by women and children. The horses shared in the excitement and were hard to control when the men dismounted to retrieve their sticks or pick up a rabbit. It was more than an hour before the men and exhausted horses gave up the wild game and went to the lake to cool off. When they returned to their families with the rabbits they had killed, they were teased by their relatives who had watched every move that was made during the hunt and now took the opportunity to tell their men what they should have done.

Captain Dodge was impressed as always with the incomparable horsemanship the Navajos displayed during the hunt. It seemed that every rider and horse were as one and that each anticipated every move of the other.

When the hunt and the visiting were over, the families began leaving to return to their homes where there was much work to be done. Captain Dodge thanked Gray Hat for inviting him and reminded him again of the iron worker and silversmith at the fort. He walked over to where Mother Red Lake was packing and thanked her for feeding

79

him. Then he mounted his horse and, with an escort of young men, galloped off toward Fort Defiance.

When they reached their homes the families began at once the work of preparing for the winter, as they felt they must make up for the day they had taken from their work to attend the rabbit hunt. Women husked corn, winnowed beans and sliced the melons, setting them in the sun to dry. Some of the men and boys repaired the winter hogans and the corrals. Others gathered huge piles of wood for the coming winter. The clan had nearly doubled in size during the past six years, and there were many children to be fed and clothed.

Near the hogan of Mother Red Lake there were now three hogans. Nazbah, as always, had rebuilt her hogan near that of her aunt, and Hesbah had brought her young Kiya' a' anii husband and built her hogan about a half mile away. The clever María had assumed the status of first wife upon the death of her older husband's Navajo wife and had moved her hogan closer to that of her foster mother. She and Hesbah continued to share their daily chores and often walked together to the hogan of Mother Red Lake, who always greeted them with an equal show of affection and gave them good advice as to how to keep their families healthy and happy. It was Mother Red Lake's custom to give the young women a little of her corn pollen to put in their buckskin pouches and to admonish them not to forget to give some to the gods every morning when they gave thanks for what they had received. "My family has prospered," she said, "because both your father and I pray and give corn pollen to the gods of the four directions every morning, as soon as we rise from our sheepskins."

The family seldom spoke of Shebah as the hard life they led had erased most of the memories of the girl from their minds. Sometimes, as she sat at her loom, Mother Red Lake would think of the times her happy daughter had sat beside her preparing the wool, and tears would come to her eyes as she wondered if Shebah were still alive and

80

what sort of life she could be living. Everyone missed She-bah during the moves to the mountain as they recalled something she had done on such moves in the past.

Since Shebah had been taken from them, all of the families sent their children in pairs, with two dogs to guard against an attack, to herd the sheep. There was little danger now, however, as the close proximity of the fort and the patrols of soldiers had stopped raids in the valley.

18

ALL WAS QUIET IN THE FORT DEFIANCE AREA until the spring of 1855. The soldiers visited and traded with the headmen and most of the Navajos felt free to visit at the fort. Some headmen, including the well-known Armijo, Zarcillas Largas, Agua Chiquito, Ganado Mucho, and Juanico, had thousands of sheep and large farms tended by their poorer relatives and slaves. All of the headmen urged their people to keep peace with the Americans and warned them not to raid the New Mexican villages in order that they might continue to prosper. Poorer Navajos did not agree with those who were rich. They continued their raids against the Pueblos, the New Mexicans, and their richer tribesmen, so that they too might grow rich and powerful.

The peaceful coexistence of Americans and Navajos was

not in accordance with Mormon plans to stop the westward expansion of the American people. They feared
they would be forced to move again if the Americans reached
the Colorado River. Gifts to the Utes, Paiutes, and some
of the poorer Navajos persuaded them to continue their
fight to hold the lands west of the Rio Grande. The Ute
chiefs rode through Navajoland asking the headmen to join
them, but the headmen refused to join with their hereditary
enemies. Besides, they were too busy increasing their herds
and enlarging their fields. In this new era of prosperity
they considered the Americans the best friends they had
ever had and had no intention of fighting their benefac-
tors.

The angry Utes and the Navajos who had joined them
struck first at the rich Navajos along the south side of the
San Juan River. They killed a few men and carried away
women, children, and livestock. Those who escaped fled
south to the protection of their American friends at Fort
Defiance. Having disposed of the Navajos along their south-
ern boundary, the Utes and their allies turned to the east
and attacked the pueblos and New Mexican villages near
Santa Fe. The soldiers came to the defense of the villages
and soon stopped the raids. The Ute chiefs soon decided
that the spoils of war were less rewarding than their former
Navajo slave raids. The war parties were disbanded and
small raiding parties, sometimes accompanied by the New
Mexicans, again struck into Navajoland.

The alliance of Utes with the New Mexicans had the
blessing of the Ute Indian Agent, as the New Mexicans had
convinced him that it was for the good of his country that
the Navajos be either exterminated or driven out of the
lands they coveted. The New Mexicans planned constantly
not only to win over the Ute Agent, but also the Governor
and the New Mexican Legislature, and to enlist the help
of Americans, Utes, Paiutes, and Pueblo tribes in driving
the Navajos out of Navajoland. They were impatient
with the slow progress of the American politicians and
alarmed at the growth of goodwill between the Navajos

and the Americans in the Fort Defiance area. They also feared that if they did not claim the lands soon, more influential Americans from the East might come to settle on the land. The New Mexicans believed that they must goad the Navajos into a war with the Americans and that the best way was to increase their raids and the Ute raids into Navajo country. At the same time as they increased their raids, they would send to the legislature reports of raids and outrages committed by the Navajos on the villages and ranches and demand that the government reimburse them for their losses.

While the New Mexicans were scheming as to how they could start a war between the Americans and the Navajos, the latter, particularly in the Fort Defiance area, were taking full advantage of their friendship with the soldiers. Many Navajos were becoming skilled as blacksmiths and silversmiths and were taking the tools and ornaments they made to their hogans. A few American traders had appeared in the area to trade cloth, tools, cooking utensils, and beads for blankets.

All that marred the friendly relationship was the action of some of the slave women who hoped to improve their position by accepting the sex-starved soldiers who gave them clothing and trinkets from the army trading post. The children they bore for the soldiers were referred to by the Navajos as stolen but were accepted by the families. The headmen spoke to Captain Dodge of the conduct of the soldiers. Gray Hat told him, "The Americans are welcome in our homes, but they must not molest our women. Our men are becoming angry and will kill any soldier they find with their women. It is best that your officers speak to the men in order to prevent another war between the Americans and my people. Some of our women think the soldiers wish to marry them and will protect them from the Navajos, but I do not think the soldiers wish to take the women to their homes when they leave this country. The soldiers must be told that this is a very serious matter and must be stopped at once."

Captain Dodge promised to speak to the officers whom he said would talk to their men. Navajo families watched their women more closely, and Navajos formed patrols to stop women from approaching the fort, but little was accomplished. The offenders became more cautious, and none of them were caught.

19

THE WINTER OF 1855-56 WAS A SEVERE ONE IN Navajoland. On Christmas Day the thermometer at Fort Defiance registered thirty-two degrees below zero. For two months blizzards swept across the land bringing deep snow drifts and forcing the people to move their herds southward toward the Little Colorado River. Thousands of sheep died in the snowbound corrals.

Gray Hat's family stayed in Red Lake Valley. The families of Mother Red Lake, Hesbah, and María joined and worked side by side in an effort to save as many sheep as possible. Men, women and children wrapped their arms and legs in grass and wool held in place with every available scrap of cloth. The men worked until they were ready to drop with their farm tools, uncovering grass and bushes to feed the hungry sheep. Branches were cut and shelters built against the hogans for the few ewes who were carrying lambs, and some of them were taken into the hogans. The rest of the animals huddled together in the corrals trying to extract a little warmth from each other. All the people worked until they were exhausted, slept huddled together until morning, and then returned to the struggle. Each morning they found more animals frozen. With tears in their eyes, they fought on until the first blizzard had subsided and the bitter cold wave had passed.

When it was over the families took stock of what animals they had left. The horses had drifted south ahead of the storm, and it was not known how many had survived. There were less than a hundred sheep left in the three corrals. Some of the other families had not fared as well as Gray Hat's family. There would not be enough sheep to feed all of the group for the remainder of the winter. Other blizzards came, but they were not accompanied by such severe cold and, as there were fewer sheep to feed, none were lost.

In February Gray Hat sent word to the other families of his clan to meet and decide what should be done. The men met at Gray Hat's hogan. A few of them rode in on horses they had somehow saved, but most of the men were on foot. Gray Hat said, "First we must have horses. Those of you who have horses will go south and find some horses to bring back to the valley. When we have horses we will go to the pueblos for sheep to rebuild our herds. We will share the sheep we now have until we are able to get some more. We will save as many of the ewes as we can."

María walked home with Hesbah and stopped to look at the few sheep left in the corral. She put her arm around her friend's shoulder and said, "It is hard to lose our sheep, my sister, but we will build up our herds again. The corrals will once more be full. When the men return with more sheep we will again see the lambs playing about and our large herds grazing in the valley. Do not cry or be discouraged. As long as we work together we will prosper."

While the men were gone to look for horses Gray Hat walked the long distance to Fort Defiance to discuss the condition of his people with his friend, Captain Dodge. The agent told him that he had already asked the Indian

Service for help, but any food they might send would not arrive until later in the summer. He questioned Gray Hat about his plans and about other Navajos in the area and as a gesture of goodwill offered the headman a sack of corn from the army warehouse. "I know the corn will not help much, as there are many mouths to feed," he said, "but our supply at the fort is not large enough to feed all the Navajos in this area." Gray Hat thanked the Captain and went to talk to other Navajos who had come to the fort in search of help. When he had left, Captain Dodge sat with his head in his hands, staring into the fireplace. He knew what was about to happen. The raids would start again as the Navajos rode out in search of food. They would not sit at home when their families were hungry.

The raids did start, mostly on the pueblos, but the New Mexicans renewed their claims of large thefts of sheep by the Navajos and demanded that the army start out immediately to punish the raiders and bring back the thousands of sheep that had been stolen. Captain Dodge was told to order the headmen to return the sheep to their rightful owners. He went to the headmen and told them that word had come to him that their people had stolen sheep from the New Mexicans and that they must be returned immediately. As the New Mexicans, as usual, had claimed greater losses than they had suffered, the Navajos could not have returned as many sheep as they were ordered to return, even if they had wished to do so. They had no intention of sending any sheep to their enemies and warned the Americans that if they chose to side with the New Mexicans they would no longer be considered friends of the Navajos. Manuelito again became the advisor and leader of the angry Indians in the Tunicha and Canyon de Chelly areas, and it was agreed that no sheep would be returned.

The spring of 1856 was one of intense activity as the Navajos increased the size of their fields to provide more food, and hunting parties went out to obtain enough meat

86

for the families. Only in an emergency was a sheep slaughtered. However, the summer was one of extreme drought and most of the low valley crops were lost. It seemed that the gods had turned against the Navajo people. Perhaps they had become too friendly with the strangers. The Americans were no longer friendly and offered no help. They insisted that the Navajos return the livestock they had stolen, but the headmen, who had seen their wealth destroyed by the Ute raiding parties and the weather, were in no mood to listen. In order to rebuild their herds they increased their raids on the pueblos and the New Mexican ranches. Captain Dodge was still accepted at their homes, but the headmen listened to him in silence and offered no comment when he urged them to stop the raids.

The Captain travelled constantly in an effort to stave off the trouble he saw approaching. He wrote many letters asking that food be sent to the Navajos but received no cooperation from his government. It seemed that war was near. The Navajos were determined to rebuild their herds, and the New Mexicans were determined to rid themselves of the Indians who held the lands they needed for the expansion of their ranches. Captain Dodge's last trip, to see how his Navajo friends were faring along the Little Colorado River ended this good man's career. His small party was attacked by the Chiricahua Apaches, and he was killed. His death was avenged by the army, which quickly moved into the land of the Apaches and started hunting them down and killing them. By the fall of 1857, most of the clan responsible for his death had been killed or driven across the border into Mexico.

The withdrawal of some of the soldiers from Fort Defiance for use in the Apache War was a signal to the Utes to raid the Navajos in the Tunicha and Canyon de Chelly areas. Ute and New Mexican raiders swept into the area but were repulsed by the Navajos, and few slaves were

87

captured. Navajo raiding parties retaliated and hit the New Mexicans along the Rio Grande. New complaints by the New Mexicans were heard in Santa Fe, and new demands were made for payment to compensate them for their losses.

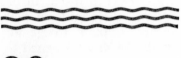

20

IT WAS DURING THE CHIRICAHUA APACHE WAR and the period of hostility between the Americans and the Navajos that Lieutenant Edwin Beale brought a camel train through Navajoland. The Americans had, for several years, been seeking a satisfactory route through New Mexico which could be used by the army and the pioneers on their way to California. It was believed that many miles could be saved if the trains did not have to swing south to follow the existing route through Tucson.

The Lieutenant left San Antonio, Texas, on June 25, 1857, travelled to Albuquerque where he loaded supplies on his camels, and then headed west along the well-travelled trail past Mount Taylor and Bear Springs to Fort Defiance. He arrived at the fort on August 26th, just fourteen days after leaving Albuquerque. The Navajos who witnessed this strange train moving through their land stared in astonishment at the "humpbacks" and spread the news of the

Kay Bennett

new animals the Americans had brought to use against them. Ample rainfall during the spring and summer of 1857 had made grass plentiful along the route and the Lieutenant wrote a glowing report of the country through which he passed. His report would have seemed strange to the soldiers who had experienced the drought of the previous year.

Gray Hat and Manuelito heard of the strange animals and rode to Fort Defiance to see the new mounts which the soldiers planned to use. From the top of a hill overlooking the fort they watched a small group of soldiers attempting to mount and ride the camels. "I wonder why the Americans have brought the humpbacks here," said Manuelito. "They cannot run as fast as our horses, and I do not think they can be ridden on our mountain trails."

"I would not want such animals in my camp," said Gray Hat. "They would be of no use to us, and I think they would bring us bad luck."

Few Navajos came near the fort to look at the camels. Word of the war in Apache country had travelled through Navajoland, and the people feared that the Americans would soon start raiding their homes. The headmen told their people to stay in the mountains where the herds could be hidden.

During the Apache War there were few soldiers left in Navajoland to interfere with Navajo and New Mexican raiding parties. However, with the defeat of the Apaches, the army returned to Fort Defiance and Fort Wingate and on September 8, 1858, formally declared war on the Navajo tribe.

Lieutenant Colonel Dixon Miles, who had been sent to Fort Defiance to organize the campaign, started out on September 9th with three hundred men, including some New Mexican volunteers, for the Canyon de Chelly where he hoped to catch the Navajos before they harvested their crops. Few of the Navajos in that area had taken part in any of the raids on the New Mexicans. They blamed the

90

Eastern Navajos for the trouble between the tribe and the Americans. Headmen had tried, many times, to explain to the Americans that there were many clans and many clan groups and that no one group could be held responsible for the misdeeds of another. However, it was easier for the military to think of the Navajos as a single group than to try to understand their complex society, and they held every member responsible for the actions of the others.

Warning of the raid reached the Navajos in the canyon the day before the soldiers arrived. The families hastily gathered their corn, even though some was still green, and with the rest of their belongings moved to the northern rim, then spread out among the hills. The soldiers descended into the upper end of the canyon and moved toward the mouth. They moved slowly, destroying all the crops that had not been carried away and set fire to hogan poles and log corrals. As the Navajos watched the destruction, they rolled rocks down on the troops and shouted insults, comparing their enemy to the sneaking coyotes and thieving crows.

The soldiers halted just before nightfall, in a wide spot at a bend in the canyon, about midway between where they had entered and the mouth. They built their fires near the center, as far from the vertical canyon walls as possible. After they had eaten, the tired men rolled up in their blankets, but no one slept. They could see hundreds of fires along the rim, and the Indians continued shouting and rolling stones into the canyon throughout the night. The following morning the soldiers resumed their march and finally reached the welcome sight of broad, open fields at the mouth. Six Navajo men who came too close were shot near the mouth of the canyon, and six women and children belatedly trying to drive their sheep to safety were captured. The captives were turned over to the New Mexicans to be sold as slaves as payment for their help in the campaign.

As soon as the soldiers were gone, men from the Canyon

91

de Chelly rode to tell their relatives in the Tunicha Mountains of what had happened. One of them rode to the camp of Gray Hat.

The headman was sitting in a small grove of oak trees talking to his wife as she worked at her loom. He rose to see who came galloping so fast across the valley, then said, "I think he is the cousin of Black Horse who lives near the Canyon de Chelly. I wonder why he is riding so fast." Mother Red Lake looked but said nothing. A lump rose in her throat and a feeling of fear swept over her. The rider raced across the field to where Gray Hat stood, and the headman held the exhausted horse as he dismounted. He told the rider to sit down, then led the horse to the corral a short distance away. Mother Red Lake greeted the rider, handed him a gourd of cool spring water and started preparing something for him to eat.

The man said, "I have ridden all night to warn you that the soldiers are killing all of our people that they can find. They are destroying all our fields and burning our hogans. They marched through the Canyon de Chelly, burning the corn and shooting at our people, but we stayed out of range of their guns and only a few of us were hit. They found many of our sheep and drove them away, and they took some of our women and children with them. It is not safe for any of us to stay where they can find us. We must all hide until the raids are over."

Gray Hat agreed. "My clan plans to stay in the mountains as long as possible," he said. "I will send word of what has happened at the Canyon de Chelly and tell all of the families to be ready to move. We will send out more scouts to watch the soldiers, and they will tell us which way the soldiers are moving."

Gray Hat's group of the Kinlichine Clan divided their sheep into small herds and scattered out over a larger area in the high mountains. The scouts kept them informed of activities around Fort Defiance, but all remained quiet as the officers planned their next campaign. On September

29, the scouts brought word that a large troop had left the fort and was riding toward Chuska Valley on the east side of the Tunicha Range. The scouts reported their progress as the soldiers moved up the valley.

The Navajos had seen soldiers riding through the valley many times during the past ten years. They had watched them from the safety of the Tunichas; however, they had never done any harm. This time, however, they saw the soldiers stopping to destroy hogans and to burn the drying cornstalks in the fields. New Mexican guides led the soldiers into small branch valleys where they had not gone in previous years and captured thousands of sheep which the Kiya' a' anii thought were safely hidden. The raids on his wife's people angered Manuelito, and he tried to enlist the help of other headmen, but they were all more concerned with moving their families to safety than fighting the Americans. Finally he persuaded a group of young men to attack the soldiers who were guarding the stolen sheep. Navajo bows and arrows proved poor weapons against the rifles of the guards, and ten of his men were killed.

Manuelito was discouraged. For ten years he had been telling the headmen that the clans must band together to fight the raiders. In times of quiet they had agreed, but when the enemy appeared, they ran and hid. With the exception of the Bitahni Clan, each Navajo family group stood alone and each headman was solely responsible for the welfare of the members. Occasionally, families of the same clan did combine forces to raid the pueblos or the New Mexican villages, but they did not band together to repel raids made against them.

The Navajo defense had always been to hide from their enemies, and for hundreds of years this strategy had proved successful. Only the richer Navajos had suffered because jealous members of the tribe often disclosed their hiding places to the enemy. In this rugged land in which there are thousands of valleys and canyons in which to hide, the army needed the help of people who were familiar with the

93

country and the ways of its people, and they found this help among the poorer class of Navajos who coveted the land and herds of their richer brothers.

As the soldiers moved through the Chuska Valley, the Kiya' a' anii remained in the mountains, waiting until it was safe to return to their prairie homes. A few headmen decided they were too close to Fort Defiance and moved their groups west of Canyon de Chelly and south to the Little Colorado River.

On November 2, 1858, the Americans moved through Washington Pass. They divided their force and moved north along both sides of the Tunicha Mountain Range. They had observed in previous years that the Navajos moved from their mountain homes to the prairies in the fall, but this year they found that their quarry had remained in hiding. The families that had planted crops in the lower valleys had already harvested their corn, beans, and melons and carried them to the mountains before the soldiers arrived. The soldiers burned the empty cornstalks and hogans and, as before, sent small raiding parties into the foothills, but without success.

When the soldiers had returned to Fort Defiance to plan their next move, Manuelito called a council of all headmen in the Tunicha and Canyon de Chelly areas. He said, "We should have followed the advice of our Mormon friends when they asked us to join the other tribes to drive the soldiers out of our land. The Mormons would have given us rifles to fight our enemies. I will take some men and ask our friends for guns, so that next time the soldiers come, we will be able to protect our families."

One of the older headmen spoke. "I do not think we should fight the Americans," he said. "It is true that they have taken many of our sheep which we stole from the Mexicans. Now that they have the sheep they have been asking us to return, the soldiers will not bother us again."

Gray Hat said, "The Americans are the allies of our Mexican enemies and will listen only to them. They have

94

never made the Mexicans return the sheep and women they have stolen from us. They captured our women at the Canyon de Chelly and gave them to the Mexicans to use as slaves. The Mexicans have stolen my daughter, and many of my friends have lost wives and children. If we wait, the Americans will take our land and give it to their Mexican friends, and we will all be killed or made to work as the slaves of our enemies. I think we should do as Manuelito says. We must all band together and fight for our land and our families."

Many of the headmen agreed to follow Manuelito, but most of them went to Fort Defiance to plead for peace. They promised to stop their raids and to return as many sheep as possible to the New Mexicans. Word of their good intentions was sent to Santa Fe and the new Superintendent of Indian Affairs, James Collins, agreed to meet with the headmen at Fort Defiance. On Christmas Day, he and Colonel Benjamin Bonneville, who commanded all the military forces in New Mexico, met with the headmen at the fort. At this meeting the two officials demanded that, in addition to the return or payment for the livestock claimed by the New Mexicans, the Navajo headmen must move all their people about twenty miles west of the boundary established by the Meriwether Treaty of 1855. This new boundary was about one hundred miles west of the Rio Grande, and the headmen were told that no Navajos would be permitted to live east of the line or to use the land for farming or grazing.

The loss of half of their grazing grounds and the demand for payment of damages under this Bonneville Treaty could not be enforced without a full scale invasion to drive the Eastern Navajos west of the designated boundary. The Navajos living on the lands the Americans had seized owed no allegiance to the headmen who had signed the new treaty and had no intention of moving away from their homes simply because a few headmen in the west had assumed the authority to speak for them and had signed another piece of paper to stop the American raids. They

95

would stay where they had always lived and continue farming and raising livestock on their lands, and if they needed food, they would raid the pueblos and New Mexican villages, just as they had done for many generations.

None of the Navajos realized that times were changing. They did not realize how fast the non-Indian population along the Rio Grande was increasing. Besides the natural increase, which was greatly augmented by the offspring of the slave women, there were hundreds of Americans moving into the area, seeking a part of the lucrative Indian trade and a contract for the delivery of supplies to meet the wants of the increasing numbers of soldiers stationed along this new frontier.

Ranchers needed more help to raise crops and livestock to sell to these people and, while the slave trade provided some help, non-Indians were needed to oversee the work of the slaves. Mexican and American cowboys were needed to care for the beef cattle which the army preferred to sheep.

21

THE WAR OF 1858 HAD NOT DAMAGED THE Navajo economy beyond recovery. Enough sheep had been saved with which to rebuild the herds. Families were spread out over a larger area than ever before and more land would be put under cultivation. It would be a simple matter to rebuild hogans and corrals, but this would take time. The burning of a Navajo home brings bad luck to the owner and many homes had been burned by the soldiers. Medicine men must be called to transfer this bad luck from the owners to the soldiers and to perform ceremonies to bless the rebuilt hogans.

Some of the headmen who had signed the treaty took sheep to the fort as payment for those which the New Mexicans said had been stolen, but not enough to satisfy their demands. They kept their sheep in small herds and cached supplies of food at many places in the mountains. Children were trained to run to develop speed and stamina in the event they had to escape from the soldiers.

The cessation of the war between the Navajos and the Americans, following the Bonneville Treaty, was short-lived, as no attempt was made to abide by the terms of the treaty. War broke out again in January, 1860. This time some of the headmen agreed to band together to fight the soldiers. On April 30, 1860, a large group of Navajos overran and nearly succeeded in capturing Fort Defiance. Another group attacked an army supply train. The New Mexicans, who had lost no time in taking advantage of the war, raised a party of fifty men, and in July they were led by the infamous Dine' Anaii to capture those families who were living in summer camps in the vicinity of Washington Pass. Manuelito had recruited a large party, and when his scouts reported the New Mexicans moving up the trail, he stationed his men in the bushes and rocks on both sides. The raiding party rode into the ambush and forty men were killed by flying arrows. Only the rear guard managed to turn their horses in time to escape.

More raiding parties swept through Navajoland, and Manuelito's men, as well as others who had banded together, were forced to go to the aid of their families. Manuelito moved his family and herds west of the Hopi villages. Some headmen followed him, and others moved to wherever they could find grass along the Little Colorado and its tributaries. By fall the tribe was spread out over more than forty thousand square miles of rough territory and had become very hard to locate.

On August 21, 1860, Colonel Edward Canby was put in charge of the expeditionary forces which were to put an end to the troublesome Navajo tribe. Three columns of soldiers consisting of more than one thousand Americans, about five hundred Indians from the pueblos, eight hundred New Mexicans and many Ute scouts swept through Navajoland. The Navajos who had elected to remain near their old homes were kept constantly on the move throughout the fall and the winter months.

Gray Hat's family moved from one valley to the next in the Tunichas as scouts brought word of the enemy moving through the mountains. The sheep became thin, and the herds smaller as the older ones died or were slaughtered for food. Mother Red Lake cached her large grinding stones as they were too heavy to carry and her husband shaped her some smaller ones. The women ground a little cornmeal wherever they stopped to eat. A light snow fell in mid-November, and the family slept huddled together in hastily constructed shelters of cedar branches wherever they stopped for the night. Kee and the other young men patrolled the area constantly and kept watch for the soldiers everywhere they went. The snow melted, and the soldiers could no longer gallop along the slippery mountain trails. Horses became lame and were shot. Navajo scouts took note of where the animals were, and their families returned to cut meat from the carcasses as soon as the soldiers had moved on. More snow fell in December, and few soldiers were seen in the high mountains, but now the Navajos were suffering from the bitter cold as well as a lack of food.

In January, 1861, Gray Hat joined a group of headmen and rode to Fort Defiance to ask for peace. Colonel Canby was convinced that this time the Navajos had been so severely punished that they realized they could not fight the American army. Peace was declared and another treaty was signed on February 15, 1861. This time the treaty stipulated that all Navajos must move west of Fort Fauntleroy which was near Bear Springs.

Colonel Canby next reported that as the Navajos had been defeated and scattered, they would give no more trouble and he recommended that Fort Defiance be abandoned. In accordance with his recommendation, the troops stationed at the fort were moved out on April 25, 1861, and the fort was turned over to the Navajos to do with as they wished. The New Mexicans considered the cessation of the war to be ill-advised and, as usual, did not recognize the Canby Treaty between the United States and the Navajos to be binding upon them. They still wanted all of the Navajo lands, and they continued to conduct slave raids against their enemy. Soon the Navajos were retaliating with raids on the Mexican villages, and the New Mexicans were again petitioning the legislature for help and demanding payment for livestock they claimed stolen. The stage was being set for another war.

WITH THE ELECTION OF ABRAHAM LINCOLN, the government adopted whatever policies seemed most expedient in dealing with peoples of the South and the West. It sought to free the Negro slaves in the South and encouraged the enslavement of Indians in the West. It sought to take lands from the plantation owners of the South and from the western tribes to give to the loyal friends of the northern politicians.

The outbreak of the Civil War resulted in the resignations of Colonel Fauntleroy, Colonel Loving and Major Sibley, who went to fight for the Confederacy. During the war they saw the homes of their people destroyed, and their people suffering from lack of food and clothing just as they had helped to make the Navajo people suffer. They saw their people forced to leave their homes and start life anew in the west just as they had sought to force the Navajos to move to the west of their native land.

Major Edward Canby was left in charge of the disorganized troops that remained in New Mexico. The first test of his troops was in June, 1861, when Brigadier General Sibley (the former Major Sibley) led a Confederate army of Texans up the Rio Grande. However, the Union army troops from California under Colonel James Carleton and volunteers from Colorado came to the aid of Major Canby and succeeded in stopping the Texans at Glorieta Pass in February, 1862, putting an end to General Sibley's plans of conquest.

During the War Between the States, the Navajos, Apaches, Comanches, Utes and Kiowas took the opportunity to increase their raids on Indian puebles and New Mexican settlements. Many New Mexicans moved to the larger towns for safety. The Navajos reoccupied all of their former lands. They planted fields and grazed their herds as far east as Mount Taylor.

In the fall of 1862, Colonel Carleton was given the rank of Brigadier General and was appointed Military Commander of the New Mexican Territory. His plan for a peaceful takeover of Apache and Navajo lands was to kill or take captive all of the Indians in the territory and to concentrate the captives in camps under guard. To put his plan into effect he decided to attack the Apaches first,

100

as they were giving the most trouble to the New Mexicans.

General Carleton ordered Colonel Christopher (Kit) Carson, with five companies of New Mexican volunteers, and Colonel Joseph West, with two companies of California volunteers reinforced by as many Pueblo Indians as possible, to lead their troops against the Mescalero Apaches. He told his officers to kill the warriors and to send the women and children to the new prison camp. Next he proceeded to establish Fort Sumner on the east bank of the Pecos River and to set aside the lands around the fort, which were known as the Bosque Redondo, for the use of the Indians he hoped to settle there. When the Apache War was over, it had netted the Americans about four hundred prisoners who were taken at once to the Bosque Redondo to be taught how to live as peaceful farmers instead of warring hunters.

In the summer of 1863, General Carleton was ready to move against the Navajos. He re-garrisoned Fort Defiance for Colonel Carson and sent another detachment to Fort Wingate near Bear Springs. On June 23, 1863, he sent word to the Navajo headmen that war was to start and that all of their people who did not wish to fight were to report to the American forts before July 20th. From the forts, he said, they would be taken to the safety of a new land set aside for them on the Pecos River where they would be given land to farm and where they could live in peace under the protection of the United States government. He promised to give the Navajos many things including food, clothing, homes, farms, farm tools and ample fields on which to graze their sheep and horses in the new land.

When word of the impending invasion reached Gray Hat, he called a meeting at his summer camp in the Tunichas. The headmen of the Kinlichine came to the meeting with many conflicting stories and plans. Some had heard that grass grew waist high as far as one could see in the new land along the Pecos River and that there were many trees to provide shade and firewood. It was said that

101

the Americans would give any family that moved to the new land a good hogan, many sheep and horses, plenty of food and new clothing. Some of the headmen did not believe these stories and suggested that a delegation be sent to inspect the new land before they moved their families. Others said the new land was too far away from their native land and said they would hide or move to the west until the Americans were gone. As usual, the clan would not plan to act as a unit.

When the headmen returned to their family groups they told their people of what they had heard at the meeting. The poorer families were eager to go at once and receive the American gifts. However, most of the headmen decided they would remain in their homeland, scattered over a large area, in small groups that could hide from the Americans until the soldiers tired of looking for them.

This time the Navajo strategy of divide and hide was not effective. Small groups of soldiers guided by Ute and Pueblo scouts started combing the mountains in August. They followed every trail and found the small mountain fields and small herds of sheep and horses. As field after field was destroyed and the livestock slaughtered or driven away, it became clear to everyone that there would not be enough food to sustain any Navajos throughout the winter months.

23

GRAY HAT KEPT HIS GROUP CONSTANTLY ON
the move as scouts reported the movement of raiding parties.
He was now fifty-one and his wife was forty-nine years of
age. They were still strong but tired quickly. Nazbah's two
boys were old enough to help, but Hesbah's children had
to be looked after. María's three small children were also a
burden. The youngest was a two-month-old baby girl. Joni
had married Kee and had one small child. The family group
consisted of the five women, their four husbands, Hosea,
Chiquito and the nine children.

Kee and Chiquito were experienced scouts who reported
the movements of the enemy. The other men hunted for
wild game. Women and children went in groups to pick
berries, piñons, and anything else edible near their camp.
Although Gray Hat moved his group often, they were never
far from their hereditary hunting and grazing areas. They
moved within a mountain area roughly twenty miles long
and five miles wide, hiding in ravines, among tumbled rocks
and in the dense growths of pines, aspens, and oak trees.

Disaster struck the group in early September. Two Zuñi

scouts crept close to where the hobbled horses were grazing, killed four, and almost escaped with two more of the animals. The men returned just in time to kill the scouts before they could escape. With only four horses left, the group was no longer mobile. Fear of discovery overcame their feelings of discouragement and everyone made haste to cut as much meat as he could carry. Hawks were already circling overhead when they abandoned camp.

Snow fell early in November enabling the fugitives to move farther away from springs and streams upon which they and their pursuers were dependent for water. The snow also made it more difficult for the soldiers to travel. By the end of November, the group's supply of cornmeal was depleted, and the remaining horses had been eaten. Now they were dependent entirely on what wild life and plants they could find.

Mother Red Lake had suffered the most. The group had stayed in the mountains where there were more places to hide from the soldiers and raiding parties and where there was more food to be found than on the prairie; however, the lack of salt which they normally obtained in the lowlands increased their feelings of exhaustion. One morning Mother Red Lake woke to find her eyes swollen almost shut and called to her husband, who lay beside her, to bring her some water. When Gray Hat brought a jug to her she bathed her face and was able to see, but her face was noticeably swollen. "It is the lack of salt," said Gray Hat. "If we could get to the prairie we could get some salt weeds. Perhaps if we chewed some they would take the place of salt crystals, but if we go to where they grow we would surely be seen."

"I wish we could find a medicine man for you, my mother," said Hesbah. "Let me put some snow against your cheeks to reduce the swelling."

The women applied snow to her face and rubbed her ankles which were also swollen. But in spite of their attentions Mother Red Lake remained despondent. She said softly, "I am too old for this life of constant running with-

104

out enough rest and without enough to eat. I believe I am going to die, and I want you to go on without me so I can die alone."

"No," said María, "Joni and I will go a little way down the mountain, and at night we can go to a place on the prairie where we used to take the sheep and gather some salt weeds."

"Very well," said Gray Hat. "Now we will go hunt for some rabbits and we will have some rabbit stew. I think you will be better if we rest here today."

María and Joni did not reach the patch of salt weeds as they were frightened by a raiding party of New Mexicans, but the men returned with three rabbits. The women made a stew and Mother Red Lake ate a little, but she was no better. Gray Hat sat beside her half the night, singing softly the old sacred songs as he asked the gods for their help, but his faith was no longer as strong as it once had been. He looked sadly around at his thin, sick and hungry group sleeping huddled together and wondered why this evil had come to his people. Finally he went to sleep only to dream of shadowy figures piling rocks on his prone body, and when the dream people finally started to cover his head, he woke struggling to escape and heard his wife moaning as she, too, slept an uneasy sleep. Gray Hat was worried more than ever by his dream as he felt it presaged the death of his wife.

When Mother Red Lake woke she was worse than the day before. "Someone bring me some water," she cried. "My eyes are so swollen I cannot see any of you." Hesbah hurried to bring water and patted it gently on her mother's face. Nazbah made a little cornmeal mush and fed it to her aunt. Mother Red Lake's eyes were now only narrow slits in her swollen face. The children stayed a little distance away, staring with large eyes at their grandmother. They forgot their fear of being surprised and killed by their enemies, as a greater fear of losing the person who had brought them

105

into the world and been by their side ever since to help them engulfed them.

It was while the women were trying to help Mother Red Lake that Kee came running into the camp. "The soldiers are coming," he gasped. "They are about a mile away and marching this way. They are on both sides of the trail leading to this valley." Everyone reached for his belongings; just as they had done a score of times before, the group rose to follow their leader to another hiding place. For a moment they forgot Mother Red Lake, who lay on the ground near the small fire, making no effort to move. Kee and Chiquito came to her and said, "We will carry you, my mother."

"No, my children," she replied. "The snow is too deep. You must go on without me. Leave some food with me and some wood by the fire where I can reach it. Now hurry or you will all be killed. Let the soldiers find me and kill me, for I am dying anyhow. Go now and save yourselves and the children, as I do not want to be the cause of their death."

"No, my mother," said Hesbah, "we cannot go without you. We cannot let anything happen to you. We will take turns carrying you."

"Do not waste time arguing with me," said Mother Red Lake. "Do you want the soldiers to catch you and kill your children? Go now before they get here. Nazbah will take my place as head woman. She is wise and will decide what is best for the family."

Finally it was decided to leave Mother Red Lake. Hesbah wrapped a blanket around her for the last time, and Nazbah set a little meat and cornmeal where she could reach it. María moved the firewood closer. "We will be back, my mother," said Kee, "as soon as the soldiers leave this area."

"Very well, my son," responded his mother, "but go now quickly." Gray Hat walked slowly down the trail. He did not look toward his wife as they moved away. All had tears in their eyes as they plodded away through the snow. Only the children looked back. A large part of their world

106

had been left behind, and their lives would never be the same again.

Gray Hat led them through the forest, then over some wind-swept rocks and back into a dense growth of high pines and scrub oak. They were all exhausted and stopped to rest frequently. The women tried to keep the children from crying and sat cradling the younger ones in their arms, trying to comfort them. They dared not stop too long. Kee and Chiquito scouted ahead and, finding no one, led the little group to the base of a rock bluff where a small grove of oak trees would provide them with firewood. They built a small fire and, when they had dried their moccasins, built shelters of pine branches, then lay down to regain their strength.

When the family left, Mother Red Lake lay listening to the crunch of the crusted snow under their feet. When she could no longer hear them, she put another branch on the fire and sat slumped against a rock, waiting for the soldiers to find her. It was very quiet as she sat there alone, straining to hear their approaching footsteps. All she could hear was the slight wind moaning through the tops of the high pine trees. She wished the soldiers would hurry, as she no longer wished to live and suffer, but no one came. She tried to hold her swollen eyelids open with her fingers so she could see, but nothing moved within the range of her vision. She was all alone for the first time in her long and useful life. The fire died down, and she put on another stick and held her hands close to it for warmth. Her body ached as she made even this slight movement, and she wished that her enemies would come and put her out of her misery.

For three days Mother Red Lake lay and suffered. Then one afternoon she heard someone approaching. She tried to see who it was but could see nothing. She braced herself against a rock and waited for the sound of a shot, but instead she heard a Navajo man speak.

"Yah tah hay, my grandmother," he said. "I saw the smoke from your fire. Are you all right?"

She tried to answer, but her mouth was swollen and she

107

could only whisper, "Yes." The man put his ear close to her and she whispered, "I am dying, my son."

He replied, "I have seen others like you, little grandmother, you need salt. Here, take these crystals and hold them in your mouth." The man went on to say that he and three other men had raided a Zuñi sheep herd and were taking some sheep and horses back to their families who were hiding along the San Juan River. "We will stay here with you tonight," he said. "We have not seen any of our enemies all day so this should be a safe place to camp. I will go and tell my friends to bring the sheep here."

He left and Mother Red Lake thought, "Am I dreaming? Did someone come and talk to me?" The salt crystals in her mouth reassured her. She had been found by friends.

The man was gone about an hour, and she drifted off to sleep. She woke again as she heard the sound of men's voices. The men greeted her warmly. They killed a horse that had become lame and made some stew. "I am putting more salt in your stew, my grandmother," said one of the men. "The stew will give you strength, and the salt will stop your swelling."

"I know, my son," replied Mother Red Lake in a husky whisper. She drank the stew and suddenly felt better. Perhaps she would not die.

The men sat around the fire eating stew and telling of the many narrow escapes they had from soldiers and raiders since they had left the Zuñi pueblo. That night they took turns guarding the camp, but all was quiet.

In the morning Mother Red Lake was better, partly from the large doses of salt and partly because of the bold spirits of the men. The Navajos she had seen during the past few months had been half-starved, dying, and running like frightened animals. It was good to know that some of her people still had the courage and fortitude to raid the camps of their enemies. Her spirits rose as she listened to the men. Perhaps the soldiers had given up already as they had in previous years and had gone back to their fort.

108

The men stayed with her another day, but on the following morning the man who had found her said, "My grandmother, we must leave you now. We have been gone several weeks and must take these sheep to our families. We are happy to see that you are better, and I think that in a few more days you will be able to follow your family. We will leave you plenty of meat and salt." The men cut up the frozen horse meat in small pieces, placed it in a blanket and hung it in a nearby tree. They filled a large buckskin pouch with salt, brought her more firewood and left her with her jug of stew near the fire.

When the men had gone, Mother Red Lake began planning how she would rejoin her family. There had been no snowfall since they had left, and she could follow their footprints. She thought how happy her family would be to see her and how she would feed them with the meat, liberally flavored with salt, which the men had given her. She busied herself cutting the meat and intestines in small strips and putting them close to the fire where the heat and smoke would dry them. She was able to stand and move about a little and new hope seemed to be effecting her cure as much as the salt crystals she kept in her mouth. The weather became warmer as it often does in December and the snow began to melt where it lay on the rocks. "I must start soon," Mother Red Lake said to herself, "or my family's footprints will disappear and I will never find them."

It had been ten days since she had been left to die and now because of the salt, plenty of food, and rest, she had regained much of her old strength and spirit. On the eleventh day she put her small grinding stone and clay jug on top of the dried meat in her blanket bundle, wrapped her small blanket around her shoulders and, with the bundle on her back, started down the trail after her family.

She walked almost a mile before stopping to rest. Her back ached again and her legs were sore. She rubbed her arms and legs to keep them from becoming stiff and, half-rested, started off again. By evening she found a shelter where her family had spent their first night. They had not been able to travel far because of the children. She saw the footprints of a party of booted soldiers that had passed nearby and wondered how they failed to see their quarry so close by.

She spent the night at the shelter and woke stiff and sore in the morning. She rebuilt the fire and sat close to it as she rubbed her legs; then she went to a nearby tree and rubbed her back against the rough bark. She cooked some meat and sat eating it and more salt as she wondered how much farther her family had managed to travel. Finally she rose and, throwing her bundle over her shoulder, started out again, following the footprints of her people.

The swelling in her hands and ankles was greatly reduced, and she did not tire as quickly as she had the previous day. The sun was bright and the wind quiet. She came to the place where Gray Hat had led his party over the bare rocks and sat down to think which way he might have gone. She hid her bundle and started searching for tracks and in about two hours found where he had led the family over a slight rise and down a rocky ravine about a half-mile from where she had left her bundle. She returned to get her precious supply of meat and decided she would camp in the ravine that night. She went a short distance down the ravine to where there were a few trees and, as the sun was setting, built a small fire between two large rocks and put a few pieces of meat in some snow water to stew.

24

AFTER THE FAMILIES LEFT MOTHER RED LAKE, they travelled slowly, ever alert for the sound of pursuit. Kee scouted ahead, and Chiquito followed a short distance behind. The men and older children helped the women as they somehow managed to half-carry and half-drag the smaller children along. They were so weak they could not cover more than two miles a day. When they reached a hiding place overlooking their old homes in Red Lake Valley, Nazbah told Gray Hat the women and children could go no farther. Gray Hat agreed and said they would stay where they were until the soldiers came that way again.

Every day the men went out to hunt. They hunted in a small circle, seldom more than a mile from camp as they feared the camp might be attacked. Two weeks had passed since they had left Mother Red Lake to die. The men had talked of going back but they feared to leave the family, even if only for a few days. They did not know that the soldiers were marching to the north and that most of the raiders were in the lowlands where they found it easier to hunt

111

Navajos than in in the rough mountain country. The little group lived in constant fear of discovery by soldiers and raiders.

Kit Carson was well aware of the plight of those Navajos who still roamed the mountains. His men had destroyed the crops and disposed of most of the sheep and horses, leaving the Navajos to live on what wild life and plants they could find. He knew it was possible for the Navajos to survive on such fare if left alone in warm shelters, but that they could not survive if they were forced to move around in the bitter cold. They would surely suffer from too little food and frostbitten hands and feet. They would, eventually, have to give themselves up or die. He knew that by now most of the old people had died from exposure and that babies were being buried along the trails because mothers were no longer able to nurse them. How much longer could the Navajos hold out? In his orders to the officers he stressed the importance of keeping the Navajos on the move.

Gray Hat's group soon adopted a routine which would provide food and at the same time warn everyone of possible attack. Chiquito was sent every day to see if any enemy might be following their footprints which were still visible in the slightly melted snow. On one afternoon he climbed a large rock, from where he could see a long way down the trail, and saw a figure moving in and out of the pine trees about a mile away. He whistled a warning to the other men and Kee, who was nearby, answered, then came to join him. "I saw someone moving along our trail," said Chiquito. "He is probably a scout."

"Did you see only one man?" asked Kee.

"Yes," replied his brother, "but there may be more. The soldiers usually send out three or four scouts." Hesbah's husband, attracted by the warning whistle, joined them, and the three men sat and watched. The figure appeared again and sat down, leaning against a rock beside the trail.

"That is no soldier!" exclaimed Kee. "It is a Navajo woman! It is our mother!" The men climbed down from

112

the rock they had been crouching on and ran quickly down the slope to where Mother Red Lake was resting. "My mother, my mother," cried Kee, "we thought you were dead."

"Hush, my child," said Mother Red Lake, "it is bad luck to speak of death. I am all right now, and I have brought you some food." They were all laughing and crying as they hugged her and held her hands.

"Our camp is just about a mile from here," said Hesbah's husband. "I will carry your bundle. Everyone will be happy again when they see you."

When they walked into camp the despondent, heartsick and despairing group came to life. They gathered around Mother Red Lake and everyone tried to touch her hands or blanket. It seemed the world had become bright again, and they even forgot their fear and their hunger. They asked question after question, and she told them of the men who had found her.

"And now, my children, let us eat," she said. "Here, Nazbah, is some salt. Put plenty of it in the stew and we will all feel better." The women filled every jug. It seemed that the salty broth was the best they had ever tasted. Gray Hat sat close to his wife, holding her hand and singing softly as he thanked the gods for bringing her back to them.

It was a few days later that a messenger from Manuelito found them. He brought word that Manuelito wanted Gray Hat and other headmen to join him west of the Hopi villages, as there were no soldiers in that area. "We cannot travel so far without horses," said Gray Hat. "My people are weak and we have small children that we must carry. If Manuelito would send us horses we would gladly leave these mountains and join him."

"When I return I will give him your message," replied the messenger. "Now I must go to look for our other friends."

When he had gone Gray Hat said, "If we had four good horses we could leave the mountains. We could travel at

113

night and avoid our enemies as they always build fires that can be seen from far away."

The prospect of moving about the mountains the rest of the winter in sub-zero temperatures was not pleasant. There were few raiding parties that cared to hunt for the Navajos during such bitter cold weather. However, Kit Carson kept his foot soldiers moving about in order to frighten the Navajos and keep them on the move and exposed as much as possible, hoping they would suffer so much that they would finally surrender.

"We will move toward the Black Mountains," said Gray Hat. "We cannot keep running from place to place all winter. If we cross Red Lake Valley without being seen, there are many places in the Black Mountains where we can hide. We will be closer to the Hopi villages and may be able to steal some horses and sheep from their herds. We will start today, as we will become weaker every day we stay here."

The little group started moving down the mountain and in a few days had reached the valley. They hid among the large rocks, not daring to build a fire. It was very cold as they sat huddled together trying to keep warm until nightfall. Everyone was tired and hungry, and it was not easy for the mothers to keep their children quiet. María's sick baby cried constantly under a blanket which partially muffled her thin cry. Toward evening a small party of soldiers rode up the valley and stopped about a mile away to cook. The hearts of the little group fell as they feared the soldiers had stopped to make camp for the night.

However, after they had eaten and had sat around smoking for an hour or so the soldiers moved on. Two of them rode close to where the little group was hidden and looked directly at the rocks behind which they were hiding. They stopped as though they intended to dismount, and María pressed the blanket over her baby's head to stifle the sound of the baby's cry. The soldiers looked toward their hiding place once more, then, apparently satisfied that no one was

114

there, rode on to join the others. When they had gone María uncovered the child, but it was too late. The baby had suffocated. María rocked the small body in her arms as tears streamed down her face. She had known for days that the baby could not live, but now that death had finally come, she felt that she could not bear the loss. The other women were crying, too, as they took the tiny body from her arms and placed it in a crack in the rocks, then covered it with smaller rocks to protect it from the coyotes.

They could not delay any longer. With the soldiers gone and darkness spreading over the valley, they left their hiding places and started across the open field. By morning they were in the cedar trees that covered the eastern slopes of the Black Mountains, and they stopped to rest before starting up a steep trail leading to the high pine forests. They went a short distance until they found a safe place to stop and build a fire. While the others sat close to the fire warming themselves, the young men stripped bark from the cedars for them to bind to their legs under their wrap leggings. Partly rested, they started up the trail again, the boys going ahead to look for rabbits.

Kee saw the smoke from a fire and cautiously approached. When he was a short distance away he saw a Navajo man, a woman and a young boy and called to them. They started to run, but when he called again the man turned and stumbled toward him. They were as destitute as Gray Hat's family and weak from hunger. They told Kee they had come from the Chaco Canyon area with other families to seek safety in the Tunicha Mountains, but had found that the mountains were no longer a safe place to stop, so had continued westward. They had lost their sheep and their horses, and many of the group that had started together had been killed or scattered in four directions.

The experiences endured by these three fugitives were the same as those of the other Navajos from as far east as the Chama River, who had fled ahead of the soldiers and raiders into the Tunicha Mountains only to find Kit Car-

115

son's patrols conducting their never-ending marches back and forth along the mountain trails. Many had continued westward into the high mesas of the Black Mountains, then turned south in search of anything edible that might keep them alive for one more day. By the time these groups had travelled so far, only the hardiest were left. These survivors moved in small groups, usually just a man and his wife and their older children, as their older relatives had died or been abandoned and their babies had died of malnutrition or been strangled. The survivors were a thin, hungry and desperate people who would not hesitate to crawl into the camps of other Navajos or into the camps of their enemies in search of food. If they had been armed with guns, nothing would have prevented them from attacking their enemies to obtain the food they so desperately needed.

Navajoland had been overrun since the declaration of war in July by the Comanches, Paiutes, Kiowas, Utes, Zuñis, Jemez and the New Mexicans, all looking for livestock and slaves. This was a time of great prosperity for these groups of predators. The United States Army paid the raiders one dollar for each sheep and twenty dollars for each horse captured and turned over to the soldiers. It had been estimated that prior to the start of the war the Navajos had more than two hundred and fifty thousand sheep and sixty thousand horses and, while the raiders only captured a part of these herds, still it was a profitable business. A more lucrative phase of this war was the taking of slaves. Athough General Carleton had issued orders forbidding the selling of Navajo captives, the raiders found little difficulty in smuggling them into the villages and ranches along the Rio Grande and disposing of them at high prices. So many raiders swept through eastern Navajoland that by December there were only a few Navajos left east of the Tunicha Mountains. These few had fled north into the La Plata Mountains or south into Apacheland.

To prolong their lucrative business, the raiders followed their quarry westward but they found the Navajos increas-

116

ingly difficult to find. The small groups without livestock and unburdened by the young and the very old found many places in which to hide and occasionally even lay in ambush and killed small groups of raiders, stripping them of all their clothes and provisions and leaving their naked bodies lying on the snow. Finally, as winter temperatures dropped and blizzards swept across Navajoland, many of the raiding parties disbanded, and the members returned to their homes. Scouts for the Eastern Navajos reported to those who were in hiding in the mountains, and many families returned to their former homes. The men banded together and were soon raiding the pueblos and New Mexican ranches.

25

GRAY HAT'S FAMILY CONTINUED ITS SLOW journey toward the Hopi villages. The food Mother Red Lake had brought was soon gone, but the men were able to catch a rabbit or two every day to keep the group alive. They walked one day and stopped to rest and to hunt the next. They saw no soldiers or raiders but occasionally met Navajo families moving westward. Light snowfall wet their clothes and moccasins and forced them to stop to dry them or their feet would have frozen. Their moccasins were coming apart and the sinew they used to repair them did not last long. They padded their feet and legs with cedar bark and rabbit skins, but in their thin and weakened condition, the sub-zero weather and cold winds cut through their clothing. They kept moving only because they did not know what else to do.

On their rest days the young women and older children looked for grasses and bushes that might have some seeds remaining, gathered the seeds and pulled up the plants to get roots to add to the stews. They looked under piñon trees for nuts which might have been missed by the birds and seeds of certain cedar trees which could be eaten.

One day when they were out looking for food they came across the bones of a horse that someone had killed months before. There were still shreds of ligaments which had dried on the bones during the hot summer. "We can boil the bones," said Hesbah.

"Yes," responded María, "and I will grind up the hooves."

Joni laid her blanket on the ground, and they laid the bones on the blanket and started carrying it back to camp when a rabbit jumped up almost at their feet and ran into a crack between two rocks. The children dropped the blanket and ran after it. The oldest boy knelt down and looked into the crack. "I can see him!" he yelled. "He is not far back."

"Be quiet," said Hesbah. "Do you want someone to hear you? Now let me see where he is."

She bent down and saw that the rabbit was crouching about five feet back from the opening. "Stay here," she said to the children, "and don't let him come out. I will get a stick and catch him."

She found a long stick and said, "Now, when I drag him out don't let him get away. Get some rocks and kneel around me and as soon as I drag him out, hit him."

She stuck the stick slowly into the crack until it touched the rabbit, then she quickly jabbed it into him and twisted it so as to entangle it in the animal's loose skin and pulled him out. Everyone hit the rabbit and María grabbed him

118

and broke his neck. They were all overjoyed, and the women had to warn the excited children again not to make so much noise.

"This has been a good day," said María, smiling for the first time since the death of her baby. "Now pick up the bones and we will show grandmother what we have found."

26

IN JANUARY, 1864, KIT CARSON'S MEN MADE another march through the Canyon de Chelly area to prevent the Navajos from settling down. The weather was very cold, and the small patrols did not go far from their base camps. They stopped frequently to warm themselves and to brew some coffee. They had no liking for this kind of warfare and hoped every day to receive orders to return to the comforts of Fort Defiance.

Chiquito was the first to see one of the patrols less than a mile from Gray Hat's camp. He ran quickly to warn the others. The men threw snow on the fire and everyone bundled up his belongings and followed his leader at a fast walk. It was difficult now for Hosea, Mother Red Lake, and María's husband to keep up. The young men and women took turns carrying the smaller children. Kee stayed behind to see if the soldiers followed his family. When the patrol stopped to build a fire, he rejoined the group.

"It will be dark soon," said Gray Hat. "I know of a small cave near here that I will take you to. I used it several years ago when I hunted deer in this area."

Gray Hat left the trail he had been following and led the little group to the cave only to find that another Navajo family had taken shelter in it. The strangers were frightened until Gray Hat approached their fire and said, "We have been running from the soldiers but our old men and children can go no farther. We would like to camp here by you tonight."

"Very well," said one of the men. "Do you have any food?"

"No," replied Gray Hat. "We plan to hunt tomorrow."

The group settled down around a fire and, as usual, took off their moccasins and leggings and rubbed their legs and feet. When their feet were warm again, they smoothed out the cedar bark and rabbit skins they used for padding and rewrapped their leggings and replaced their moccasins. Hosea was tired and the warmth of the fire made him sleepy. As he sat rubbing his sore feet he nodded and finally fell asleep. Mother Red Lake woke him and told him to put his moccasins on before he went to sleep. The old man said he would, but he soon dozed off again, his bare feet close to the fire.

Kee, Chiquito, and Hesbah's husband sat about two hundred yards away from the camp, listening for sounds of pursuit. They heard Ute scouts at a distance communicating with each other by wild animal cries, and then suddenly Kee saw figures moving in the darkness nearby. He ran silently back to the camp and told everyone they must run and hide as their enemies would be there in a few minutes. No one stopped to gather together their few possessions. Kee quickly put out the fire and slipped away into the woods. The others disappeared in all directions into the darkness. Hosea woke, still barefooted, and, without thinking, ran after them. He stopped only when he cut his foot on a sharp rock and sat down next to a tree to try and see the extent of the injury.

120

He heard someone moving near him and he lay as flat as possible on the snow, hoping he would not be discovered. In the darkness there was not much danger unless a soldier came within a few feet. Then he heard a sob and knew it was one of the children. He called softly and Hesbah's son stopped, then came to him. The boy sat down beside him in the darkness.

"We must get farther away," said Hosea. "When it is light, they will look for us." The two rose and walked as quietly as possible, intent only upon putting more distance between themselves and their enemies.

By sunrise the icy snow had so numbed their feet that there was no feeling left. They sat down to rest but were afraid to build even a small fire. They sat rubbing their feet and their legs, cold and hungry. Hosea said, "We must find our family. I think they will return to the cave to get the things we left there. I must have my moccasins and my leggings." He continued to rub his feet, but there was no feeling. The deep cut was no longer bleeding and the flesh had turned blue. He noticed that the sole of one of the boy's moccasins had been lost during their flight and that the boy's foot was bleeding. To add to their troubles a light snow started falling, and although this would conceal their tracks from the soldiers, it would also hide the tracks of the family which they must rejoin. Hosea unravelled the edge of his blanket and, using the woolen thread, bound grass around their feet. "We must go to the cave now," he said, "but we must be careful as the soldiers may still be there." Their sense of direction was good; they moved toward the cave, stopping every few minutes to look and to listen, but all was quiet.

That afternoon Kee found them and led them to another cave where the family had taken shelter. Everyone was there except for the men who were looking for Hosea, Hesbah's boy, Joni and her small son. Gray Hat soon found Joni and brought her to join the rest of the family. The stranger Navajos they had camped with were not found.

121

Unencumbered by old people and children, they had run faster than Gray Hat's group and were far away.

Mother Red Lake looked at the haggard faces of Hosea and the boy as they limped into camp. From their faces her eyes shifted to their feet. "Your feet are frozen," she said to Hosea. "Where are your moccasins?"

"I left them at the cave," said Hosea. "When the soldiers came, I ran off without them."

"Oh my son, my son," cried Hesbah as she examined her boy's feet. "Your feet are frozen." She rubbed the boy's feet with snow to try to bring back the circulation.

"I will boil some cedar branches," said Mother Red Lake.

The women beat some cedar branches to a pulp and boiled them in a jug. They cooled the liquid quickly in the snow and patted it on the frozen feet. They were worried as the feet remained an unhealthy blue and yellow color. They continued rubbing them and applying the cedar liquid, but it was too late. The feet began to swell, and the pain in their legs grew until both Hosea and the boy fainted.

Gray Hat sat beside his old Hopi friend and during a short period of consciousness spoke to him. "Lie quiet, my friend," he said. "We will stay here with you."

Hosea replied, "I will never leave this place. I wish that I had returned to the Hopi people so I could have died there instead of in this cave. Now that my life is finished, I want to thank you for letting me live with you for so many years, and I want to ask one more favor. Please bury my body. Do not leave it where others may find it."

His voice died away, and they could not understand what else he had tried to say. Tears were in everyone's eyes. The stocky little man had never complained during the years he had lived with them and had always been ready to lend a hand in all of the family's activities. Now, instead of passing the last years of his life quietly weaving and telling stories to the children he loved, he had been subjected to

122

months of hunger and suffering and was dying in a strange cave far from his home.

Hesbah's son was dying, too, and she was helpless to prevent his death or to ease his pain. Her tears fell on his discolored swollen feet as she sat and rubbed them hopelessly.

Again, that afternoon, the soldiers came searching in the direction of their hiding place. Kee gave the alarm and everyone made ready to run. Hosea regained consciousness again as they put him in the back of the cave and Gray Hat told him they would return. They put Hesbah's son with Hosea and covered the small entrance with rocks, then gathered their few belongings and followed Gray Hat down the trail. Hesbah plodded along, her two little girls by her side, her senses numbed by the loss of her son. The girls pulled at her dress and asked why their brother was not coming with them, but she could not speak. She just patted their heads and rearranged their blankets about their shoulders. When the smallest one tired, she picked her up and carried her a little way and was a little comforted by the feel of the small body in her arms.

When they stopped to rest, Gray Hat said to Hesbah's husband, "I think you and Chiquito should return and pick up the blankets and jugs the children left at the high cave, but be careful as the soldiers may still be between us and the cave. As soon as we find a hiding place, Kee will come back to meet you and tell you where we are. Without the blankets others in our party may die."

The young men left the little group and headed back the way they had come. If all went well they would only be gone a few hours. As they neared the cave, they met a wild-eyed Navajo yelling and laughing as he ran down the trail. "I am looking for the soldiers," he yelled. "If I find them I will climb a high tree where their bullets will not reach me. I will show them that I am smarter than they are."

"No, don't do that," said Chiquito. "They will shoot you down."

123

"No they won't," said the man. "You will see when I find them." He ran off down the trail, still laughing and talking to himself.

Chiquito and Hesbah's husband left the trail and continued on their way. The crazy man had made so much noise they were afraid he had been heard and that the soldiers would come looking for him. They heard a Ute scout signal and an answering signal, and then they heard a soldier a short distance away, speaking to his men. Then they heard the loud laugh of the Navajo and saw him about a mile away, sitting on a branch of a lone pine tree about fifty feet above the ground, yelling for the soldiers to try and get him. The soldiers saw him too and, although they could not understand what he was saying, they ran toward him. When he saw the soldiers the Navajo cursed them in what broken Spanish he knew. "You are like dogs barking at a squirrel," he yelled, throwing some twigs down at them. "Your bullets cannot reach me."

One of the soldiers took aim and fired. Chiquito and Hesbah's husband saw the man fall, his body hitting against the branches as he fell. He hit the ground with a thump, almost at the feet of the soldiers. A Ute scout laughed and said, "This one will not run again."

"No," said the sergeant, "his troubles are over. I wonder how many more of his people will go crazy before this war is over."

A stout soldier walked over and turned the body over with the toe of his boot. "I wish they would all climb the trees so we could kill them. I am tired of marching around through these mountains. If I had known I would have to walk around all winter in the snow, freezing half to death, I would not have joined the army."

"Look around now," ordered the sergeant. "There may be more Navajos near here. This one must have run off from his friends."

The patrol split and went in four directions, two of them passing close to where Chiquito and Hesbah's husband

124

lay hidden, but after about an hour they reassembled and sat down under the tall pine and brewed a pot of coffee, and as they drank, they stared at the dead body and wondered why the Navajo had acted as he did. When they were ready to move on, one of the soldiers took a knife that the Navajo had tied to his waist with a strip of buckskin. "I will keep this as a souvenir," he said.

Chiquito and Hesbah's husband waited until the soldiers were gone. They noted that the soldiers were following a trail to the south instead of moving in the direction their family had fled; then they walked on to the cave. They found nothing disturbed. Hosea's moccasins and leggings still lay where he had left them, half covered by the new snow. The young men left them where they lay, for they believed Hosea was now dead and feared to touch any of his former belongings. They found the two blankets the frightened children had left behind and their two jugs. "We must hurry," said Hesbah's husband. "Kee will think the soldiers have captured us. We have been gone longer than we expected."

Kee was waiting for them when they returned. He told them Gray Hat was taking the family to another place where they might find some deer. As they walked along, they told Kee of the crazy man who had climbed the tree. Kee said nothing but he wondered how much longer they would be able to withstand the fear, the hunger and suffering and the pain of seeing those they loved dying around them.

27

AT THE NEW CAMP THE LITTLE GROUP SAT, mending their clothing in silence. Even the children were strangely silent. The loss of Hosea and Hesbah's son was almost more than they could bear. Gray Hat tried to turn their minds to other matters by talking of the deer hunt he had planned. "We must leave early," he said, "so we will be well hidden near where the deer sleep before the sun rises tomorrow. I have been there before, and I know where the deer stay at night. We will kill them as soon as it is light enough for us to see."

Early the next morning he led the three young men to the place where he remembered deer had been when he had hunted in the area a few years before. The men crept silently toward a thicket at the end of a small valley in which the deer had long been accustomed to graze. Small pines and bushes blocked their view in the semi-darkness, and they heard nothing stirring about. When they were close to the thicket they hid and made ready their bows and waited. As the valley became lighter they saw something move, and a doe stepped out of the trees and stood between two bushes, looking nervously from side to side.

No one moved and she stepped out into the open and began pawing at the snow to uncover a little grass to feed on. She was directly in front of where Kee was hidden. He rose to his knees and shot. His arrow struck her in the neck and she plunged back into the thicket, followed by Kee and the other hunters. The small branches struck them in the face, but they did not feel them as the thought of deer meat pushed all other thoughts out of their minds. The frantic doe tried to leap over a large rock, but her strength was failing and she fell back. Chiquito shot from a few feet away and the doe quivered and lay still. There were no other deer in the thicket and no signs that other animals had been there since the last snowfall.

"When I was here before," said Gray Hat, "we found a large buck and ten does with their young in the valley."

"Everyone hunts for deer now," said Kee. "The soldiers shoot every one they see. They can kill them from a longer distance with their guns than we can."

Even the appearance of the deer in the camp failed to cheer the women. They cut up the animal, saving every scrap of meat and intestines and every shred of skin and ligaments. Now they could repair their moccasins properly, and they would have additional strips for their leggings. Gray Hat and María's husband worked on the skin, scraping it and rubbing it with the brain of the doe to keep it soft. Gray Hat prayed as he worked, but he had no faith in the efficacy of his prayers as he had no corn pollen left to give to the gods. He hoped that they would understand that his people were starving and would forgive them. The gods seemed far away and seemed to have lost interest in their people.

While the others were working, Hesbah's husband and Kee went out to scout around. They had seen the patrol they had run from turn south, but there might be other patrols in the area.

When they were gone, Mother Red Lake left the other

127

women to cut and dry the deer meat and went over to where Gray Hat was working. She watched him for a while then spoke of a matter which had been uppermost in her thoughts since the death of Hosea. "I have been thinking," she said. "Winter will be gone in a few more weeks, and it will be easier for our enemies to move about in search of us. They seem determined to kill us all because we did not go to their new land when they told us to go. Perhaps we should have gone to the fort instead of running away. If we had gone, Hosea and my grandson might still be alive. We are many miles from the Hopi villages and some of us will not be able to walk so far. We need a long rest and good food. I am discouraged, my husband, but I will do whatever you think best and so will the rest of the family."

Gray Hat replied, "Yes, my wife, you are right. If we were all young and strong we might escape. I have been wondering how to contact the Americans to tell them we are willing to go to their new land on the Pecos River. If we show ourselves, they will shoot us before we can speak."

Although the young women, too, had often thought it had been a mistake to run instead of surrendering to the Americans, no one cared to put her thoughts into words. Their children were cold and hungry, and they feared they might die. Without seed to plant or sheep, the future remained dark even though the soldiers left. However, not even Hesbah or María, who had seen their children die, offered any complaint. They would remain with their family and go where their leader decided to take them, even though he led them to their deaths.

That evening, as the family sat around a small fire eating deer meat, Gray Hat brought up the matter of surrendering to the Americans. "I have been thinking that we should not have run when the Americans said they would take us to a new land," he said. "I did not think they would follow us about all winter." No one spoke and he continued, "Our children should have a warm place to sleep and good food to eat if our clan is to survive.

128

Perhaps in the new land we will find comfort and can give our people the kind of life that is best for them. The difficulty now is how to meet with the soldiers and how to tell them we are ready to give ourselves up, as they will shoot as soon as we expose ourselves to them."

"I agree with our leader," said María's husband. "We cannot keep running from our enemies. If we give ourselves up they will feed us. Perhaps we can plant our fields, rebuild our herds and live in peace in the new land."

"Yes," said María, "I have been thinking that I am the one to speak to the soldiers. Many of them understand Spanish. I do not think they will shoot me if I shout to them from a distance in the Spanish language. I will tell them we wish to give ourselves up and go with them to their new land."

"They will capture you and make you their slave," said Joni.

"If we see two soldiers leave their companions to scout in the woods we will try your plan," said Gray Hat to María. "The rest of us will hide close by and kill them if they try to harm you. Next time we see the Americans we will take you to them to speak for us."

Other Navajo families in equal or worse distress than Gray Hat's group were also ready to surrender to the Americans but feared to approach the soldiers. Many had worn out their moccasins and bound up their feet with grass and bark that had to be constantly adjusted. Their feet were sore, and many left blood stains on the snow as they stumbled around looking for food. They dug roots, boiled old bones and hides, and on good days managed to kill a rabbit to keep them alive another day. They grew thinner and thinner as they moved about, ever fearful of being discovered and killed by their enemies.

28

IT WAS A SUNNY MORNING IN EARLY FEBRUARY, and some Navajos who had given up before the start of the war were washing the Fort Defiance laundry a short distance from the barracks. As they started to hang up the clothes they were startled by a desperate, half-starved Navajo man who crawled out from behind a rock and shouted to them to tell the soldiers that he wished to give himself up. Fortunately, the guards did not shoot and he was told to come to the fort. He was taken to Kit Carson, and through an interpreter, told the Colonel that there were many Navajos who wanted to surrender but were afraid to approach the fort or speak to the soldiers.

Kit Carson at once gave orders for his men to stop firing at the Navajos. He told his men to bring those Navajos who surrendered back to the fort under escort so they would not be attacked by raiding parties. Navajos at the fort were sent out with small patrols to spread the word that it was safe for those who remained in hiding to come to the fort.

By the end of February army reports say about two

130

thousand sick, half-starved, ragged Navajos had surrendered and were camped around the fort ready to be taken to Fort Sumner. They were given firewood from the army stockpile and a little food was issued to each group as it came in. The women thankfully accepted the food but sent their men to ask for salt. Some of the Navajos were given shoes and army blankets, but there were not enough of either to care for all the prisoners who were in need. The surrender of so many Navajos at once had not been anticipated and no provision had been made to feed or clothe them. Navajos were also turning themselves in at Fort Wingate, but that fort was equally unprepared to care for such a large crowd of ragged, half-starved people.

Colonel Carson decided he must move all the prisoners to the Rio Grande where food could be obtained. He planned to use all wagons available and to send the captured sheep and horses along with the prisoners. However, most of the Navajos would have to walk, and in their weakened condition, it would take many days to march the one hundred and seventy miles from Fort Defiance to the Rio Grande.

On March 4, 1864, the prisoners were lined up to start the long walk to Fort Sumner. With them went five hundred horses and three thousand sheep. As the supply of cornmeal was almost depleted, the soldiers issued a small amount of wheat flour to each family. The women accepted the flour, but most of them did not know how to prepare it for their families. They made a cold gruel in the same manner as they made cornmeal mush and the result was that many of the weaker and sicker Navajos were soon doubled up with stomach cramps and dysentery. Those who ate the uncooked flour before starting were lucky, as they were left behind at the fort to recover.

Others who ate flour during the march fell along the trail and had to be shot by the soldiers as there was no room in the wagons and no extra horses to carry them.

131

Freezing weather accounted for many deaths as there was little time to rest or to stop and build fires to warm the marchers. It was essential that the prisoners be kept moving until they reached the Rio Grande.

After the first day of the march, coyotes began to follow the party and hawks and crows circled overhead, waiting to pounce on and tear apart the bodies of those left in the wake of the long column. The horses weakened and were no longer able to carry the old and the sick. As they fell they were slaughtered and the meat divided among the marchers. Some of the old people were left behind. Their relatives gave them a little food and marched on. The old ones sat by the side of the trail, watching hopelessly as the column passed them by and disappeared from sight behind the rolling hills.

The small children, for whom there were no horses, were somehow carried by men and women as they struggled to keep up until they reached the river. The long trail was marked by the bones of animals and the bones of the murdered and frozen Navajos. As the column neared the Rio Grande the soldiers rode ahead and returned with food and horses. Finally, what was left of the column moved into a camp on the bank of the river. Here the people were fed and allowed to rest before starting on the second half of the three hundred and fifty mile march to Fort Sumner.

In spite of the suffering and tragedies they had endured, no one left the column. They still believed that when they reached the new land, their troubles would be over. They would have the new hogans the Americans had promised, their own fields of beautiful corn and beans and squash, and herds of sheep and horses. In the new land they would live in peace and security, protected from their enemies by the soldiers. If they could persuade the gods to follow them, they would live again as they had before the war. Many Navajos worried about the lack of communication with the gods during the past three years. With-

132

out ceremonials, how could they rid themselves of the spirits of unfriendly animals and the human dead which were with them? In the new land, the medicine men could again perform the powerful rituals needed to resume contact with the gods and, with their help, everyone would be able to resume the place assigned to him and live in peace and prosperity.

The prisoners resumed their march to Fort Sumner in April. The weather was still cold, but more blankets had been provided and more horses were available for those who could not keep up with the column. A few died, but the majority were able to complete the second half of the journey.

Other groups were on their way to Fort Sumner, and by late spring, more than five thousand Navajos had arrived and were spread out for fifty miles along the Pecos River. The promised hogans had not been built, and the prisoners were forced to live in pits covered with hides and scraps of canvas supplied by the army. Clans banded together and sent delegations to the fort to beg for food and clothing, but there was little food to be had. General Carleton had made no provision to feed so many hungry prisoners.

The general hoped that by fall his prisoners would be growing their own food and would no longer be dependent upon the army. His plan called for clearing thousands of acres of land, breaking it with plows, and irrigating it with a system of canals that would bring water from the Pecos River. The General put Captain William Calloway, an officer experienced in irrigation, in charge of the project. The Captain prepared plans and put the Navajos to work, digging a main canal to divert water from the river to the proposed farmlands.

As there were only fifty garden spades available, the Navajos took turns digging. Somehow they managed to complete the main canal, twelve feet wide and six miles long, in one month. When the main canal was completed,

133

they dug small lateral ditches to lead the water from the main canal to the plots of land which were to be farmed. Small plots were allotted to each family group and everyone, men, women and children, went to work digging out the tough mesquite roots with their bare hands, as few spades, picks, or other farm tools were available.

By midsummer three thousand acres of land had been cleared and planted, and corn was beginning to sprout. It seemed that the problem of food for the prisoners had been solved.

29

WORD OF THE PAUSE IN THE FIGHTING TO permit Navajos to come to the forts did not reach those who were hiding in the mountains as quickly as it had reached those in the hill country and the nearby valleys. No patrols came to the mountains where Gray Hat's group had camped. Kee and Chiquito kept watch from vantage points along the more commonly used trails, but saw no one. All of the men hunted and returned at night with a rabbit or two, but with no word of seeing any strangers. The women hunted for other foods, but stayed close to the camp. The days passed and they wondered what had happened to the soldiers. Had they all returned to their fort?

March winds brought a blizzard with a little snow, but

the family was now well sheltered, and their fires kept them warm. Their moccasins and leggings had been repaired, and they were ready to run again if any danger approached. Now that the decision had been made to surrender, all plans of travelling farther to the west were abandoned.

"Perhaps we should send a party to Red Lake Valley," said Gray Hat. "There were always soldiers marching up and down the valley." After some discussion, it was decided that Kee, Chiquito, María and her husband would go.

"Without the children we can reach the valley in two days," said Kee.

"Yes," said María's husband, "we should leave at once. I have been thinking that raiding parties will be looking for us again now that the snow is melting."

The four left camp the next morning. The sun was warm, and they walked rapidly down the trail. By noon they had gone about five miles. Kee and Chiquito went ahead of María and her husband, looking for signs which might indicate that their enemies were in the area. Shortly after noon, Chiquito, who was in the lead, heard someone coming along the trail and hastened to hide behind some rocks to see who it was before he gave the alarm. It was a Navajo woman leading a horse on which two children were riding. As soon as he was sure no one was following her, Chiquito jumped out of his hiding place and struck the horse in the forehead with his axe. The horse reared, throwing the children into some bushes, and the woman fled a little way into the woods before turning to look back. Chiquito struck the horse again, killing it. The woman, hearing no sound of pursuit, slipped back through the trees to see what had happened to her children and, seeing only one Navajo man, she cried, "What have you done? You have killed my horse and now who will carry my children?" As she spoke she gathered her children, who were about eight or nine years old, to her to see if they had been hurt when they fell. Kee joined them and the woman became less belligerent. She sat down and started to cry.

135

"Where is your husband?" Kee asked.

She replied, "My husband went south to steal another horse for us, but he and his brother were killed, and I am taking my children to Black Hill to look for my father. Now my horse is dead, and I cannot go on without a man to hunt for me." She and the children started crying again. Their men had been killed just a few weeks before and now they had lost their horse.

"My family is hungry," said Kee. "We have many children to feed. I will ask my father to bring his group here to cut up meat." María and her husband finally reached the scene and the Black Hill woman repeated her story. Kee left and walked as quickly as possible back to Gray Hat's camp. While he was gone Chiquito, María and her husband started cutting up the horse. The Black Hill woman watched for a while, then joined them and told her children to help.

It was late the following afternoon when Gray Hat's family arrived. The Black Hill woman told Gray Hat her story and as she spoke of her husband she started crying again, her tears falling on the meat she was cutting. "I don't know what to do," she said. "I cannot go on. Will you let us join your group?"

"We are going to give ourselves up to the Americans," replied Gray Hat. "The soldiers will feed us and then take us to the new land on the Pecos River."

"Yes, I know," said the Black Hill woman. "My people talked about going to the new land last summer, but our leader said we should stay in our homeland. The Mexicans and the Hopis came and killed our sheep and stole our horses, and my people ran in every direction to save their lives. I think most of them escaped, but I do not know where they are now."

"You may stay with us," said Gray Hat. "My wife will tell you what to do." Mother Red Lake told the Black Hill woman and her children to help the other women cut and dry the horse meat. Gray Hat and Hesbah's husband went to look for a place nearby where they could camp.

136

The following morning Chiquito, Kee, María and her husband continued their walk toward the Red Lake Valley. As they neared Fort Defiance, Kee went ahead to see if there were any patrols in the valley. He sat down on a high, rocky point overlooking some black basalt peaks south of the fort. It was late in March, and here and there snow lay in spots shaded from the afternoon sun. A year ago he would have seen herds of sheep and horses grazing in the valley, but now nothing was moving. Late in the afternoon he saw a mounted patrol of soldiers returning to the fort from the south. He saw that two Navajo men were riding with the patrol. "They are the Dine' Anaii," he said to himself. "They have always guided our enemies when they come to attack us." Kee did not know that the Dine' Anaii were already at Fort Sumner. Their headman, Crooked Foot, had been the first to accept the American offer of free gifts and had moved his people from Mount Taylor to the Bosque Redondo before war had been declared. His small clan had helped to build the fort and were well treated by their former allies.

The patrol followed the small stream below Kee and stopped for a few minutes to water their horses, then continued on toward the fort. Kee decided to stay where he was until morning. The wind was cold, so he withdrew from the edge of the cliff and built a small fire in a small ravine among the pine trees. He wrapped his blanket around his shoulders and sat waiting for the morning. In the morning he returned to his former vantage point. About mid-morning a group of ten Navajo men, women and children appeared, walking along the stream which led toward the fort. About the same time he saw the same patrol of six soldiers and their two Navajo guides, coming to intercept the Navajo group, but no one ran and the soldiers did not fire. The groups met and talked for a while, then the Navajos continued walking toward the fort and the patrol rode away to the south.

The peaceful meeting puzzled Kee. Was the war over? Apparently it was safe for the Navajos to show themselves

137

again. He decided to speak to the group and, after making sure no soldiers were in sight, he walked quickly down the mountain to meet them. The leader explained that the soldiers were riding around telling the Navajos that they would not be shot if they came to the fort to give themselves up. "I will go with you," said Kee, "and ask the Americans if I may bring my family to the fort."

As they neared the fort, he saw several other Navajo families camped outside. The group he was with sat down a short distance away from one of the families while Kee and their leader went to talk to them. They were told to go to a warehouse building to ask the officer in charge for food. Kee accompanied his new friend to the warehouse where several soldiers and Navajos were working under the direction of an officer. When they spoke to the officer, he called his interpreter over and the man asked them what they wanted. They told him they had just arrived at the fort and wanted some food. After finding out how many persons were in their party, the officer told his men how much meat and cornmeal to measure out. "You can get firewood at the army woodpile," he said.

Kee told the interpreter his family would like to come to the fort, and the officer told him to bring them in. "You must hurry," he said. "If they are not here in ten days the soldiers will start looking for your people and will kill everyone they find."

Kee stopped long enough to eat some cornmeal mush then started back to tell his family what was happening at the fort and what the officer had told him. He found María, her husband, and Chiquito where he had left them. They had been worried but had decided to wait another day before leaving. They had seen no one from the fort.

When they reached Gray Hat's camp, Kee spoke to his father. "The Americans have stopped the war so that the Navajos that want to stop fighting can come to their fort and give themselves up. Many of our people have given up, and the soldiers have taken them to the new land. The officer told me that we must give ourselves up in ten days, or the soldiers would start looking for us again. We have eight days left and, as it will take our family four or five days to walk to the fort, we should start tomorrow."

"Very well, my son," said Gray Hat. "We have all agreed that we must surrender. We will start tomorrow."

Everyone was excited. The many months of suffering and running were nearly over. No longer would they have to live in fear of discovery and sudden death. The thought of leaving their beloved country saddened them but did not outweigh their desire for food and safety, which the Americans had promised them. Even though they dreaded the move to a strange country, it was better than the starvation and death which awaited them in their homeland. The adventure which lay before them gave them a new interest in life.

30

IN THE MORNING THE BLACK HILL WOMAN and her children were gone. They had taken as much dried meat as they could carry and slipped away without waking anyone. Even Hesbah's husband, who had been guarding the camp, had not seen them leave. "Well," said Gray Hat, "I suppose she changed her mind and decided to go back and look for her people. We do not have time to look for her. We have enough food to last until we reach Fort Defiance where the soldiers will feed us. I hope she finds her people."

As Gray Hat's group made ready to leave camp, they heard someone running toward them and they quickly hid in the woods. The Black Hill woman's children ran into the deserted camp. They shouted, and Hesbah's husband answered from his hiding place. They ran to him crying, "Our mother fell into a ravine and we think she is dead."

"Be quiet," he said. "Do you want someone to hear you? Now, tell me what happened."

"We were running," said the boy. "We were afraid you might catch us and take our meat. Our mother said we would go through the woods and hide, but it was so dark we could hardly see one another and then she ran through some bushes and disappeared. When we followed we saw she had fallen, but we did not hear her and the darkness hid her from us. We waited until it was light and saw her lying below."

"I will go back with you and see what I can do," said Hesbah's husband. He called to the others and, when they had reassembled, the children repeated their story. Gray Hat said, "I will go with you, and we will see what we can do."

The Black Hill woman's children took the two men to where their mother had fallen. She was sitting at the bottom of a rock cliff about twenty feet high. She had unwrapped one legging and sat looking at her leg. Gray Hat called in a low voice and asked her if she was all right. "I have broken my leg," she replied.

"Sit quietly and we will come down to you," said Gray Hat. They found a cleft in the rocks and climbed down. Gray Hat examined her leg and saw that it was broken. He cut a branch from a tree and made several smooth sticks. Then, with the help of Hesbah's husband, he pulled and straightened her leg until he felt the ends of the bone come together. He placed two smooth sticks on each side of her leg and bound them tightly with her legging. There was sweat on the woman's face when they had fin-

140

ished, but she had not fainted or made any sound. "We must leave you here," said Gray Hat. "We cannot carry you all the way to the fort."

"Please let my children stay with me," whispered the Black Hill woman.

Gray Hat turned to the children and asked them if they wished to stay. The boy said, "I will stay with my mother. I know how to hunt rabbits. I will stay and take care of her." His sister said she would also stay with her mother.

"Very well," say Gray Hat to the woman. "You have enough meat to last several weeks. If you do not move about, your leg should be well enough to walk on in a few weeks. I am sorry I have to leave you here, but I must take my family to the fort."

Gray Hat and Hesbah's husband left the Black Hill woman sitting at the base of the cliff and returned to their families. Everyone was ready to go on to the fort. They picked up their bundles and followed their leader along the trail. Kee went ahead and Chiquito followed a short distance behind to give the alarm if any of their enemies appeared.

31

GRAY HAT'S PARTY WALKED FOR FIVE DAYS, stopping often to let the children rest. As they neared the fort, everyone was fearful, as the area they travelled through was that which they had seen overrun by raiding parties. The young men stayed well ahead and behind the little group as they walked through the high pine trees until they reached the open country. Once in Red Lake Valley, they followed the small stream which flowed through the valley until they came within sight of Fort Defiance.

Around the fort they saw a hundred campfires burning and a great crowd of Navajos walking about as they visited with friends they had not seen for many months. As Gray Hat stood looking for a place to camp, a young man came to greet him. He was of the Kinlichine Clan and was happy to see one of the headmen of his people. "Yah tah hay, my father," he said. "It is good to see you. My wife is camped over there. Will you join us?"

"Thank you, my son," replied Gray Hat. "Are there any more people of our clan here?"

"I have not seen any," answered the young man. He went to shake hands and speak with Mother Red Lake and then with the rest of his clan relations; then he walked with them to where his wife was cooking over a small fire. His wife greeted them warmly, gave Gray Hat and Mother Red Lake a little cornmeal mush and apologized for not having enough to feed the rest of the group.

While the women sat and talked, Gray Hat, Kee, and Chiquito went to the post warehouse to get some food. Kee reminded the officer he had been there before and told him he had brought his father and his family to give themselves up. The officer told his men to weigh out eighteen pounds of cornmeal, one pound for each person, ten pounds of wheat flour, five pounds of beans, and to give the group a half of a sheep. The soldiers put the rations in front of Gray Hat and then handed him a small bag of salt. Kee shouldered the mutton and Chiquito picked up the other rations and followed their father back to their camp.

Mother Red Lake and the women were glad to receive so much food. They had eaten rabbit, horse meat, roots, and seeds for so long that the mutton and cornmeal would

142

be a real treat for them and their families. Hesbah opened the cloth flour sack and took a little out. She showed the white powder to Mother Red Lake and asked her if she had ever seen any food like it before. The woman they were camping with interrupted them. "It is flour," she said. "The soldiers and Navajos who work in the fort showed us how to prepare it. The flour will make you sick if you eat it before it has been cooked. I will show you how to mix it with a little water and cook it on a hot rock."

Mother Red Lake said, "Very well, you can show my daughter. I will make some cornmeal mush and María and Joni can cut up some meat to roast. We have not tasted roasted sheep meat for many months."

While the women were eagerly preparing the other food Hesbah sat with her new friend, watching her prepare the flour bread. The woman repeated the stories she had heard from those who had arrived before of how the first group of Navajos that had given themselves up ate the flour dry or mixed with a little water and became so sick with stomach cramps that they rolled around on the ground and could not even sit up. "I heard that many of our people died," she said. "After that everyone was told how to cook the flour."

While she talked, she flattened a piece of dough in her hands and cooked a tortilla, sprinkled a little salt on it and handed it to Hesbah. Hesbah broke off a very small piece, gingerly tasted it, then put it in her mouth and chewed it. "It has no taste," she said. "Why do the soldiers eat this instead of cornmeal?" She broke off another piece for her mother, then gave the rest to María and Joni. The children asked for some and were given small pieces by their mothers. No one liked the wheat flour bread, but they ate it, as no food should ever be wasted.

While the women prepared the food, the men walked to a nearby hill where most of the other men had congregated and sat down to listen to what they had to say. The talk was of the Bosque Redondo and what they would receive

143

when they got there. Most of the headmen doing the talking were skeptical of the American promises of herds and farmlands, but none said they would not go. Gray Hat was doubtful, too, but when Kee asked him what he thought he said, "We must wait and see, my son. None of us knows what the Americans will do when we reach the new land. Perhaps their word is good, and perhaps they promise us many things so it will be easier to make us move from our lands that they have been trying to take from us for so many years. Let us go now, as I think your mother has food prepared. We will say nothing of what we have heard."

The men did not voice any doubts they had as they sat around the fire. Everyone ate too much and it was not long before the children complained of stomachaches. Mother Red Lake sent Chiquito to the black rocks they had passed to get some sage she had seen growing there. She boiled some sage tea and made the children drink a little of the bitter brew.

In the morning everyone felt better. The women visited with their neighbors and heard countless rumors of what the Americans were going to do with them. Among the women, too, there were those who had doubts of receiving gifts from their enemies in the new land. Others, believing the promises, looked forward to new hogans, herds of sheep, new dresses and iron pots in which to cook tasty foods for their families. None of them, the fourth group of Navajos to be taken to Fort Sumner, wanted to leave their homeland. They had all resisted until they had no choice. To stay meant death for themselves and their children.

Mother Red Lake spoke to her husband of what she had heard. "If the Americans are going to give us so much," she said, "why do they not give it to us now and let us stay here? I think they speak two ways and will give us nothing in the new land."

"I too have no belief in their promises, my wife," replied Gray Hat, "but we cannot stay here. They will not let us raise crops or sheep. We can run and hide from the soldiers, but without food we cannot survive. We have no

144

choice but to go with them and to hope that they will feed us."

The following morning the soldiers drilled in front of the fort. The officers believed that a show of force would convince any Navajos who might still be planning to leave that it was useless to resist. Everyone watched with interest as the soldiers drilled in a small area. The Navajo women admired the uniforms and the rhythmic way in which the soldiers marched and turned. The Navajo men gathered together on the hillside criticized their every move and the way the sergeant shouted his orders. "They are just showing off to frighten us," said Chiquito. "If we had their guns and their horses, we could kill all our enemies and move back to our old homes."

"Be careful what you say," cautioned Kee. "Some of the Navajos around here might carry your words to the soldiers to get more food. We cannot trust our own people."

The soldiers drilled for about a half hour, then formed a long line facing the Navajo encampment. An officer stood in front of them with his interpreter and spoke to the crowd. "You will all start marching to the new land tomorrow morning," yelled the interpreter. "All of you men come here as you must help to load the wagons which will carry the food." When the men were assembled, the officer told them some of the rules they must follow on the march. "The head man of each family will be given rations every night. Tonight you will draw food for tomorrow," he explained. "When we start marching tomorrow everyone must stay in line. We cannot have you leaving the group. We will leave at sunrise." When he had finished speaking, the officer selected twenty of the young men to help load the wagons and turned them over to a sergeant who led them into the fort.

32

PREPARATIONS FOR THE LONG WALK WERE simple. Moccasins had been repaired or footgear had been made from blankets. There was nothing to pack except what food had been issued for the day and a few cooking jars. There was no extra clothing or extra blankets. Everyone rose early, finished eating shortly after sunrise, and sat holding bundles of the meager family belongings as they waited to be told what to do.

Mother Red Lake had divided the food for the others to carry. In her bundle she had put her small grinding stone and cooking jar. Gray Hat and Hesbah's husband would carry the water jugs. Every item was important.

About an hour after sunrise the wagons were driven out of the fort and lined up a short distance down the trail. A detachment of twenty-four soldiers mounted their horses and took positions along the line of march. An interpreter told the prisoners to line up behind the wagons. Some of the soldiers moved among them, forming them into a long line in front of the fort. As soon as they were in their places, everyone sat down in order to conserve strength for the long walk. An officer rode along the line with his interpreter, pointing out those prisoners he thought would be unable to keep up with the column and told them to find a place in the wagons. He had horses brought for the families with small children. When this had been attended to, he rode to the head of the column and gave orders to start moving.

Gray Hat's family was given a position near the head of the column. The little group lined up behind the wagons with Gray Hat in the lead. Hesbah's husband followed the group, leading a thin horse which carried the two small children and a few bundles of the family's food.

When the officer in charge waved his arm, the wagon drivers cracked their whips, horses whinnied and lunged forward and the creaking wheels began turning. Soldiers rode up and down the line, shouting as they ordered the prisoners to get on their feet and start moving. Finally the long line of about seven hundred people was in motion, and a thin cloud of dust rose and moved along with them. At the rear of the column came a herd of a thousand sheep urged on by mounted Navajo herders from the fort.

Hesbah stepped out of line to look back at the long line of people which stretched out about a half mile behind and a soldier quickly rode up and told her to stay in line. Excitement was in the air and sadness too. There were tears in many eyes and a feeling of hopelessness in many chests as they started the long march away from their beloved land, which they would never see again.

Although it was now mid-April, the air was still cold and snow still lay in the ravines. The column moved slowly, little more than a mile an hour, and halted every two hours to permit the prisoners to rest. They were weak from months of hunger and suffering but at this leisurely pace they could all keep walking at least for a while. At noon the column was halted, and while the soldiers were being fed by the army cook, the Navajos sat and ate the cornbread and boiled mutton the women had prepared that morning.

Soon they were on their way again, walking along the old trail which wound through the sagebrush covered hills and valleys eastward toward Bear Spring and Fort Wingate. They walked about ten miles the first day and halted near some cedars where the prisoners could get wood for their fires. An interpreter told them to come to the wagons to draw cornmeal and to go to the rear of the column to draw their meat rations for the following day.

While Gray Hat and Kee went to draw rations for the group, the other men gathered firewood, and the women started the evening meal. When they had eaten, all of them repaired their moccasins, then wrapped their blankets around their shoulders and lay down on the ground, close together for warmth, and were soon asleep. The soldiers took turns standing guard, as they thought some of the prisoners might decide to leave the group under cover of darkness.

In four days they had reached Fort Wingate and camped near the sacred Bear Spring. Gray Hat told the children of how many bears came to the spring to drink, but that night they saw only the horses and sheep being watered.

The next morning a few more Navajo families who had turned themselves in to the soldiers at Fort Wingate joined the other prisoners and took their places at the rear of the column. The road they followed was the well travelled one leading to Albuquerque. The column moved along the foot of the red sandstone bluffs, stopping at small streams which at this time of year were still carrying water from the melting snows.

A week after leaving Fort Defiance, they came in sight of the snow-capped Mount Taylor. Some of the men had seen the mountain before, when they had ridden with raiding parties to the Rio Grande. Two families in the group had formerly lived near the base of the sacred mountain, but to the rest this was their first sight of the mountain which legend said marked the southeast corner of the land created by the gods for the Navajo people. Gray Hat said, "When we see any of our sacred mountains we should stop

148

and pray. Perhaps if our medicine men would go to the top and pray, the gods would listen and return to their people." As they walked along, he sang very softly the chant which is sacred to the mountain.

On the night they camped near the base of Mount Taylor, many of the Navajos met to pray and in the morning they stood facing the mountain and threw a little corn pollen toward it, while they listened to the men who knew the sacred chants ask the gods for their help.

Gray Hat passed his pouch of corn pollen to the members of his family, and they followed his example as they put a little of the sacred pollen in their mouths, a little on their heads, and threw a little toward the mountain. The soldiers watched them and laughed, but they did not interfere.

The following night a family slipped away from the camp and returned to their old home near the base of the mountain. Two soldiers were sent to look for them but soon returned, as no time could be lost in moving the prisoners to the Rio Grande. Already the officers saw that there would be a food shortage before they reached the river. Horses and sheep were becoming thinner and some were dying along the trail. Those that died were speedily butchered and the meat loaded in the wagons.

The older people were showing signs of weakening, and their faces began to show signs of suffering as they plodded along, determined to keep up with their families. Mother Red Lake rode more often, while the small children walked or were carried by their mothers and fathers. María's husband was suffering the most, but he kept moving and said nothing. María noticed that he was stumbling more often and that his face was gray with weariness and pain, and she walked by his side, wishing that she could do something to help him. That night a baby died and was buried in some rocks near where the group was camping. María dreamed that she had broken a leg, and she saw herself sitting by the side of the trail, watching the column moving away. She considered the dream a bad omen and watched her husband closely as he rose and ate. As they

149

took their place in the line, he wavered and fell, and she bent over to speak to him but he was unconscious. Kee and Chiquito carried him to the wagons, but there was no longer room enough for another person. "Lay him on the ground by that cedar," said one of the soldiers. "You can not carry him."

"I will stay here with him," said María. "We will follow you as soon as he is well."

"We cannot let anyone stay behind," said the soldier. "Our orders are to keep everyone with the column until we reach Fort Sumner. Now get back into line and leave him here." As they hesitated, not knowing what to say, he pointed his gun at them and called to another soldier to come and help him. The soldier took María by the arm and led her back to Gray Hat's group. Kee and Chiquito followed helplessly. They told Gray Hat of what had happened, but he could do nothing. The column continued moving, and after everyone had passed, one of the soldiers rode back and shot the still unconscious man.

María cried, "He was a good husband, always kind and gentle to me and my children. What can I do?"

"Yes, my child, he was a good man," said Mother Red Lake. "Ever since you brought him to live with us he has been like a brother to me. We will all miss him." There were tears in every eye as they walked along in silence, thinking of their dead friend. Another valued member of the family was gone.

33

THE LONG COLUMN OF NAVAJOS MOVED ON
past the Laguna Indians' pueblo and the New Mexican
frontier village of Cubero into the sand hills which extend
as far as the Rio Grande. When they reached the rolling
sand hills, the prisoners removed their moccasins and
walked barefooted in order to save them for use when they
came to rocky terrain. Their feet were sore from the constant chafing of torn and ill-fitting moccasins and improvised blanket wrappings, and it was a relief to walk barefooted for a while.

Mother Red Lake was suffering from pains in her back
and legs. Each morning Hesbah rubbed her to remove
some of the stiffness before they took their place in line.
The other women divided her bundle and carried her few
belongings with their own, but still Mother Red Lake
could hardly keep going. The horse that had been given
them for the children to ride had fallen, and she could no
longer ride when she needed a short rest. Finally one morning Mother Red Lake's strong will failed to overcome her

pain and she said, "Let me lie here, my children. You must go on without me."

"No, no, my mother," cried Hesbah. "Let me rub your back and you will be all right. The soldiers will shoot you if we leave you behind." Leaving María and Joni to do what they could for her mother, Hesbah ran to look for the interpreter. He was standing near the wagons and Hesbah stopped to try to compose herself, then approached him and said, "My mother is not feeling well today. Will you let her ride in a wagon for a little while?" The interpreter looked at her for a minute, then turned his back and walked away. Hesbah burst into tears as she walked back to her family and told her father what had happened.

"I will go and speak to him," said Gray Hat. "Perhaps he will listen to me."

"The soldiers will not listen to any of our men," said Nazbah. "They just like to order us around."

As the family group stood talking about what they might do next, the interpreter rode up and spoke to Gray Hat. "One of the women that was in the last wagon died last night," he said. "Your wife may take her place if you hurry and put her in the wagon before we move on."

Hesbah, Kee and Chiquito half carried their mother to the wagon and helped her climb over the side; then Hesbah breathed a sigh of relief, and the tight feeling of terror that had gripped her left. Once more her mother had been saved from a horrible death.

Mother Red Lake sat in the wagon and for a time looked at her hands and feet as she struggled to realize just what had happened. One minute she had been lying on the ground, unable to rise, and now she was jolting along in a wagon. She was weary in mind and in body, and it was hard to concentrate. She looked back at the dusty haze which partially obscured the marching figures of her people and wondered if what she saw and the squeak of the wagon wheels which she heard were real, or if they were a part of a dream. She dozed, awakened, and dozed again, and as

153

she slept the wagons moved slowly along, carrying her farther and farther away from her homeland.

Mother Red Lake retained her place in the wagon the following day and began to feel a little better. "Perhaps I will be able to stay with my family until we reach the new land," she thought as she looked back at the others. "Perhaps we will all be strong and healthy again when this long walk is over." She sat and planned what she would do for her family once they reached their new home. She would feed them all they could eat and the children would never be hungry again. She would make them all new clothes and new moccasins. As she planned, her interest in life returned and her spirits rose; but as she looked again at the thin, ragged, and half-starved crowd stumbling along behind, her spirits sank and she wondered how many would survive until they reached the land of plenty. She watched as a prisoner lagged behind and the soldiers pushed him back into line with their gun barrels.

Finally the column climbed the last hill west of the Rio Grande, and the marchers looked down into the valley. A thick fringe of trees lined the banks of the river as far as they could see, hiding the water from view. Above the river the high Sandia Mountains dominated all of the land to the east. The officer led the group down the long, sandy slope and halted them on the bank of the river at a campsite selected for all previous groups of prisoners destined for Fort Sumner.

When they reached the water, everyone waded in. The soft sandy bottom felt good, and the cold water seemed to wash away the pain and fever. After they had washed their feet, the women splashed water in their faces, then left to start preparing the evening meal for their families.

A detachment of officers and men rode into the camp from Albuquerque to inspect the prisoners and consult with the column leader as to what would be needed to continue the march to Fort Sumner. Fresh horses would be needed, and more wagons for the prisoners and for supplies to be taken to the fort must be provided. A large herd of sheep for the army and their prisoners at the fort would be sent along with the column. Noting that some of the prisoners had no blankets, one of the officers promised to send a few Mexican blankets to the camp. The greatest problem was footgear to replace the ragged moccasins and improvised blanket wrappings the Navajos were wearing. Army shoes were too stiff for the sore and swollen feet of the prisoners unless heavy socks were provided. Orders were given to release sheepskins from the army stores and to give them to the prisoners for the fabrication of moccasins, along with unbleached muslin which they could use to bandage their feet.

It was decided to keep the Navajos in the camp on the Rio Grande for four days to give their feet a chance to heal and for them to gain more strength before starting on the second half of the long walk to Fort Sumner.

34

FINALLY ALL WAS READY AND THE COLUMN moved away from the river, crossed the valley, and started up the rocky canyon road which led through the mountains to the high mesas east of Albuquerque. The officer in charge set a slow pace and the rested Navajos moved along in better spirits and with renewed hope. Mother Red Lake rode in one of the wagons, and the small chil-

dren were mounted on fresh horses. The days were warm, but the prisoners walked with their blankets over their heads and, in dusty places, drawn across their mouths. The warm weather was drying the road, and on the mesas the stifling dust became daily more of a problem. Strong winds sweeping across the high prairie land carried clouds of stinging sand and dust to add to the discomfort of the marchers.

In a few days Navajos were again tiring and a few weakened and died, but the rest moved on, determined to stay with the column to the journey's end. It was two weeks after the column left the Rio Grande that they reached the valley of the Pecos River. The crowd of Navajos, looking eagerly down into the valley that was to be their new home, saw first, at the end of the road, the adobe buildings of Fort Sumner. It was mid-afternoon and the sun shown on the buildings and on the waters of the Pecos River which flowed in front of the fort. A bright flag waved in the wind over one of the buildings. They could see Navajos, the Dine' Anaii, constructing the adobe walls of other buildings at the fort. In the nearby fields they saw a thousand Navajos working along irrigation ditches and many soldiers walking or riding about as they supervised the activity.

An officer and some men rode out from the fort to meet the column and to tell the column leader where to take the new arrivals. As they waited, the newcomers looked up and down the valley for their new homes but all they saw were small tepee-like shelters, made of sticks covered with torn canvas and sheepskins, scattered about the fields. Where were the fine hogans they were to occupy in this new land? The column moved on to an area in the rolling hills about a mile from the fort, and the interpreter told the prisoners they would camp there that night. A wagon brought several barrels of water from the river for them to drink and use to cook with. The water seemed very bitter and at first they spit it out but, as there was no other, they drank it sparingly. Some of the sheep they

157

had brought with the column were slaughtered, and the rest were driven to the army corrals. Cornmeal was issued and soon fires were burning, and the women busied themselves preparing food for their weary families. There were few who slept soundly that last night of the long march. They were at the end of their long journey and wondered what the Americans would have in store for them in the morning.

The following morning ten Navajo headmen came to see the new arrivals. The prisoners were told that the members of each clan were to go with their clan leader and that he would take them to the group he represented and be responsible for them. The clan leaders took positions a little away from the crowd, and the people picked up their belongings and went to shake hands and take their positions behind their leader. The headman of the Kinlichine Clan was glad to see Gray Hat and his family and greeted them warmly, as Gray Hat was a respected headman of a large group of the clan. "It is good to see you, my brother," he said. "We cannot talk here, but tonight I will tell you of all that has happened since I arrived a month ago, and all that the Americans have told me."

Gray Hat's group and the other family of their clan walked with the leader up the river valley for about three miles until they came to the Kinlichine camp. There were about four hundred members of the clan assembled in a small area along the side of a sandy hill. Some of the families were living in holes they had dug into the hill and covered with weeds and grass. Others had erected crooked poles and covered them with sheepskins. All of the shelters were makeshift, as materials were not available to construct the type of hogans they were used to living in. There were no straight pine poles or cedar branches, but there was mud along the river banks and later they could build hogan walls like they could see being constructed for the houses at the fort. In this camp there were families that

158

had once been rich and families that had been poor, but here all were equal, for all were equally destitute. Only the clan leader stood above the rest of the group.

The clan leader told Gray Hat that he would go with him to get some cottonwood poles from a pile some of his people were cutting at the river bank, and that they would also go to the army warehouse to get some sheepskins, as the soldiers would not issue the poles or skins unless he was there to make his mark on a piece of paper. Kee, Chiquito, and Hesbah's husband went with them to carry back whatever they were able to get. As they walked along, the leader told Gray Hat that the shelters they were living in were temporary and that they would soon have houses to live in. The soldiers would teach them how to build adobe houses like the ones at the fort and would bring poles for the roofs from the mountains. The houses would be built side by side in a long line. Gray Hat looked at the barracks buildings which were similar to those he had seen on the New Mexican ranches but said nothing. He would have preferred to live far from his nearest neighbor but these houses were better than living in the shelters his people now occupied. It was a great disappointment to him when the leader told him that he would not be given a herd of sheep and horses. All sheep were to be kept in one herd which would belong to the clan but no one could kill an animal unless the army officer gave his permission, and no horses would be given to any of the Navajos.

While the men were gone, the women talked to their clan relatives. Somehow every family group had expected to receive its own farms and its own herds of sheep and horses, and had never imagined they would have to live crowded together, work together on a community farm, and care for a community herd of sheep. No one could have any pride of ownership in the farm or herds that they shared with the rest of the clan. All the women were dissatisfied and wished that they had never come to this new land. They thought of the high, pine-covered hills of their

159

mountain farms, and of how pleasant the summers had been in the old days. They did not like the hot, treeless plains, they did not like the makeshift shelters, they did not like to be ordered about, they did not like the bitter water they had to drink, but most of all, they did not like to live so close to their neighbors.

Mother Red Lake chose a place on the side of the hill about fifty feet away from the nearest shelter and the young men built two small shelters with the poles and sheepskins they had brought from the fort. The weather was warm and, for the time being, everyone would sleep on the ground outside. When they had finished, the family sat around a small fire, eating and discussing what each had seen or heard since their arrival. Gray Hat said nothing, but soon rose and joined the other two headmen of the Kinlichine Clan at the fire in front of their leader's shelter. "It will be the responsibility of us four men to do what we can for our people," said the leader. "We can do little now, as we are at the mercy of our captors. I have asked for more food and clothing for our people, and the officers have told me that they will soon receive the things we need and that they will be given to us as soon as they arrive. They also have told me that we must produce more food, that we must prepare more fields and plant more crops because there are now six thousand of our people here, and what has been planted this year will not be enough for all of us."

"My family will help," Gray Hat assured him. "What can we do?"

"I will show you a place to be cleared and planted to-morrow," said the leader.

The next morning the clan leader took Gray Hat's group to the clan farm and set rocks at the corners of the plot assigned to them. He gave them three spades and an axe to clear the land and showed Gray Hat where the ditches should be dug to lead the water from a main ditch that ran along one side of the plot. Kee and Chiquito started digging a small ditch while Hesbah's husband worked with his wife, María, and Joni. Mother Red Lake would stay in camp to take care of the children and to cook for the others.

The plot assigned to them covered about ten acres, on which there were many mesquite bushes that must be grubbed out. The women and children pulled up the bushes while Hesbah's husband dug around the larger ones, loosening up the dirt around the tough roots so the others could pull them out. There were several yucca plants in the plot which they grubbed out and set aside, for the roots would be used to make soap for washing hair. The women were pleased, as they had not been able to wash their hair with yucca soap since leaving the Rio Grande. They would all wash early the next morning before starting work, as it was bad luck to wash in the evening.

It was now June and too late for the newcomers to plant, so when their plot was cleared and the irrigation ditches dug, they were sent to help in the other fields where the corn was already a foot high and the melon vines were starting to run among the stalks. Some of the men were sent to work in a field that had been planted with wheat under the supervision of the soldiers, who were more familiar with the cultivation of this grain than the Navajos.

When the corn bloomed, the women gathered the pollen and carefully dried it alongside their shelters where it was protected from the wind. Everyone thanked the gods for the coming crop and gave pollen to them, but despite the gifts and the prayers, shortly after the corn had tasselled and the small ears had started to form, the fields were struck by corn worms which ate the ears away and destroyed much of the crop. Later, in October, half of the nearly matured wheat was destroyed by severe storms. The Navajos watched in despair, as they saw the crops they had almost given their lives to produce, being destroyed. It was clear to everyone that the gods did not look with favor on this alien land and were punishing them for leaving the

161

land they had been given. Some of the older people began talking of leaving and going back to Navajoland.

Although everyone was discouraged, they were not yet defeated. They would pray again, and they would plant again early next year; meanwhile, the army would feed them. But now it was estimated that there were eight thousand prisoners at the Bosque Redondo, and it was not easy for the army to acquire enough food for so many hungry people. Appropriations to buy food were made, but contracts were given to friends by government and army officials and prices climbed higher and higher as the contractors and ranchers sought to make as much money as possible from the desperate situation.

The days when Congress would think nothing of granting billions of dollars to help the so-called underprivileged people around the world had not yet come. In 1864 it was difficult for Congress to justify an appropriation of even one hundred thousand dollars to help people in the United States, so due to lack of money, misuse of the money made available, and lack of interest by the government, hundreds of Navajos died of starvation and disease as they fought desperately to force the alkali-impregnated soil of the Bosque Redondo to yield some sort of crops which would sustain them.

In desperation, General Carlton ordered that rations be cut in half and that no more than twelve ounces of cornmeal or flour and eight ounces of meat per day be given to each prisoner. The Navajos felt that this cut in rations was just another promise which the Americans had broken and just another means of weakening them so they would die. They had not been given the new hogans, herds of sheep and horses, fields of their own or new clothing. They had been crowded together in shelters that were little protection against the cold winds, made to work in the fields like slaves with few tools to work with, and now even their food ration was cut. Some families picked up their belongings and slipped away from the camp, hoping to find

162

their way back to their old homes. But in spite of their many grievances, most of the Navajos stayed and went to work to produce another crop. By the end of January, 1865, they had six thousand acres of land planted with corn, wheat, melons, squash, beans and peas.

The leader of the Kinlichine and his headmen tried to keep up the spirits of their people by repeating to them the promises made to them at their meetings with the fort commander, but most of the Navajos no longer believed in American promises.

On January 1, 1865, the growing complaints of the prisoners were partially stilled by the arrival of the long-awaited shipment of blankets, cloth, ploughs, farm tools, scissors, knives and beads. The shipment was not as large as expected, as only about thirty thousand dollars worth of goods were actually delivered to the fort, although the appropriation to buy them had been one hundred thousand dollars.

Gray Hat's family was given about thirty yards of un-bleached muslin for clothing, four lightweight blankets, a pair of large scissors, two butcher knives, and a bag of bright-colored beads. The headmen told the women they would be shown how to make clothing for their families, but many of the women simply cut off lengths of material, one for the front and one for the back and tied them to-gether to wear as a flimsy manta style dress. Mother Red Lake spoke to her husband about the cloth which provided no warmth. "If you will get the women some wool and some poles we can use to make looms, we will weave some blankets and make some warm clothes for our families," she said. "The blankets and material the Americans have given us will not keep us warm and are so flimsy they will soon be worn out." Gray Hat spoke to his leader and along with the leaders of other clans went to the fort commander to request wood for the looms and wool for weaving. Their request was willingly granted and wagons were sent to the

163

Capitan Mountains a hundred miles to the southwest for poles and additional firewood.

They returned in about two weeks, and soon looms were erected and the women were busy, weaving the traditional mantas and blankets for their families. Mother Red Lake, Nazbah, and Hesbah sat at their looms most of the daylight hours, weaving the yarn being carded and spun by the young girls. First they wove a blanket with black and white designs for each of the men and boys, then they started manta dresses for themselves. They unravelled the red and blue yarns from their old mantas and blankets and incorporated them in their new garments to make broad, colored stripes across the top and bottom. In a few weeks everyone had discarded his old ragged clothing and walked around with the pride their race had always felt in being well-dressed.

During the seven months of captivity, even Mother Red Lake had regained her health, but not her peace of mind. Now as she sat at her loom she could forget, at least for a while, the squalor of the camp and the hum of the many voices around her. Old legends she had learned from her mother and from Hosea came to her mind, and she repeated them to the children as they sat around her. Occasionally Nazbah and Hesbah took their turns at telling the old stories of their people which they had been taught.

After the January planting, the clan leader sent Kee with some other men to help construct more adobe buildings at the fort, Chiquito, to the blacksmith shop and Hesbah's husband, to the slaughter house to help cut up the meat. All three young men drew extra rations for their work and acquired a great deal of experience which they put to good use in later years.

A small church was built at the fort, and young priests were sent by the Bishop of New Mexico to start a school for the Navajo children. At a meeting with the post commander, the clan leaders were asked to send all of the young children to the school so they could learn to speak the American language. The headmen went from campfire to campfire, speaking to the women and telling them of the new school. Most of the women were not in favor of sending their children away even for a day. Who would protect them from the soldiers? Was this another move to take the children out of sight and kill them?

The headmen finally convinced a few of the mothers that no harm would come to their children and on the first day of school a crowd of about a hundred children, accompanied by their mothers, assembled before an adobe building which was to be used as the school. A long-gowned priest stood before them and spoke to them in Spanish, as he thought they, like the Pueblo Indians, understood a little of that language; but everyone sat in silence staring at him as he walked around, his long gown swinging and his arms waving as he sought to convince them of the value of an education.

Finally he opened the door of the building and motioned for the children to go inside. Everyone crowded forward, and finally, an interpreter who had been watching walked over and told the crowd that only the children were to go inside. The crowd drew back, and the mothers refused to be parted from their children until the interpreter told them they could wait outside to see that no harm came to the children. After much discussion, some of the older children went into the classroom. Some of the women took their children and left, and the others sat down to wait.

Inside the school the priests had constructed long benches for their students, and the frightened children were told to sit down. When all was quiet, the long-gowned man walked back and forth in front of them, talking, but no one understood him, though they watched his every gesture and his long gown as it swung about. Occasionally he would go to a table and pick up a card on which there was a letter of the alphabet, but the letter and his pronunciation were meaningless to the children. Finally he asked one of the boys to stand up, but when he took the boy by the arm the child burst into tears as he thought he had been chosen as the first to be killed. The other children started edging toward the door to escape. The priest hastily released the boy and opened the door so the children could rejoin their mothers. When all was quiet, the interpreter said they were to come back the next day.

María had sent her ten-year-old boy with Nazbah and her fourteen-year-old son. The girls had been kept at camp to help with the weaving and the cooking, and Nazbah's oldest son was helping unload some wagons at the warehouse. When they returned to the camp, everyone was interested in what had happened. The two boys, who by now had forgotten their fear, assumed an attitude of great importance as they explained to their sisters and elders what had happened. They explained in great detail how the priest was dressed and how he had talked, and how he had shown them pictures of black sticks on white paper. "When we left the interpreter said we should come back tomorrow and learn more about how to speak like the white man," said Nazbah's son.

"Can you talk a little of the white man's language now?" asked Mother Red Lake.

"No," said the boys, "but we will learn tomorrow." Although María had spoken both Spanish and Navajo since she was a small girl, she knew it would not be easy for the boys to learn to speak like the Americans. She knew it would be good for them to learn the language of their captors so they could understand what was being said, but she remained quiet as she knew Mother Red Lake did not approve. She would encourage her son when they were alone.

Spring came early to Fort Sumner, and in March the fields were green with young corn and wheat and the other crops the prisoners had planted. "It will be nice to have young corn to eat," said Hesbah.

"Yes," replied María, "and melons. I will drink melon

166

juice instead of this bitter water. Every time I take a drink I think I will be sick." The spring brought birds to the cottonwood trees, and their singing seemed to brighten the camp. It seemed that the worst was over and that soon there would be fresh food to eat.

However, a new cloud hung over the Bosque Redondo. The Comanches, who had been making small raids on the Navajo herds at the north and south ends of the reservation, were becoming bolder. Larger parties of raiders were starting to strike close to the fort, and the soldiers seemed helpless to stop them.

35

THE POWERFUL COMANCHE TRIBE AND THEIR Kiowa allies had opposed the establishment of Fort Sumner from the beginning, as they feared the army might interfere with their raids into Texas and Mexico. For more than a hundred years they had driven stolen herds from the south along a well-established trail to sell to the people along the Rio Grande and eastern Colorado. Now the Americans and their hereditary enemies, the Navajos, were taking their lands and forcing them eastward.

At first the Comanches confined their raids to the wagon trains moving between Albuquerque and Fort Sumner, but the trains were heavily guarded and finally, in 1865, they

167

decided to make an effort to move the intruders off of their lands and west of the Rio Grande. Small raiding parties attacked the Bosque Redondo north and south of the fort and drove off or slaughtered the Navajo herds. As there was little or no resistance, larger war parties which included some New Mexicans began entering the reservation in the vicinity of the fort itself. The alliance of some New Mexicans with the Comanches was based on trade relations which had existed for many years; trade in livestock, liquor, arms and ammunition, which both of these peoples found profitable to their way of life.

As there were only four hundred soldiers at the fort, a few guns were issued to the Navajos, and they were told to take their bows and arrows with them when they herded the sheep to use in driving off the raiders. However, the Navajos were no match for the mounted raiders armed with guns in this open country, and many of them were killed before they could run to the safety of their camps.

During 1865 and 1866 the raids occurred every week, and the Navajos lived in constant fear of attack. They grazed the sheep closer to the main encampments and refused to permit their women to go with the herds. They posted guards and brought the sheep back to the river every time a dust cloud appeared on the horizon. Their herds became smaller and the animals thinner, and more animals had to be bought from the ranchers to feed the prisoners.

The Dine' Anaii moved about among the other clans and found many of the prisoners eager to listen when they spoke of getting them jobs as sheepherders, house servants and mistresses in the New Mexican villages and ranches. This small clan of less than a hundred members had been allies of the Spanish, the Mexicans and the Americans and always the enemy of their own people. For more than two hundred years they had acted as scouts and had profited from the slave trade along the Rio Grande. Now the miserable conditions along the Pecos River gave them the oppor-

168

tunity to renew this lucrative business by recruiting the dissatisfied Navajos and, with the help of the New Mexicans, smuggling them off of the reservation. Many hungry Navajos willingly left the Bosque Redondo hoping for better food and better living conditions in the service of the New Mexicans.

In spite of the Comanche raids and the shortage of food, the Navajos still had hope during the spring of 1865. The fields were green with growing crops, and men, women and children suffering from malnutrition were still able to dig and hoe and irrigate in the fields with smiles on their faces. The corn bloomed and tasselled and tiny melons formed on the vines, but then the plants began to wither and the corn worms reappeared in the newly-formed ears, and much of the crop was destroyed.

The loss of their crops two years in a row was almost more than the people could bear. Women and children sat and cried, and the men met together to make plans for leaving the prison camp. Voices of the medicine men became stronger as they warned the people that they must return to the land the gods had given them or they would surely perish in this accursed land. The people listened and many slipped away, choosing possible death rather than the misery of life and eventual death in this desolate land far from their homes.

Although the army could not take care of the prisoners already at the Bosque Redondo, General Carlton ordered more soldiers from other forts in the territory to patrol the area between Fort Sumner and the Rio Grande in order to intercept the escapees and bring them back. The General also knew that many Navajos still roamed the New Mexico Territory as free men and that their presence might retard the westward spread of ranchers and miners. He persuaded some of the headmen at the Bosque Redondo to go and speak to the groups who were beyond the reach of the army and to warn them that they must turn themselves in at once. His messengers returned with reports that

169

there were still many New Mexicans and Ute raiders in search of slaves and livestock in Navajoland and that the Navajos were still scattered and in hiding from the raiders.

36

THE BEGINNING OF SEEMINGLY ENDLESS INVES-tigations of the Bosque Redondo started in July, 1865. A new Indian agent, Theodore H. Dodd, was appointed and, about a year later, officially commissioned by President Johnson to act for the Navajo people on the reservation. He immediately went to St. Louis and, with Congressional approval, ordered more tools and clothing for his charges.

In spite of Agent Dodd's efforts, the crop raised in the spring and summer of 1866 was little better than those of the two previous years, and the Navajos remained on re-duced army rations.

In the fall of 1866, General Carlton was replaced by General Getty and orders were issued to transfer control over the Navajos from the War Department to the Depart-ment of Indian Affairs; however, the transfer was not actually made until 1868, as the latter did not want the responsibility and did not have sufficient funds to feed so many Indians.

General Getty arrived in time to witness the next of the horrible experiences suffered by the prisoners at the

170

Bosque Redondo. Smallpox struck the reservation during the winter of 1866-67, and many of the Navajos died from this new plague.

Gray Hat's family, like every other family on the reservation, lost all hope of raising food on the reservation after the crop failure of 1866. Short rations of tainted food and bitter alkali water, which gave them dysentery, further weakened their bodies and their will to cultivate the fields in which nothing would grow.

Medicine men did what they could to treat the people. Accompanied by some of the younger men, they went to the mountains a hundred miles away, travelling at night to elude the soldiers and raiders, to obtain herbs to treat the sick. They brought back the roots of water plants to treat those who had contracted venereal diseases from the soldiers, pine pitch for the treatment of sores, and mountain tea for a variety of sicknesses, but still the Navajos died because the gods would not help.

Mother Red Lake brewed herbs and doctored her family, but medicine was no cure for malnutrition; they grew thinner and more listless as the days passed. She had not been well during the winter and had spent too much of her waning strength caring for the sick all around her. Many of the Navajos were dying from smallpox which threatened to destroy the entire tribe. Firewood was scarce and the cold winter winds seemed to penetrate even several thicknesses of blankets. As she watched the smallpox killing her people, Mother Red Lake wondered if she, too, had contracted the disease. She watched her body for the appearance of the red spots but none appeared. Finally, she became too sick to help the others, and Nazbah and Joni stayed with her while the other members of the family worked at the fort or went in search of weeds to burn in the shelter to keep her warm.

One morning her throat became so inflamed and swollen she could scarcely swallow. Hesbah brewed some sage tea, and she let a little trickle down her throat. The warm tea relieved the soreness a little, but it did not go away and

171

became worse toward evening. She drank a little tea, keeping some in her mouth, until she finally went to sleep. In the morning she could hardly breathe, but the sage tea again reduced the swelling so she could speak.

"I am worse," she said huskily to Nazbah. "This time I will not recover. I have urged Gray Hat to leave this place and hoped to live to see my old home once again. Our land was good to us. We had fine horses and many sheep when I was young. You must keep telling Gray Hat to leave this place and take our family back to where they belong."

Nazbah and Joni sat and listened. They could do nothing to save her. In the old days, perhaps, a ceremonial might have saved her, but here there were no gods to call to.

The following morning Mother Red Lake was dead. She had lost all desire to live and had not even struggled or tried to call out for help as she choked. The family cried helplessly outside the shelter as Nazbah and Hesbah prepared their mother's body for burial.

The post commander had designated several places as cemeteries, marking them with posts, close to the hills and above the irrigated farm lands. The burial area assigned to the Kinlichine and the nearby clans was about a mile from the camps in which they lived. Nazbah asked some of her relatives to help dig a grave in the frozen ground, and after they had finished and blackened themselves with ashes to ward off evil spirits, they carried Mother Red Lake's body to the grave, quickly covered it and left without looking back.

After the burial the shelter in which Mother Red Lake had died was burned, and a new shelter was built a short distance away.

That night as the family sat in silence around their small campfire, they wrapped their blankets more tightly around their heads to shut out the sounds of the coyotes who came nightly to fight over the bodies of the dead.

The death of his first wife made Gray Hat more determined to leave the Bosque Redondo at the first opportunity.

172

All of the prisoners had the same desire, and plans of escape had, for the past year, become almost the only topic of conversation when the men worked in the fields or sat around the campfires in the evenings. The headmen discussed plans for the removal of their clans as they could not run off and leave the rest of their people with no one to represent them. The new Indian Agent, Dodd, spoke well but promised nothing when the headmen asked him if they could be released to return to their homeland. There were many rumors that, now that their old enemy was gone, the new general would soon let them return to Navajoland. However, there was no change at the Bosque Redondo. In the winter and spring of 1867, the unwilling Navajos were again forced to plant and cultivate crops, some at the point of the soldiers' guns, and by February they had planted nine thousand acres which no one expected to harvest.

It was in the spring of 1867 that Manuelito and Ganado Mucho arrived with small groups of their people. Although they had been under constant attack by the New Mexicans, Utes and Hopis for four years and had lost many of their women to these slave traders, they soon realized that their lives as fugitives were preferable to those of the prisoners.

After visiting with the Kiya' a' anii headman, Manuelito came to speak with Gray Hat. Manuelito was still a strong, well-built man of about forty-eight who walked proudly around the camps in striking contrast to the thin, half-sick and discouraged prisoners. He was very angry at the Americans and asked Gray Hat why he had remained and let his people be so mistreated. Gray Hat had no answer. How could he tell of the hope they had felt during each planting season, of the many promises of better food and clothing which had been made, of the rumors that had been circulating for the past two years that they would soon be sent home?

Many Navajos had left, but those who remained had lived from day to day for four years on hopes and promises, watching their friends and relatives die from disease, ex-

173

posure, maltreatment, food poisoning and the guns of the Comanche and New Mexican raiders as they waited for their headmen to perform some miracle which would permit them to leave and return to their old homes.

37

LIVING CONDITIONS AT THE BOSQUE REDONDO were miserable, but for many of the Navajos without hope, life still went on. Marriages were arranged, babies were born and people died, just as they always have through good times and bad everywhere in this world. Infant mortality was high and life expectancy lower than it had been in the old days, but it would have taken many years to completely destroy the group unless their jailors resorted to more severe measures than those usually condoned by human beings.

It was in the fall of 1867 that Chiquito spoke to his father of marriage. He had choosen a pretty young woman of the Dibezhiini Clan whom he had seen working in the fields. There had not been many of the elaborate marriages which the Navajos loved for the past fourteen years and Chiquito, like many other young men, had not been urged to take a wife because he had been needed to help protect and provide for Gray Hat's family. Now he was no longer

Kay Bennett

needed. The children, with the exception of Joni's seven-year-old son, were well able to tend to the family chores.

Gray Hat had no objection and told his son he would speak to the young woman's parents the next day. He discussed the marriage first with Nazbah. "Yes," she said, "your son should marry but what can we give the girl's parents? We cannot go to them empty-handed."

"I do not know," answered Gray Hat. "In the old days we could have given them some fine horses and sheep, but now we have nothing. All of our people are destitute, and I do not think they will expect much. Other young men are being married, and their families have no more than we. Still, I am a headman and they will expect more."

"I can give a blanket," said Nazbah almost in tears. "They will have to be satisfied with that. Oh my husband, when will we be able to leave this terrible place? How can the children marry and raise families? How can they ever be happy in this desolate land?"

Gray Hat had no answer. He drew his blanket around him and went to sleep.

The next day Gray Hat walked over to the camp of the Dibezhiini Clan and sought out the parents of the young woman Chiquito had spoken of. The girl's parents were flattered. They knew Gray Hat was one of the headmen of the Kinlichine and felt it quite an honor to have such an important guest at their shelter. They gave him a little to eat from their meager food supply and asked his opinion as to when they might be allowed to return to their old home. While they talked, Gray Hat looked at the young woman who sat in the shade of the shelter, listening to the talk of her elders. He could see she was healthy and very pretty. He also approved of her parents who were well-mannered and soft-spoken. Finally he came to the real purpose of his visit. "I would like for my son to marry your daughter," he said. "He is a good son and will take care of her when we leave this terrible place." He paused and the

176

young woman spoke before her parents could make any comment.

"I will not marry your son," she said. Her parents were shocked. They turned and frowned and the girl looked sullenly at the ground. They were surprised at Gray Hat's proposal and sat for a few minutes trying to collect their thoughts before answering.

"I will talk to my daughter," said her father. "Perhaps she will change her mind. Our lives here are so strange that she scarcely remembers how happy our family once was. I will come to see you tomorrow." Gray Hat rose and thanked them for feeding him, then returned to his own camp. He did not like the young woman's manners but, as her father had said, life here was not normal and he would not oppose the marriage if she changed her mind.

While Gray Hat was looking over the girl and her parents and making his proposal, Nazbah and the other women of the family were making somewhat guarded inquiries about the girl Chiquito was planning to marry. "She is one of the young women that are slipping off at night to visit the soldiers," reported Hesbah. "She flirts with all the guards and they bring her food from their storehouse."

"Yes," said Nazbah. "I too have heard that she is not liked by the older women of her clan. It is just as well if she refuses to marry Chiquito. She would not make him a good wife."

Gray Hat told Chiquito of his talk with the girl's parents and told him to stay in camp as the girl's father would come to visit them the next day.

When the Dibezhiini clansman arrived, Chiquito took his place a little distance away from his elders. Nazbah gave their visitor some tea and made him welcome. After a short talk about other matters he said, "My daughter will not listen to me or to her mother. I have told her she should be honored to have you speak for her. I can see your son is a fine man, and I would be pleased to have him

177

join our group, but I do not want you or him to be unhappy with us. It is best that you find another woman for him."

Both of the girl's parents were very unhappy, but there was nothing they could do. The young women who were mistresses of the soldiers considered themselves better than their parents and no longer dependent upon them for the necessities of life. They could now disobey their parents without being turned out to starve.

Chiquito was very unhappy, and so were some of the other young men. They blamed the soldiers for what was happening to some of the women. "The soldiers are no good," said one of them. "I notice they are always ready to shoot us because we have no guns but when the Comanches come, they run to their fort. I have never seen any soldier shoot at a Comanche. They leave us to fight with bows and arrows so we will be killed and they can take our women."

"Yes, that is true," replied another young man. "But what can we do? It would be easy to kill the guards at night but if we kill one, we will all be shot the next day."

"I think we should kill some of the guards," said Chiquito. "I am tired of being pushed around in the fields. I have heard that the soldiers are bringing new diseases to our women, and I think we should kill the guards who are responsible."

For several days the young men talked, and the more they talked the angrier they became. Finally a plan evolved by which the guards could be killed with little risk to the prisoners. They would stage a Comanche raid at night and blame the killing on the raiders. They would wait until the new moon so the darkness would be complete.

On the night of the next new moon they divided into pairs and crept up on two of the guard posts. They killed five of the guards with their knives, then assembled a short distance away and started imitating loud Comanche yells as they ran away from the camp. They ran a short distance,

178

then circled back and returned to their homes where they wrapped themselves up in their blankets and pretended to sleep.

The detachment sent from the fort found nothing except the dead bodies of the soldiers. The next day about twenty soldiers rode out to follow the trail of the raiders, but they could find no trail. Officers and interpreters came to question the Navajos about the raid, but no one could give them any information. The women who had been with the guards said nothing, as they knew they too would be killed if they testified against their people.

The young men kept their secret well and vowed they would kill more of the guards if they did not leave the women alone.

38

IT WAS NOT LONG AFTER THE RAID STAGED BY Chiquito and the other young men that Nazbah was called to help with the delivery of a baby. The young woman had lost her mother during the smallpox epidemic. Hesbah and María went with Nazbah as the birth of a baby, even in the prison camp, was always of great importance to the clan.

They found the young woman, attended by three of her relatives, lying on a sheepskin in the shelter. The young woman was in labor and her attendants were taking turns pressing down on her stomach to force the baby down.

Nazbah took charge at once. She put her cool hand on the young woman's hot forehead and spoke gently to her. "It is almost time for your child to be born," she said. "We will make you some cornmeal mush to keep up your strength. You must kneel up now so the baby will fall on this soft sheepskin." Two of her relatives held the young woman as she knelt and Nazbah pressed down. In a few minutes the baby was born, and as soon as the infant fell, Nazbah picked it up and slapped it on the back. The baby cried and María proceeded to cut and tie the natal cord.

"It's a boy," they all cried as they crowded around, almost forgetting the child's mother. Hesbah laid the exhausted woman on a sheepskin and fed her a little of the cornmeal mush while the other women washed and admired the baby boy. Finally they wrapped him in a rag and gave him to the mother.

Nazbah and her two helpers said goodbye and started for their home. Hesbah said, "That baby does not belong to a Navajo man. No Navajo ever had yellow hair."

"I know," said Nazbah. "He is the son of one of the soldiers. I do not know why any woman would wish to have children for our enemies."

"The women get extra rations from the soldiers," said María. "I would rather die from starvation than even speak to such evil men." They were all depressed. The Navajo moral code permitted Navajo men to have children by alien women but it did not sanction Navajo women having children by alien men. Since the coming of the Americans, first at Fort Defiance and now here in the concentration camp, Navajo women had borne children for the white men, even though they knew they would not be permitted to stay with their own clan and would have to seek refuge with another clan. It seemed that life at Fort Sumner was destroying many of the beliefs which had kept the tribe strong throughout the years.

180

"We must leave this place," said Nazbah to Hesbah. "You must help me to convince your father that we must leave at once. I would rather be killed quickly on the trail leading away from here than stay and die slowly. I cannot bear to see our children growing up as the slaves of the Americans."

"My husband says that Gray Hat plans to leave," replied Hesbah, "but he will not lead his people to their death. He thinks that soon we will be allowed to leave in peace."

"The Americans have spoken of letting us go for more than a year," replied Nazbah. "I hope the day will come soon. Some of our women are killing their babies at birth rather than trying to raise them in this horrible place. I think if we stay here much longer, there will be none of us left to leave."

39

THE CONDITIONS AT THE BOSQUE REDONDO deteriorated rapidly during the winter of 1867-1868. The cost of maintaining the Navajos had always been resented by the local people, and as it became better known through speeches made by rival politicians, the project became even more unpopular with all the voters. Finally, after two years of argument, the Department of Indian Affairs agreed to accept the responsibility for taking care of the prisoners and the War Department agreed to turn them over to that civilian department. Shortly thereafter, investigations of the reservation were again made which revealed the same miserable condition of the Indians, their exploitation by politicians, officers and government officials, and the utter impracticability of maintaining so many people in such a small and agriculturally worthless area. It was finally decided, much to the relief of the local voters, to let the Navajos return to their homeland.

On June 1, 1868, a treaty was drafted by Lieutenant General Sherman and Colonel Tappan who had been sent by President Andrew Johnson to act as peace commissioners. The treaty was accepted without question by the desperate Navajo headmen. They all assembled at the headquarters building, eager to sign any paper which would permit them to leave. As they filed by the table presided over by a group of army officers, each headman was asked his name, and as the name given to him by the Americans was entered, he made his mark. Twenty-six headmen made their marks, whereby they agreed to the provisions of a treaty which had been explained to them but which they only partially understood. Agent Dodd signed the treaty as agent for the Navajos.

A copy of the treaty follows:

THE UNITED STATES-NAVAJO TRIBE TREATY OF 1868

Signed June 1, 1868   Ratified July 25, 1868   Proclaimed August 12, 1868 — Articles of a treaty and agreement made and entered into at Fort Sumner, New Mexico, on the first day of June, one thousand eight hundred and sixty-eight, by and between the United States, represented by its commissioners, Lieutenant General W. T. Sherman and Colonel Samuel F. Tappan, of the one part, and the Navajo Nation or Tribe of Indians, represented by their chiefs and headmen, duly authorized and empowered to act for the whole

182

people of said nation or tribe, the names of said chiefs and headmen being hereto subscribed, of the other part, witness:

ARTICLE 1. From this day forward all war between the parties to this agreement shall forever cease. The Government of the United States desires peace, and its honor is hereby pledged to keep it. The Indians desire peace, and they now pledge their honor to keep it.

If bad men among the whites, or among other people subject to the authority of the United States, shall commit any wrong upon the person or property of the Indians, the United States will, upon proof made to the agent and forwarded to the Commissioner of Indian Affairs at Washington City, proceed at once to cause the offender to be arrested and punished according to the laws of the United States, and also to reimburse the injuries of said persons for the loss sustained.

If the bad men among the Indians shall commit a wrong or depredation upon the person or property of anyone, white, black or Indian, subject to the authority of the United States and at peace therewith, the Navajo Tribe agrees that they will, on proof made to their agent, and on notice by him, deliver up the wrongdoer to the United States, to be tried and punished according to its laws; and in case they wilfully refuse to do so, the person injured shall be reimbursed for his loss from the annuities or other money due, or to become due to them, under this treaty, or any others that may be made with the United States, and the President may prescribe such rules and regulations for ascertaining damages under this article as in his judgement may be proper; but no such damage shall be adjusted and paid until examined and passed upon by the Commissioner of Indian Affairs, and no one sustaining loss whilst violating, or because of his violating, the provisions of this treaty or the laws of the United States shall be reimbursed therefor.

183

ARTICLE 2. The United States agrees that the following district of country, to wit: bounded on the north by the 37th degree of north latitude, south by an east and west line passing through the site of old Fort Defiance, in the Cañon Bonito, east by the parallel of longitude which, if prolonged south, would pass through old Fort Lyon or the Ojo-de-Oso Bear Spring, and west by a parallel of longitude about 109 degrees 30 minutes west of Greenwich, provided it embraces the outlet of the Cañon-de-Chelly, which cañon is to be all included in this reservation, shall be, and the same is hereby, set apart for the use and occupation of the Navajo tribe of Indians, and for such other friendly tribes or individual Indians as from time to time they may be willing, with the consent of the United States, to admit among them; and the United States agrees that no persons except those hereinso authorized to do so, and except such officers, soldiers, agents and employees of the Government, or of the Indians, as may be authorized to enter upon Indian reservations in discharge of duties imposed by law, or the orders of the President, shall ever be permitted to pass over, settle upon, or reside in the territory described in this article.

ARTICLE 3. The United States agrees to cause to be built, at some point within said reservation, where timber and water may be convenient, the following buildings: a warehouse to cost not exceeding twenty-five hundred dollars; an agency building for the residence of the agent, not to cost exceeding three thousand dollars; a carpenter and blacksmith shop, not to cost exceeding one thousand dollars each; and a schoolhouse and chapel, so soon as a sufficient number of children can be induced to attend school, which shall not cost to exceed five thousand dollars.

ARTICLE 4. The United States agrees that the agent for the Navajos shall make his home at the agency building; that he shall reside among them and shall keep an office

184

open at all times for the purpose of prompt and diligent inquiry into such matters of complaint by or against the Indians as may be presented for investigation, as also for the faithful discharge of other duties enjoined by law. In all cases of depredation on person or property he shall cause the evidence to be taken in writing and forwarded, together with his findings, to the Commissioner of Indian Affairs, whose decision shall be binding on the parties to this treaty.

ARTICLE 5. If any individual belonging to said tribe, or legally incorporated with it, being the head of a family, shall desire to commence farming, he shall have the privilege to select, in the presence and with the assistance of the agent then in charge, a tract of land within said reservation, not exceeding one hundred and sixty acres in extent, which tract when so selected, certified and recorded in the "land-book" as herein described, shall cease to be held in common, but the same may be occupied and held in the exclusive possession of the person selecting it, and of his family, so long as he or they may continue to cultivate it.

Any person over eighteen years of age, not being the head of a family, may in like manner select, and cause to be certified to him or her for the purposes of cultivation, a quantity of land, not exceeding eighty acres in extent, and thereupon be entitled to the exclusive possession of the same as above directed. For each of the land tracts so selected a certificate containing a description thereof, and the name of the person selecting it, with the certificate endorsed thereon that the same has been recorded, shall be delivered to the party entitled to it by the agent, after the same shall have been recorded by him in a book to be kept in his office subject to inspection, which book shall be known as the "Navajo Land Book."

The President may at any time order a survey of the reservation, and, when so surveyed, Congress shall provide for protecting the rights of said settlers and their improvements, and may fix the character of the title held by each.

The United States may pass such laws on the subject of alienation and descent of property between the Indians and their descendants as may be thought proper.

ARTICLE 6. In order to insure the civilization of the Indians entering into this treaty, the necessity of education is admitted, especially of such of them as may be settled on said agricultural parts of this reservation, and they therefore pledge themselves to compel their children, male and female, between the ages of six and sixteen years, to attend school; and it is hereby made the duty of the agent for said Indians to see that this stipulation is strictly complied with; and the United States agrees that, for every thirty children between said ages who can be induced or compelled to attend school, a house shall be provided for such activity, and a teacher competent to teach the elementary branches of an English education shall be furnished, who will reside among said Indians, and faithfully discharge his or her duties as a teacher. The provisions of this article to continue for not less than ten years.

ARTICLE 7. When the head of a family shall have selected lands and received his certificate as above directed, and the agent shall be satisfied that he intends in good faith to commence cultivating the soil for a living, he shall be entitled to receive seeds and agricultural implements for the first year, not exceeding in value one hundred dollars, and for each succeeding year he shall continue to farm, for a period of two years, he shall be entitled to receive seeds and implements to the value of twenty-five dollars.

ARTICLE 8. In lieu of all sums of money or other annuities provided to be paid to the Indians herein named under any treaty or treaties heretofore made, the United

186

States agrees to deliver at the agency house of the reservation herein named, on the first day of September of each year for ten years, the following articles, to wit:
Such articles of clothing, goods, or raw materials in lieu thereof, as the agent may make his estimate for, not exceeding in value five dollars per Indian, each Indian being encouraged to manufacture their own clothing, blankets, etc.; to be furnished with no article which they can manufacture themselves. And, in order that the Commissioner of Indian Affairs may be able to estimate properly for the articles herein named, it shall be the duty of the agent each year to forward to him a full and exact census of the Indians, on which the estimate from year to year can be based.
And in addition to the articles herein named, the sum of ten dollars for each person entitled to the beneficial effects of this treaty shall be annually appropriated for a period of ten years, for each person who engages in farming or mechanical pursuits, to be used by the Commissioner of Indian Affairs in the purchase of such articles as from time to time the condition and necessities of the Indians may indicate to be proper; and if within ten years at any time it shall appear that the amount of money needed for clothing, under this article can be appropriated to better uses for the Indians named herein, the Commissioner of Indian Affairs may change the appropriation to other purposes, but in no event shall the amount of this appropriation be withdrawn or discontinued for the period named, provided they remain at peace. And the President shall annually detail an officer of the Army to be present and attest the delivery of all the goods herein named to the Indians, and he shall inspect and report on the quantity and quality of the goods and the manner of their delivery.

ARTICLE 9. In consideration of the advantages and benefits conferred by this treaty, and the many pledges of

187

friendship by the United States, the tribes who are parties to this agreement hereby stipulate that they will relinquish all right to occupy any territory outside their reservation, as herein defined, but retain the right to hunt on any unoccupied lands contiguous to their reservation, so long as the large game may range thereon in such numbers as to justify the chase; and they, the said Indians, further agree expressly:

1st. That they will make no opposition to the construction of railroads now being built or hereafter to be built, across the continent.

2nd. They will not attack any persons at home or travelling, nor molest or disturb any wagon trains, coaches, mules or cattle belonging to people of the United States, or to persons friendly therewith.

3rd. They will not interfere with the peaceful construction of any railroad not passing over their reservation as herein defined.

4th. They will never capture or carry off from the settlements women or children.

5th. They will never kill or scalp white men, nor attempt to harm them.

6th. They will not in future oppose the construction of railroads, wagon roads, mail stations or other works of utility or necessity which may be ordered or permitted by the laws of the United States; but should such roads or other works be constructed on the lands of their reservation the Government will pay the tribe whatever amount of damage may be assessed by three disinterested commissioners to be appointed by the President for that purpose, one of the said commissioners to be a chief or headman of the tribe.

188

7th. They will make no opposition to the military posts or roads now established, or that may be established, not in violation of treaties heretofore made or hereafter to be made with any of the Indian tribes.

ARTICLE 10. No further treaty for the cession of any portion or part of the reservation herein described, which may be held in common, shall be of any validity or force against said Indians unless agreed to and executed by at least three-fourths of all the adult male Indians occupying or interested in the same, and no cession by the tribe shall be understood or construed in such manner as to deprive, without his consent, any individual member of the tribe of his rights to any tract of land selected by him as provided in article (5) of this treaty.

ARTICLE 11. The Navajos hereby also agree that at any time after the signing of these presents they will proceed in such manner as may be required of them by the agent, or by the officer charged with their removal, to the reservation herein provided for, the United States paying for their subsistence en route, and providing a reasonable amount of transportation for the sick and feeble.

ARTICLE 12. It is further agreed by and between the parties to this agreement that the sum of one hundred and fifty thousand dollars appropriated shall be disbursed as follows, subject to any condition provided in the law, to wit:

1st. The actual cost of the removal of the tribe from the Bosque Redondo reservation to the reservation, say fifty thousand dollars.

2nd. The purchase of fifteen thousand sheep and goats, at a cost not to exceed thirty thousand dollars.

189

3rd. The purchase of five hundred beef cattle and a million pounds of corn, to be collected and held at the military post nearest the reservation, subject to the orders of the agent, for the relief of the needy during the coming winter.

4th. The balance, if any, of the appropriation to be invested for the maintenance of the Indians pending their removal, in such manner as the agent who is with them may determine.

5th. The removal of this tribe to be made under the supreme control and direction of the military commander of the Territory of New Mexico, and when completed, the management of the tribe to revert to the proper agent.

ARTICLE 13. The tribe herein named, by their representatives, parties to this treaty, agree to make the reservation herein described their permanent home, and they will not as a tribe make any permanent settlement elsewhere, reserving the right to hunt on the lands adjoining the said reservation formerly called theirs, subject to the modifications named in this treaty and the orders of the commander of the department in which said reservation may be for the time being; and it is further agreed and understood by the parties to this treaty that if any Navajo Indian or Indians shall leave the reservation herein described to settle elsewhere he or they shall forfeit all the rights, privileges and annuities conferred by the terms of this treaty; and it is further agreed by the parties to this treaty that they will do all that they can to induce Indians now away from the reservation set apart for the exclusive use and occupation of the Indians, leading nomadic life, or engaged in war against the people of the United States, to abandon such a life and settle permanently in one of the territorial reservations set apart for the exclusive use and occupation of the Indians.

In testimony of all which the said parties have herein agreed hereunto on this the first day of June, one thousand eight hundred and sixty-eight, at Fort Sumner in the Territory of New Mexico, set their hands and seals.

W. T. Sherman
Lieutenant General, Indian Peace Commissioner

S. F. Tappan
Indian Peace Commissioner

Barboncito,		Serginto	his X mark
chief	his X mark	Grande	X
Amijo	X	Inoetenito	X
Delgado	X	Muchachos Mucho	X
Manuelito	X	Chiqueto Segundo	X
Herrero	X	Cabello Amarillo	X
Largo	X	Francisco	X
Chiqueto	X	Torivio	X
Muerto de Hombre	X	Desdendado	X
Narbono	X	Juan	X
Narbono Segundo	X	Guerom	X
Ganado Mucho	X	Gugadore	X
		Cabasin	X
Council:		Barbon Segundo	X
Riquo	his X mark	Cabares Colorados	X
Juan Martin	X		

Theo. H. Dodd, United States Indian Agent for the Navajos

ATTEST:

Geo. W. G. Getty, Colonel Thirty-seventh Infantry, brevet Major General U. S. Army

Chas. McClure, brevet major and commissary of subsistence, U. S. Army

B. S. Roberts,
Lieutenant Colonel
Third Cavalry,
brevet Brigadier General
U. S. Army

J. Cooper McKee,
brevet Lieutenant Colonel,
Surgeon U. S. Army

James F. Weeds, brevet
major and assistant
surgeon, U. S. Army

J. C. Sutherland,
interpreter

William Vaux, Chaplain,
U. S. Army

40

TWO WEEKS AFTER THE SIGNING OF THE
treaty, seven thousand Navajos were ready to make the
long march back to their homeland. With them went about
fifteen hundred horses and about two thousand head of
sheep and goats, all that was left of an estimated two hundred fifty thousand sheep and sixty thousand horses the
Navajos had owned at the start of the war of 1863.

Word of the signing of the treaty, which the Navajos
considered an agreement to let them go to their old homes,
spread throughout the camp almost before the last headman had made his mark. Everyone started bundling up his
meager belongings, checked his clothing and particularly his
moccasins. Everyone, except the very small children, remem-

192

bered the long walk which now must be made again before they reached their homeland.

Gray Hat explained that all the prisoners would leave at once. The army planned to have fifty wagons ready to carry the food, but those who could not walk would have to ride on the horses.

"You must ride a horse," said Nazbah. "It is not fitting that a headman should walk."

"Yes," said Kee. "All of the rest of us can walk. Even my young son can keep up with the column."

"We will see," replied Gray Hat. "Tomorrow we will see how many babies, small children and old people that cannot walk are in our clan and how many horses are needed."

Nazbah had kept Mother Red Lake's small grinding stone that she had carried during the years they had run from the soldiers. "I will take this small stone back with me to the land our mother loved," she told Hesbah as she added the stone to her bundle, "and these small rocks shaped like sheep. Mother Red Lake always said they would bring us good luck and many sheep. Perhaps they will make our herd increase. Perhaps all our ewes will have twins."

On the morning of June 18, 1868, the people started filing out of the Bosque Redondo. All day long, group by group, they joined the column until it stretched out for a distance of about ten miles. The worried looks on their faces as they sat waiting turned to smiles of relief as they were herded into place and started walking away from the camp where they had spent so many miserable days.

Agent Dodd rode near the head of the column and behind him followed a wagon for his wife and two children. The long column was escorted by four companies of cavalry to protect it from raiding parties and to see that all the Navajos kept going until they reached Fort Wingate. Officers and soldiers rode up and down the line, yelling at stragglers and telling the people to stay in line.

193

The Kinlichine Clan was about midway in the long line. Before they rose to take their place, Gray Hat took a little corn pollen from his pouch, put a little in his mouth, a little on his head and threw a little toward the sun as he prayed for the gods to help them to return to their native land. He passed the pouch around and the others followed his example and repeated, "May we walk in beauty back to our land. May we have beauty around us as we walk." As they left the camp it seemed that a great load slid off their shoulders and their spirits lifted. There was sadness too, as they thought of Mother Red Lake buried and left behind in this alien land.

Gray Hat walked along, leading his horse. He talked more than usual, as he assembled his thoughts to meet the changing conditions which lay ahead. "Do not expect too much," he said to his family. "It is enough that we are going back to our old home. Four years ago we came to this evil place expecting fine homes, fertile fields and herds of sheep and horses. We found nothing but poorness and death. Now we are promised that the army will protect us from raiding parties and that they will give us farm tools, seeds, clothing and sheep and goats and that our young men will be taught carpentry and blacksmithing, but we must not believe such promises. We must all plan to work hard, and we will prosper by our own efforts as we did in the past."

The young women listened and made plans for new hogans with thick adobe walls like they had seen at the fort. The men thought of riding alone across the hills and along the mountain trails where they could absorb in silence the beauty of the land and the sky. In time the nervous tension born of the crowded, noisy camp would be replaced by their native calmness and dignity. Once again they would be able to follow the plan their gods had given them, and when they did resume their place in the well-ordered plan of nature, their lives would again be good.

As they walked along, the old beauty way chant which they had almost forgotten came to many of the people, and

194

they repeated it in silence as they trudged along, trying to shut out the noise and discomfort. Dust rose from the many marching feet and sand blew in their faces. They drew their blankets across their mouths but the dust stuck to their sweating bodies and rimmed their red eyes. Mothers with cradle boards on their backs covered their babies' heads with cloth and hoped that they would sleep.

The column moved about ten miles a day and halted just before sunset to allow the women to cook the meager rations. Water was scarce and was used sparingly to wash the caked dust from their faces.

On July 5, the column reached the Rio Grande. As they waded out into the shallow stream, they shouted with joy. Never had water felt so good to tired and dirty bodies. They drank the muddy water and it tasted sweet after drinking the bitter alkali water of the Bosque Redondo. The men washed out their water jugs and filled them with the river water. They felt they had rid themselves of the last reminder of the prison camp.

As they washed themselves, the young Dibezhiini girl that Chiquito had wanted to marry walked by Gray Hat's group and smiled at Chiquito. Now that they were leaving the prison camp she had changed her mind. Chiquito turned away and would not look at her. He, too, had changed his mind. He would look for a wife when they were back home again.

Two days' march after leaving the Rio Grande, a few families slipped away from the column. Officers and interpreters reminded the people of their promise to go to the new reservation which started at Fort Wingate and not to try to make their homes anywhere between the fort and the Rio Grande. More guards were posted at night but still a few more families left, and the headmen could do nothing to prevent them. However, most of the Navajos stayed with the column, and by August they were camped around Fort Wingate. Winter was approaching, it was too late to plant, and they had no sheep. To survive through the

195

winter they must stay near the fort and draw rations from the army until spring. Conditions were so crowded around the fort that the army was forced to move some of the people to the vicinity of Fort Defiance and issue rations from there.

Gray Hat's group was among the ones that were marched to Fort Defiance. They were home again. All around them were the familiar cedar and piñon-covered hills leading to the cool pine-covered mountains. Gray Hat selected a campsite about two miles north of the fort. He left Hesbah's husband in charge and walked with his two sons up the mountain. It was good to be back in the land they loved. That night they lay near a spring under the tall trees, breathing in the sweet smell of the pines. As they lay, each man with his own thoughts, in the old familiar surroundings it seemed as though the years that had passed must have been a bad dream from which they had just awakened. The same sweet water was flowing from the same spring, the same rock outcroppings were around them, the same stars shone through the same trees above them and the same cool, pine-scented air blew across their faces. Kee shook his head to clear his mind. What had happened? What had all the punishment endured by his people accomplished? Here they were, back where they had started, weaker and poorer but still back where nothing else in nature had changed. Five years had been taken from his life and the lives of his people to prove to them that the Americans, when banded together, could destroy the unorganized Navajos and that in the future they must submit to the wishes of the white man's government.

41

THE FALL OF 1868 WAS PLEASANT. FAMILIES travelled to the nearby hills to pick piñons and berries and to renew their stocks of medicinal herbs. It was good to be back in familiar surroundings. The families were still crowded around the fort, but not as crowded as they had been at the prison camp, and they could come and go as they pleased.

The winter of 1868-69 was a hard one, as so many winters are in Navajoland. The army was not prepared to feed the large crowd that remained around the fort, and often there was not enough food for everyone. New Mexicans brought corn by oxcarts from army warehouses in Albuquerque and cowboys drove in herds of beef cattle purchased in Texas, but still there was never enough food. The Navajos supplemented the army ration by hunting rabbits and gathering wild plants, and some of the young men stole livestock from the pueblos to help feed their families.

Finally the long winter was over, and as soon as the snow started to melt, the Navajos started moving away from the forts. Seed corn, beans and squash and a few farm tools were issued from the army warehouse, and the Navajos began at once to plant in the low valleys. They planted large fields, and as the weather moderated some, moved to the mountains to plant in the mountain valleys.

Bad luck was still with many of the families. A late frost, drought and a grasshopper plague destroyed many of the crops in the low valleys.

Gray Hat's family did not sit idly by at their camp near Fort Defiance. They were all anxious to return to their old homes in the valley.

"It is too late to plant this year," said Nazbah, "but we can still gather piñons, acorns and berries. There are cactus apples and many seeds in the hills and the mountains that we can store. The Americans have never given us enough to eat and unless we are prepared, we will again go hungry. Let us go look at our old home and while we are there, we can gather some food to bring back."

"Very well," said Gray Hat. "We will wait until ration day, then leave."

On ration day they were issued beef and took time to cut it in thin strips and to dry it close to the fire. The weather was very hot in the valley. Most of the families had moved into the cooler Cañon Bonito and Black Canyon. Others had moved a little farther from the fort to the shade of piñon and cedar trees near Gray Hat's camp. Many, like Gray Hat's group, made ready to visit their old homes for a few days.

When the meat was dried, Gray Hat's families swung their bundles over their shoulders and started for Red Lake Valley about twelve miles away. It was good to be walking among the familiar hills and trees again. The children had grown up in exile but still remembered the land around their old homes.

Nazbah's boys were now young men, eighteen and nineteen. They admired Kee and stayed with him as much as possible. Kee had promised to help them make strong

198

bows and arrows and to teach them to hunt in the mountains. Hesbah's daughters were fourteen and sixteen. María's daughter was twelve and her son fourteen. He was a quiet boy who preferred the company of Gray Hat to that of the other boys. The two were good friends and spent much time walking or just sitting and talking about many things. The old man told his eager listener of the old days and of the ancient legends of the tribe. Joni's eight-year-old son was too thin and he tired easily. She worried constantly about his health and kept him near her.

The little group walked slowly, pointing out to each other the familiar landmarks. When they reached their old fields and grazing grounds they saw that the grass had grown thick during their absence. "I hope we can get some shovels from the fort," said Hesbah's husband as they looked out over the field. "We should plant as early as possible in the spring." They passed by the spot where Mother Red Lake's hogan had stood and silently wiped the tears from their eyes. At this moment they all realized their loss more than at any time since her death. María moved closer to Hesbah and held her hand as they walked on.

About a mile farther up the valley Nazbah stopped and said, "I will build my hogan here." She walked to a nearby piñon tree and broke off a small branch and sniffed it. "I had almost forgotten how good it smells," she said. "This tree will protect our home and bring back our former prosperity." The place she had selected was where the early sun would shine on her hogan in the morning and where the afternoon sun would add its warmth during the winter months. A small hill on the north side would partially protect it from the winter wind.

"Yes, this a good place," said Gray Hat.

"I will rebuild where I lived before," said Hesbah. María chose a different location for her hogan, as she

199

had no wish to live among the memories of her dead husband.

"Where will you build your hogan?" Nazbah asked Joni.

"I think I will build near María," she answered. "There is a place against the rocks where it will be easy to build a corral for our sheep. Maybe the Americans will give us some sheep soon."

While Kee and his son went with Joni to select a place for her hogan, the others looked around and planned what was to be done. The old hogan and corral poles had been burned and nothing remained except two grinding stones that Hesbah and María had buried before they left. More poles would have to be brought from the mountains and, as there were no horses to do the work, the men would have to drag them. There were plenty of rocks but these, too, would have to be pushed by hand and raised to make the hogan walls. Branches must be brought and earth piled on them to form a roof which would shed the rain waters. The construction of new hogans would take a great deal of time. It was decided that the men and boys should stay and build the hogans and corrals so all would be ready when the families returned in the spring. Gray Hat and the women would return to the fort to draw rations and would bring food to the men.

Chiquito was very restless. He felt that he was too old to live in his foster mother's hogan. He should have a wife and a home of his own. He thought of the Dibezhiini girl, then quickly shut her out of his mind. Perhaps he would find someone else at Fort Defiance. Meanwhile, he would help his relatives build their homes.

On ration day at Fort Defiance, Gray Hat was not allowed to draw rations for the men and boys at Red Lake Valley. The officer in charge explained that everyone must be present to draw his own rations. To avoid giving more than one ration to each person the people were herded into a large corral and as they filed out, each was given food for a week. Even though each person drew only one ration, there was never enough food for all those who waited in the line.

Gray Hat and some of the others walked to Red Lake Valley where the men were working and told them the bad news. "Next week," he said, "you will have to stop work and come to the fort to draw your rations."

"We will find enough to eat here," said Kee. "We would like to have some cornmeal, but we can do without it for a week. We will send the boys to look for food while we work."

Every two days they added six more poles to the pile. It was slow work. When they had twenty-four straight pine poles on hand, they started rolling stones to the hogan sites for the walls. They worked for three months until they had completed the hogans and corrals. The women came every week to help and to gather food. Two days of every week were lost as they walked to and from the fort to draw their rations.

Snow fell in early December, and the men stopped work in the valley and remained near the fort to help bring in wood for the fires.

January and February of 1869 were bitter cold months, and the fires had to be kept burning night and day to keep the makeshift shelters warm. There was never enough food, and the young men hunted rabbits every day to supplement the army rations.

Kee made bows out of oak for all the boys and taught them to hunt. In late November, Gray Hat had led Kee, Chiquito and Hesbah's husband on a deer hunt, and they had killed two fat does, which were a welcome addition to the family diet. Kee had taken the deer sinews, softened them with the brains and used them to reinforce the new bows. Thus reinforced, the bows were effective at a distance of about a hundred feet. The boys practiced daily and soon became expert with their new weapons.

Gray Hat brooded over the past a great deal. Daily he

became more convinced that the future would remain dark for his people unless they returned to their old ways. The great ceremonials were out of the question at this time, mainly because of the shortage of food to feed the crowd and sheep with which to pay the medicine man and his helpers. No ceremony could be successful but could even bring bad luck if the people gave no gift of value in exchange for the gift of knowledge brought to the ceremony by the medicine man. Only small ceremonies could be held for which small payments could be made.

Gray Hat and the other headmen spoke constantly to their people against any further raids. "The raids have brought us bad luck," he said to his clansmen. "The gods do not want us to bring Mexican slaves to our land. They created this land for the Navajos, and they will punish us again if we bring any strangers here to live with us. We must not even bring the sheep or any other possessions of these alien people here if we expect the help of the gods." Most of the Navajos listened, but some who refused to leave their old homes east of the new treaty boundary continued their raids on the New Mexican and Pueblo Indian villages.

It was during the winter months at Fort Defiance that Chiquito met Hanabah. Her family had built a shelter about halfway between the fort and the shelters of the Gray Hat family. She was a few years older than Hesbah's daughters but they had become friends, and on ration days she and her mother and father walked with Hesbah's family to the fort. Her family was of the Miidiisgizhni Clan. Hesbah liked the pretty young girl and made plans to have her and Chiquito meet. Chiquito had already noticed her, as he had several others, but most of those he watched were much younger than he, and the older women already had husbands. Hesbah spoke to Hanabah's mother in secret and found a ready acceptance of her brother. "My husband and I are alone," she said. "It would be a great help to us if we had a strong young man like your brother

202

with us." She spoke to her husband about the proposed match and he, too, was in favor of a marriage with the son of a headman. The problem was how to throw the two together.

An unusually large catch of rabbits gave Hesbah the opportunity. She invited the Miidiisgizhni family to eat roasted rabbit with the Gray Hat family. As the women sat and talked, she directed most of her questions at the girl, for she knew Chiquito who sat listening to Gray Hat and the girl's father would be watching. On the next ration day, Hesbah feigned a sore back and asked Chiquito if he would come with her family and help carry her rations. Chiquito walked with Hesbah's husband and the girl's father. The three found much in common as they talked of the spring planting and speculated upon how many sheep they would receive.

During the next few weeks Chiquito found several opportunities to stop and ask Hanabah's father for advice and finally he spoke to Gray Hat. "My father," he said, "It is time I marry. Your wife's sons are grown, and I am no longer needed at her hogan. You know the woman I wish to marry. She was here with her mother and father. Her father is a fine man and, as he has no sons, he needs help in his fields. Will you speak to him for me?"

"Yes, my son," replied Gray Hat. "I already approve and so does the rest of our family. The women have spoken of nothing else for many days. I will speak to her father and I am sure he will accept. Hesbah has already told me the girl will not refuse."

The following day the marriage was arranged. Nazbah was upset because she had nothing to give the bride's family. "I will send my sons to help build the hogan," she said, "and later when we have some wool I will weave them a blanket. It is not right that a son of a headman go empty-handed to the home of his in-laws."

Four days later the couple was married. Everyone was happy, but thoughts turned to weddings of former days.

203

For Chiquito, this occasion so dear to the Navajo people would necessarily be a simple affair. On the day of the wedding, Hanabah's mother cooked some white cornmeal mush in an earthen jar, then poured it into a basket and handed it to her daughter to carry. Another basket of dry cornmeal and a water jug were placed in front of the couple.

A medicine man from the Miidiisgizhni Clan took charge. He told Hanabah to pour water over Chiquito's hands, then had Chiquito do the same for Hanabah. He then placed the basket of mush in front of them and, taking corn pollen, made a line across the mush from east to west and from south to north, to form a cross. As he spread the sacred pollen he prayed for the happiness of the young couple. He handed the pollen to Chiquito, who sprinkled it along the lines the medicine man had made. Hanabah's turn was next. She sprinkled the pollen along the same lines. She was followed by Gray Hat and Nazbah, and then by her own parents.

The medicine man told Chiquito to scoop up a little of the mush with the fingers of his right hand from the east end of the cross and eat it. He told Hanabah to follow Chiquito's example. "Now," he said to Chiquito, "take some from the south, then from the west, and lastly from the north." Chiquito did as he was told, and Hanabah followed him.

When they had eaten mush and pollen from the four directions, they scooped out a bit from the center of the cross. The medicine man told them they must eat all the mush that remained in the basket while they listened to the advice of their elders. While they ate, he repeated the good advice he had given to many couples before. "Now that you are to live together," he said, "you must take care of each other. Chiquito, if you abuse your wife, the gods will punish you. In order for you to have success in life, your marriage must be good. You must not be jealous of one another. You must respect each other, and you must not argue. Hanabah, you must always prepare good food for your husband. You must keep your home clean, and you must never scold."

Gray Hat also spoke to the young couple at length, and the wedding was over. In the old days many old men would have spoken about the care of the horses and sheep and of how the children should be raised, but now there were few old men.

Chiquito stayed with his new in-laws, and Gray Hat's family returned to their camp. From now on Chiquito was a member of his wife's family and would be considered a member of the Miidiisgizhni Clan.

42

ALL WINTER THE FAMILIES THOUGHT OF planting. The days seemed to pass very slowly as they impatiently waited for the warm days of spring. Late in March the weather moderated, and the snows melted in the lower valleys. April winds started drying the soil, and the family decided they would plant. It was earlier than they had planted in the past, but they had grown used to the Bosque Redondo climate and had forgotten that frost could still be expected in this high country as late as May.

Gray Hat's group drew two garden spades and a quantity of seed corn, beans and squash seed from the army warehouse. They waited until ration day, then, with all their belongings, moved to Red Lake Valley.

"We will bless our new homes first," said Gray Hat. "Bring the cornmeal and come with me, my wife." At Nazbah's hogan he sat down in the center, holding his pouch of corn pollen. Nazbah sat next to him, holding a ceremonial basket in which she had placed the white cornmeal she had ground. The rest of the family sat on each side. He started singing in a low voice the song of the hogan. As he sang his children joined, but the grandchildren remained silent. They had never heard or did not remember the old song.

When the song was finished, Gray Hat repeated the blessing with prayer:

"May our hogan stand with blessing.
May our hogan stand with beauty.
May our hogan stand without evil."

Then as he continued repeating the prayer, Gray Hat stood and walked to the east roof log. He put a little of the sacred pollen on the log above the doorway. Nazbah put a little cornmeal on the same spot. Then he and his wife repeated the blessing at the center of the south, west and north roof logs. When this was completed, Gray Hat passed his corn pollen pouch around, and each person put a little in his mouth, a little on his head, and threw a little into the air as they each made a wish for the house's occupants. Hesbah said, "May you have many sheep and horses." Kee said, "May you always have corn."

When he had completed the blessing of Nazbah's hogan, Gray Hat repeated the blessing of the home ceremony in the hogans of María, Hesbah, and Joni.

When they planted, everyone worked in the field. There was no joking or laughing. The spectre of starvation which had been with them for so many years was still a very real

206

Kay Bennett

presence in the minds of both children and adults. The men took turns digging holes about six inches deep, while the others broke up the clods, planted the seeds and covered them carefully. They planted about four acres and, if all went well, would harvest enough crops to feed them all during the year to come. They saved some of the seeds to plant in their field in the mountains.

When the planting was done, the men and boys again hunted for rabbits and prairie dogs and the women searched for wild carrots, onions, celery, and the other edible plants that grew in the hills and mountains. Gray Hat and Nazbah did not join in the search for food. The long years of suffering and privations had taken their toll, and it was difficult for the old man to climb about on the mountain trails. He walked slowly in the valley and made daily trips to the field to pray for the crops. Some days he sat, a lonely figure in the middle of the field, for hours, chanting the ancient corn song and asking the gods for their help.

The weather continued warm, and early in May the corn sprouted. The dark green stalks were a sign of a healthy crop. Everyone formed the habit of going to look at the green field before leaving to search for food in the mornings.

It was in mid-May that a cold blanket of damp air enveloped the valley and frost settled on the tender shoots. For three nights the frost returned, and when the cold wave left, the sprouts were black and withered. Everyone sat and cried helplessly as they looked at the field from which they had expected so much. Finally Kee stood up and said, "We will plant again. It is not too late to grow a crop. I will go to the fort and get some more seed."

That afternoon he and his two nephews left. The officer at the fort knew what had happened and was as worried as the Navajos. It seemed that the army would have to feed the Indians for another year. He gladly gave Kee the seeds he had come for and wished him good luck.

208

When Kee returned, the family repeated the hard work they had done earlier, and soon the planting was finished. When they had finished replanting in the valley, Hesbah's family and María, with her children, moved to the mountain as it was time to plant in their mountain field.

In July the field in Red Lake Valley was green again, but much of the moisture had left the ground and the stalks were not as healthy as they had appeared before. The family pulled weeds and grass that threatened to choke the stalks, and piled a little more earth around each one to try to keep the ground from drying out. The drought continued, and although the corn tasselled, the stalks were thin and unhealthy. The family prayed every day for rain, and occasionally their hopes were raised by clouds which appeared in the west. But the strong dry winds which came with the clouds drove them away before they dropped any moisture.

As though the long drought was not enough, a plague of grasshoppers settled on the valley to feed on the withering corn. Every day the families took small cedar branches into the field to knock the insects off the corn and stamp them into the ground. They made little headway against the thousands of grasshoppers, but it was better to fight than sit and watch their crop being destroyed. Ears that were nearly matured were taken from the stalks to be eaten rather than being left to the insects.

In the end, scarcely enough corn was saved from the four acres to make a hundred pounds of cornmeal. The field in the mountains fared better, and in September the family harvested a good crop of corn and beans and squash. Still, there would not be enough for everyone until the next year. They would have to rely on the army again for food.

The young men in all the drought-hit areas talked of raiding the pueblos, but their elders preached against any

209

more raids which might bring army reprisals. Knowing of the enmity which existed between the Americans and the Mormons, some men conducted raids on the Mormon herds. However, Mormon country was far away, and without horses, raids were difficult to carry out.

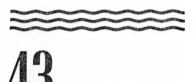

43

AFTER THE LOSS OF THEIR CROPS, THE NAVAJOS almost gave up in despair. It seemed that all of the gods were against them. Only the arrival of the sheep once more raised their spirits and gave them new hope for the future.

It was in November, 1869, that the first of the long awaited sheep were driven into the corrals at Fort Defiance. Word that the herds were on the way had been given the Navajos on the previous ration days, and everyone had assembled days ahead of time around the fort to see them arrive and to make certain that each got his share.

Gray Hat's group had camped near the fort three days before. No one was left behind in Red Lake Valley. The crops that had been harvested were left unguarded, as the sheep were of primary importance to the family.

As they watched the herds being driven into the corrals, everyone wondered how many he would get. There were many sheep, but there were also many people. "I wonder how many sheep we will receive," said Nazbah as she tried to picture the size of the herd they would be driving back to their home.

"I don't know," said Kee. "The big-stomached officer will tell us."

Finally the officer in charge went to the corral where the rations were issued, and the interpreter told the people to line up at the corrals where the sheep were being held. Two sheep were issued to each person and quickly dragged away. The soldiers and Navajo employees at the fort worked fast, and in five days all of the sheep had been distributed.

Gray Hat and his group were among the first in line at one of the corrals. Nazbah's sons went first, and Kee helped them drag their sheep a short distance away from the gate. After a few more sheep had been taken to join them, it was not too difficult to get the others away from the corral. When Gray Hat's group had drawn the twenty-five ewes and the ram they were entitled to, the members of the family gathered around them and drove them away. They kept moving until they were about two miles from the fort, then sat down to rest and admire the animals. Everywhere they looked, they could see other families with small herds of sheep. Some had only four, others had ten or twelve.

The sheep were thin from the long drive which had originated north of Santa Fe but none were old, as the old and the sick had died on the way. "It will not be long before they are fat again," said Nazbah as she stroked one of the animals. "There is plenty of good grass in the valley. We must take good care of them."

"Yes," said Hesbah. "It will take several years to build up our herd. I wonder how many of the ewes will lamb in the spring."

"I wish it was spring now so we could shear them and get some wool for our blankets," said the impatient Joni.

"We can each take one and clip it," said María. "We can keep it in the hogan until the wool grows again."

211

"Yes," said Nazbah, "that is what we will do. We can each weave a blanket to trade at the fort."

The little group drove their herd slowly, stopping often to let the sheep eat. It was dark by the time they herded them into one of the corrals they had prepared at their home. In the morning everyone gathered around the corral to look at the sheep. It was good to have even this small herd. The sheep gave them a feeling of security which had been missing from their lives for many years.

Gray Hat walked with the girls when they let the sheep out of the corral and took them a few hundred feet away to a good spot of grass. The calmly grazing sheep brought his world back into focus, and for the first time he could see that his people might some day be able to return to the good life they had once enjoyed. Later the Navajos were each issued one more sheep or a goat, and thirteen more animals were added to the Gray Hat herd.

44

THE WAR BETWEEN THE STATES AND THE WAR between the United States and the Navajo Tribe had little effect upon the lives of the people on Don Pedro's ranch. During the past ten years Don Pedro had turned the supervision of ranch and mines over to his son, and in 1869 the only duties left to him were those pertaining to family finances. At seventy-eight years of age, Don Pedro was still proud of his erect, slim figure and of his well-fitting clothes which María had the house servants keep freshly laundered for him. Once a month Don Pedro rode to Chihuahua on business and to visit with a doctor who had been his lifelong friend, but lately the trips had seemed to tire him.

With few duties to attend to, Don Pedro spent more time sitting in the pleasant courtyard, talking to María. She had been born on the ranch forty-two years before, and had never had any interest other than the welfare of its master. She knew every field and hill as well as Don Pedro and all of the more than two hundred servants who worked in the fields and at the mines. The two sat in the courtyard almost every evening and discussed the affairs of the ranch and of Mexico. Sometimes Don Pedro spoke of the United States, which was pressing down upon the northern boundaries of their country. Don Pedro had always been kind to María, and her devotion and loyalty to him were absolute.

Sometimes Shebah joined them and Don Pedro spoke of her people. He told her that the Navajos had been captured and kept under guard by the United States Army. He told of when they were released to return to their former homes, and he spoke of the war underway in Texas and Mexico against the Comanche Tribe.

Shebah tried to picture the country in which she had spent her childhood, but the pictures were hazy and she could not recall the faces of her family. After twenty-four years the ranch had become her home, and routine weaving, housekeeping, and rides with María about the ranch had become her way of life. The son she had borne for Don Pedro was now twelve years of age and had fallen heir to the job of polishing his master's leather and silver, and of caring for his master's horse. María had given him the Spanish name of Fernando, but Shebah had called him Keedah since birth.

At thirty-five years of age Shebah was a beautiful wo-

214

man. Her large-eyed, high-cheeked oval face framed by jet black hair was serene and proud. Like María, she wore her hair fastened at the back of her head by a silver clasp and allowed it to hang down her back to her waist. María had taught her to sew, and she had copied her friend's style of blouse and full skirt, discarding her woven manta. She had long ago given up all plans for escape, and had no desire to return to her people.

Doña Isabella was also growing older, and her disposition did not improve with age. She continued to be dissatisfied and unhappy with life on the ranch, and no longer cared to accompany Don Juan to the mines. Except for her daily rides into the hills, she stayed in her part of the ranch house and spoke to no one except her own house servants. Her dislike for her father-in-law had deepened, and she was careful to avoid the old man. Her husband's trips to the ranch were always unpleasant, as he consistently refused to interfere with the established order of his father's life.

Her dislike for María and Shebah matched her dislike for Don Pedro because of the favoritism he showed them. She believed they were slaves to be told what to do, not ladies to be sat with and spoken to, as though they were members of the family. "They act like they are your father's wives instead of his mistresses," she complained to her husband. "They walk around dressed in fine clothes, giving orders to the other servants as though they were the owners of this ranch. I notice the Indian woman never works at her loom except when she wishes to amuse herself and her son, your illegitimate brother, rides your father's horse as though it is his own."

"My father told Fernando to exercise the horse," replied Don Juan. "He has not been feeling well enough to ride the past few weeks. I am worried about his health."

"I am not," said Isabella. "Your father is an evil man, a disgrace to your family name, and he is becoming worse in his old age. I wish we had never come here to live

215

with him. We should have stayed in the cities like the rest of the family."

Don Juan had heard his wife's complaints many times, and had learned to control his temper and to be patient with her. "I could not have deserted my father," he said. "Someone had to help him and, as I am the oldest son, it was my duty. As I have told you before, my family cannot give up the ranch and the mines and besides, I would have never been happy working in the city."

"I have never been happy here." said Isabella. "However, my happiness has never concerned you."

Don Juan sighed. "A person can be happy anywhere if he so wishes," he said. "You have disliked my father since the day you came here, and it has been this dislike that has made your own life unhappy. He is a good man and wanted to be your friend."

It was in the spring of 1870 that Don Pedro died. Don Juan stopped all work in the fields and closed the mines so all the servants and supervisors could attend the burial. A priest came from Chihuahua to perform the last rites, and prominent officials came with him to pay their respects to the family. Don Pedro had been a very important man, and his family had widespread contacts in Mexico.

María and Shebah washed their patron's body and dressed it in Don Pedro's finest clothes. They and the rest of the house servants were very busy, as the house had to be thoroughly cleaned and the beds made up with Don Pedro's best linens for the important guests who would spend the night at the ranch. Doña Isabella had her servants prepare the guest rooms on her side of the house and ordered food prepared in both of the kitchens. As hostess, she would have no time to attend to housekeeping duties, and left them in the capable hands of María and her own housekeeper.

About two hundred ranch and mine workers and their families camped near the bunkhouse. The servants were all sad and a little apprehensive. Don Pedro had been a good master and had never permitted any overseers to mistreat them. Now, although Don Juan was well liked, there would be a change. It was well-known that Don Juan's wife did not wish to stay on the ranch, and perhaps she would persuade her husband to sell it. Even though Don Juan stayed, nothing would be the same as it had been when the old master was alive.

45

LESS THAN A WEEK PASSED AFTER THE GUESTS had left when Doña Isabella sent for María and Shebah. "I will take over the care of the house now," she told them, "and as I have my own housekeeper and my own servants, I will not need either of you here. The field overseer will find room for you with the other servants and will tell you what to do."

María was shocked and her temper flared. "I have taken care of your father-in-law's house for thirty years," she said. "When he was alive I did everything possible to make him happy and comfortable. Is this the way I am to be repaid by his son's wife? Shebah stood silently by as her friend spoke. She and María had discussed what might happen when their patron was gone, but they had thought they would be kept as house servants and would work for Doña Isabella's housekeeper. Now to be sent to work in the fields with lower class servants hurt their pride.

That evening they sat and talked. "We can take three horses from the corral and go to my people," said Shebah. "We will be welcome at my mother's home."

"I will not work in the fields," said María. "I will not be treated as a slave. I can read and write, which is more than the overseer can do. I will go with you, my sister, for I can no longer consider this place my home. We will pack some food and some of our clothes tonight, and in the morning we will go to the corral and get the horses. No one will suspect, as everyone knows we often go for rides and Doña Isabella had changed nothing yet. We will not be missed until we are too far away to be caught and brought back."

Early the next morning they went to the corral and as usual, joked with the cowboys, as the men saddled their favorite horses. They rode back to the ranch house, filled their saddle bags with food and strapped their blanket rolls behind the saddles. Then, as though nothing unusual were happening, they rode at a slow trot toward the fields. When they had passed the field hands, they urged their horses into a fast trot and were many miles from the ranch by nightfall.

They planned to ride until they intercepted the Chihuahua-El Paso trail, then to follow that trail to the Rio Grande. They would follow the river north, obtaining the food they needed at the small towns scattered along the river. They knew they could not travel through Apache country, as they had heard many stories of how strangers were killed by Apache warriors. They would somehow circle around the land of the Apaches and find Shebah's people. Shebah and her son could easily pass as Mexicans until they reached the land of the Navajos. Neither woman realized they would have to ride seven hundred miles before they found Shebah's people, but if they had known, the distance would not have deterred them. It was better

218

to die on the trail than to stay and work in the fields for a vindictive mistress.

The fugitives were not missed until Doña Isabella sent for them after her two o'clock lunch. She had lain awake much of the night, planning the changes she would make in the house and the household. She had decided that her first move would be to rid her house of the insolent María and sullen Shebah. They had both been spoiled by Don Pedro and seemed to think she had no right to be in her own house. She would move them and that Indian boy out immediately.

She sent one of her servants to bring them to her, but they were not in the house. After some questioning, a servant said she thought she had seen them out riding. "They will never ride our horses again." Doña Isabella said to herself. "They will soon realize they are servants and that servants do not go riding whenever it suits their fancy. They will be kept too busy from now on even to think of riding." Upon further inquiry at the bunkhouse, the cowboys confirmed the story that the three had ridden away from the corral early that morning.

It would be dark in about an hour, and Doña Isabella pondered what to do. She was glad to be rid of the women. They would always be a source of trouble at the ranch. She feared her husband would not approve of her decision to send them to the fields. She had the right to choose her own house servants but perhaps Don Juan would not agree to send them to the fields and would find other work for them to do. It was better to let them go. She would say nothing more and would send no one to bring them back. Don Juan could do as he wished when he found they were gone.

46

MARÍA, SHEBAH AND KEEDAH TRAVELLED THE two hundred miles from Don Pedro's ranch to El Paso in six days. They were all expert riders, and their mounts were in excellent condition.

They camped on the Rio Grande, then moved at a leisurely pace northward along the river. They stopped at many small ranches along the way. When questioned as to why two women and a boy travelled alone, María's reply was that her husband had been killed, and they were going to live with relatives at Albuquerque. The travellers were always made welcome and were usually given messages to carry to friends they would pass on their way. Their good manners and clothing impressed the simple, hospitable people wherever they stayed.

At Socorro they joined a wagon train, and the two women rode in one of the wagons while Fernando rode alongside. The wagons moved slowly, about ten miles a day, but the women were in no hurry, and were anxious to learn as much about Albuquerque and the roads west as possible from their companions. Travel up the Rio Grande had presented no problems, but they had no idea how far they would have to travel before they reached Shebah's people. They must find out which trail to travel, where they might get food and water and how great the distance before starting westward. They feared to ask questions about travel west of Albuquerque, as they might arouse suspicions as to why two well-bred Mexican ladies wished to go alone into Indian territory.

María was not happy about leaving the Spanish-speaking people along the Rio Grande. Her doubts about making a new life among the alien Navajos had grown stronger day by day. Perhaps she should stay in one of the New Mexican villages, but what could a lone woman do to support herself? She could marry. Women were scarce in all the frontier towns, but she did not want to walk into a town and marry the first wifeless man who came along. No, it would be best to obtain some sort of employment while she looked around.

When they reached Albuquerque, they went to deliver a message to one of the families. They were welcomed and asked countless questions about the family's relatives down the Rio Grande. On the second day of their stay with their new friends, María asked the wife about the possibility of finding employment in Albuquerque. She told the woman that Shebah and her son must go on to the home of relatives near Cebolleta about sixty miles farther west. The woman took her to a dressmaker who owned a small shop. When María told her she was a good seamstress, the shop owner employed her immediately, as her business had grown too large for her to handle.

Shebah was sorry to part with her friend. During the twenty-four years she had stayed at the ranch of Don Pedro the two women had become closer than most sisters. Shebah knew that life would be different with her people and was a little doubtful of her own ability to adapt herself to a life she had almost forgotten. She had worried

222

Kay Berndt

a great deal about María and now this sudden solution, although it meant parting forever, had resolved the problem.

Neither Shebah nor María slept the night before they parted. Finally, after one more tearful embrace, Shebah and Fernando mounted their horses and rode away on the well-marked trail which led to Fort Wingate. They carried several days' supply of food and two canteens of water in their saddle bags. Their new friends had told them of the trail which led to Cebolleta, and had advised them to wait and go with the wagon train which travelled as far as the western forts once a month. However, Shebah had no intention of travelling with the soldiers. She and her son would travel alone. Their horses were rested, and if they had no trouble, they would reach the land of her people in six or seven days.

It was now mid-May and the weather was perfect for travelling. "We will soon be in the land of our people, my son," said Shebah. "From now on we will speak only in Navajo. I wish we were not dressed in Spanish clothes. The Mexicans and our people have always been enemies."

"I wish we had stayed with María," said Keedah. "The Indians may not like me."

"Yes, they will," replied Shebah. "You are my son and my father is a headman of the Kinlichine Clan. My mother will be happy to see both of us."

They passed through Cubero. There were many sheep grazing around the village, and the sheepherders waved to them, thinking they must be the guests of one of the ranchers. They saw the high Mount Taylor, but Shebah did not recognize the mountain which legend said marked the corner of the land given to the Navajo people.

About halfway to Fort Wingate, they saw a cloud of dust approaching and rode behind a hill while a wagon train from the fort passed by. Near the continental divide, two Navajo men stared at them, then left the trail and rode away. Shebah shouted, but if they heard, they paid no attention.

224

Soon they saw the high Tunicha Mountains, which Shebah recognized immediately. Her mind was flooded by old memories. "My home was in those mountains," she told Keedah. "I hope my family is still there."

It was late in the afternoon when they started across the Chuska Valley toward a trail which she knew passed over the Tunichas alongside Chuska Peak. They saw a small rock house on the trail and stopped for food and water. A wagon stood just outside and two wagon horses were tied in a small grove of cedars. "We will stay here to-night," said Shebah. "We will cross the mountain to-morrow, and we should be at my mother's home tomorrow night."

They rode to where the horses were tied and dismounted. "Stay here with the horses," said Shebah. "I will go and see if we are welcome." She knocked on the wooden door and a tall white man opened it. His uncombed yellow hair stood out in all directions. His great yellow beard and mustache were stained and dirty. He wore filthy cloth trousers and a buckskin jacket. His small, close-set blue eyes stared at Shebah as she stood staring back at this wild-looking creature.

The man was one of the many itinerant traders who came to Navajoland after the release of the Indians from the Bosque Redondo concentration camp, hoping to grow rich on this new Indian trade. They brought sacks of flour, pots and pans, beads and knives to display to the Indians, but it was well known that they traded in whiskey, guns, and ammunition. They were a sordid breed who overlooked their own shortcomings and believed they were superior to the people with whom they traded.

The trader and Shebah stood looking at each other for a long minute, then he smiled and said, "Ha, what a pretty Spanish woman has come to visit me." He motioned for her to come in the house. Shebah stood where she was and spoke to him in Spanish, but he did not understand. She motioned to her mouth as though she were eating, and he nodded his head and again motioned for her to enter.

When Shebah stepped inside the door she looked around. She saw some sacks of flour piled on the earth floor and pots and pans hanging from the walls and roof. There were several stout wooden boxes and on one were a few Navajo blankets. A small iron stove and a pile of dirty cloth blankets in one corner completed the furnishings.

The trader stepped outside and looked around. He saw Keedah with the horses and said, "So, you and the boy have come for food." He came back and loaded a large pistol he had been cleaning and laid it on a sack of flour. Then he went to the door and barred it. Shebah did not like the way he was grinning at her and decided she had better leave. She went to the door, but he moved quickly. He grabbed her arm and put one dirty hand over her mouth. She struggled and managed to bite him. He hit her hard on the side of her head, and threw her to the floor and raped her. She came to as he rose laughing hoarsely. As he turned to go toward the stove, Shebah rolled to where he had laid the gun and, holding it in both hands, shot him squarely in the center of his back.

Keedah heard the shot and ran to the door. "Mother, Mother," he cried, as he tried to open the door, "are you all right?" Shebah rose and shakily managed to unbar the door. The frightened boy came in and his eyes went first to the man lying on the ground. A pool of blood was already forming alongside the motionless body. Keedah stood and stared, then turned toward his mother who was sitting on a sack of flour. Shebah said, "The man attacked me, my son; I had to kill him." She rose and they went outside where the cool air cleared her head. She knew that if the Americans came, they would kill her and her son. She must hide the man's body so no one would know that he had been killed.

Shebah told Keedah to take some water from the barrel alongside the house and give it to the horses; then she went back into the house and looked at the body. Finally she decided to take a little food, and partially filled an

226

empty flour sack. She looked in the wooden boxes but found nothing she wanted. She saw a metal box half uncovered in the man's bedding and took the silver pesos she found in it. She also found a fine silver concho belt and a few other Mexican ornaments. She also decided she would take the pistol. She wrapped what she had taken in one of the Navajo blankets and laid it by the door.

There was a coal oil lamp and a can of coal oil near the bedding. She emptied their contents on the man, his bedding, on the firewood near the stove and on the wooden logs that formed the roof. Then, taking some red coals from the stove, she fanned them into a blaze and, when the fire was well started, picked up her bundles and left. She walked to the trees where Keedah was waiting, let the trader's horses loose and told her son they were leaving. After they had gone a short distance, she turned to look back and saw the house was ablaze. There were a few sharp explosions and sparks flew as the roof fell in. "Come," she said to Keedah. "We must get away from this place. You must never mention that we stopped here or what happened. If anyone finds out, the soldiers will hunt us down and kill both of us."

They rode through the semi-darkness until they reached the foothills, then followed a canyon trail until the country became too rough to continue. "We will camp here," said Shebah. "In the morning when it is light we will go on." They washed in the trickle of water that flowed down the canyon, then gathered their blankets about them and went to sleep.

Shebah slept fitfully as the picture of the dead man kept returning. Finally she fell into a deep sleep, only to dream that the man rose out of the flames which were consuming his body and walked toward her. As his flaming figure moved closer and closer, she tried to flee but her legs refused to move. She screamed and woke. It was morning, and Keedah was already with the horses by the small stream.

Shebah prepared some food for them to eat; then Keedah saddled the horses and they started up the mountain trail. They climbed all morning and passed a few hogans, but they did not stop and no one spoke to them. Near Chuska Peak, Shebah decided she would change clothes before they went on to meet the family.

She brushed her hair, put on a tan blouse and a full tan calico skirt. Over her blouse she put on a black velvet vest with silver buttons, which had belonged to Don Pedro. Keedah had always patterned himself after his father. He liked to keep his clothes as clean and well brushed as possible. Now he brushed his black trousers, which were showing signs of wear, and put on a clean tan shirt. He shook the dust from his black, loosely-woven vest and wiped off his polished black boots. Then he brushed off his flat-topped, broad brimmed black hat with its bright, beaded band and placed it back on his curly black hair. They were ready to go.

"We will hide what I took at the trader's here," said Shebah as she looked among the large rocks. "Here is a place that will do. Bring that blanket here, my son." Keedah brought the blanket bundle and they shoved it into a crack in the rocks and covered it with smaller rocks. "Now, look around, my son," said Shebah. "Some day you may need these things. We will wait a few years before we return for them." Keedah looked around at the beautiful mountain and the tall pine trees. Already he loved this strange country.

Shebah, too, felt better in this high country. The great mountain, the pines, and the bright blue sky high above made her feel very small. The scented mountain breezes enveloped her and seemed to carry her weightless body through the branches of the pines and across the small green fields and off into the vast unknown. She stood, calmly letting the forces of nature have their way until Keedah's voice called her back.

228

"What do you see, my mother?" he asked. "You have been staring at that trail for a long time."

"Never mind, my son," Shebah said gently. "Now we are ready to go on. We will make a new life here and will never again think of what has passed."

They rode along the mountain trail until they reached a small valley and stopped by a spring to eat. "This is where I would like to live," said Keedah. "I can plant corn, and there is plenty of green grass for the sheep. I can build you a house here by the spring. I will build you a house with many rooms, my mother. Do not worry, for I am strong and I will take care of you." Tears came to Shebah's eyes as she looked at her handsome son standing so straight and unafraid as he planned what he would do for her. He seemed so young.

"I know you will," she said softly. "You are very wise. Some day you will be a leader of my people."

It was late in the afternoon when they rode into the valley where Shebah expected to find her family. The first people they saw were two young men hoeing weeds among the small sprouts of corn. Shebah waved and shouted, "Yah tah hay, my brothers." In her excitement, she supposed the young men to be Kee and Chiquito, forgetting for the moment that they had aged just as she had during her long absence.

The young men stared and Nazbah's younger son asked his brother, "Who are those people?"

"I don't know," replied his brother. "They have fine horses. They look like Mexicans, but what are they doing here, and why does the woman speak in Navajo? They are going to our shelter. I think we should go and see what they want." They left the field and walked quickly to where their mother was sitting at her loom. Hesbah and María had seen the strangers, and now they also walked over to Nazbah's shelter.

Shebah and Keedah dismounted and Shebah went to where Nazbah was sitting. After a few moments during

229

which Shebah looked questionably at the three women and the young men she asked, "Is this the camp of Gray Hat?"

Everyone remained silent, then Nazbah answered. "Yes, this is the camp of my husband, but he is not here."

Shebah said, "Oh, then you must be my aunt. Where is my mother?" Everyone looked at her in astonishment, then Hesbah asked, "Who are you?" Shebah smiled as she replied, "I am Shebah, daughter of Mother Red Lake. I have come back to find my family."

Hesbah went to her and embraced her. "I can see now that you are my sister," she said. "Forgive us for not recognizing you. It has been a long time since you were carried away, and we never expected to see you again."

"Both women began to cry as they held each other close. Hesbah took Shebah by the hand and said, "Come sit by me. I will get you something to eat."

They sat and talked for a while, and Nazbah told Shebah the two young men were her sons. "They are fine young men," said Shebah. "For a moment I thought they were Kee and Chiquito. Where are my brothers?"

"Kee is with Gray Hat," replied Nazbah, "and Chiquito is with his wife's family by the white rocks." María sat next to Shebah and offered her some mountain tea. Hesbah told her sister of their mother's death at Fort Sumner. "We all expected to die in that horrible place," she said, "but now we are back and all is well again. You look as though the Mexicans treated you well, my sister. Is she not pretty, María?"

"Yes," said Shebah. "They gave me plenty to eat and only asked that I weave for them."

Shebah suddenly remembered that Keedah was still with the horses. The boy had been waiting patiently for more than an hour. She called to him, and when he came she said, "This is my son, Keedah." The boy went around, gravely shaking everyone's hand.

"He is a fine boy," said María. "Look at his curly hair.

230

We should call him Chischillie. Sit here, my son, and I will give you something to eat." Hesbah had never quite recovered from the loss of her son, and tears came to her eyes again as she patted Keedah's hand, but she said nothing.

Joni and the children had been out with the sheep, and now they came and drove the small herd into the corral. Hesbah introduced them, and they all shook hands with their pretty new aunt. Hesbah's daughters took Keedah to look at the sheep, and the other children went with them. They were all very proud of the twenty new lambs. Keedah, who was accustomed to seeing herds of more than a thousand sheep, wondered why this family had so few, but he said nothing. He smiled and admired the animals and answered the children's questions about his clothes. "I have to wear them because they are all I have," he told them. "My mother has promised that she will make me some clothes like yours."

Nazbah said little. She was not pleased to have Shebah return with such fine clothes and horses. Had she returned in ragged clothes, sick and hungry like the rest of them, Nazbah would have welcomed her and cared for her. It did not seem right that one member of the family should have prospered while the others were enduring so much suffering and hardship. Why should this well-fed woman and her son ride in on fine horses while her sick husband had to walk?

Gray Hat, Kee and Hesbah's husband returned shortly after the sheep had been driven into the corral. They were carrying four rabbits. Hesbah ran to meet them. "My sister has returned," she cried excitedly.

Gray Hat raised his head and asked, "Your sister? Who do you mean, my child?" When Hesbah explained, the old man said, "How can it be? The Mexicans took her when the Americans first came to our land. I was a young man."

"It is true, my father," said Hesbah. "She escaped from

the Mexicans and has come home. She has brought her son with her. Come and meet her."

Kee and Hesbah's husband stopped and waited as Shebah came to greet her father. Gray Hat stood and looked at the strange woman in Mexican clothes. Shebah put out her hands, and he took one and shook it formally. Tears came to her eyes as she said, "Are you not glad to see me, my father? I have come a long way because I thought I would always be welcome at your home."

"It is your clothes," he replied. "We have suffered many years, and now you come wearing the clothes of our enemies."

"I will burn them, my father," said Shebah, "as soon as I can weave a manta. I did not wish to return in these clothes, but I have nothing else to wear."

"Very well," said Gray Hat. "You may stay with us."

"It is better that she stay with her sister," said Nazbah. "There is no room for her here."

Shebah's feelings were hurt. She had expected her father to throw his arms around her. She sensed that her aunt was not happy to see her, either. What had happened to her people? They used to laugh and joke, but now they were so quiet, and they hardly ever smiled. Even the children were sober and did not run around, laughing. Something terrible must have happened to them, thought Shebah. Even the slaves on Don Pedro's ranch laughed and joked with one another.

Hesbah broke into her thoughts saying, "Come with me, my sister; there is plenty of room at my shelter." Shebah told Keedah to bring the horses, and he followed them to where Hesbah had built a shelter of pine and cedar branches. Hesbah's daughters walked along with Keedah and showed him where to tie the horses in a grove of scrub oak trees. Keedah removed the saddles and started brushing the animal's coats with some dry grass.

Kee joined him and stroked the horses. "You take good care of your horses," he said as he picked up some grass to help the boy. "They are fine animals."

232

"Yes," replied Keedah. "They are my friends. They are thin now, but if we can stay here and rest, they will soon fill out again."

"You and your mother can stay as long as you like," said Kee. "This is your home now. I will show you where there is some good grass where your horses can graze."

Shebah and Keedah slept in the little grove of oak trees with the rest of the family, and in the morning Hesbah shared her food with them. Shebah said, "My sister, I would like to weave a manta. I will not be happy until I can discard these clothes. Do you have some wool I can use?"

"Yes," said Hesbah. "My husband will bring you some poles for a loom. We do not have much wool, but we have enough for you."

"We will help you," said Hesbah's daughters. "We will prepare the wool for you to weave."

"Come with me, my sister," said Hesbah. "We will look for some plants to put in the stew." The two sisters walked along as they had done as children, looking for wild plants, only now they did not run about throwing stones and laughing. As they walked, Hesbah told her sister of what had happened during the past years and, as she talked, all of the sadness and suffering she had endured flowed from her.

She told Shebah of the terrible days and nights when the family had run from the soldiers and almost starved to death, how the Navajos had died of hunger and the bitter cold. "We ran until we could run no more," said Hesbah, "and when we gave ourselves up, we were forced to walk four hundred miles to a camp in a desolate land where no crops would grow. We would all have died there, but two years ago the Americans let us go. They brought us back here and gave us the sheep you saw. We each received three sheep. We are not eating them because we cannot get any more. We lost most of our crop last year, but we expect to harvest corn and beans and squash in

233

our fields here and in Red Lake Valley in a few more months. We are weaving blankets to trade for horses, so our men will not have to walk. The men go twenty miles to the fort to get food from the Americans. Gray Hat cannot walk very far as he is too weak, and someone must hunt for meat every day."

As Hesbah poured out her story and told Shebah her troubles, Shebah was shocked. Don Pedro had spoken of the war and the prison camp. He had told her that the Navajos had been set free in their own land, but she had never pictured them as being ragged and destitute. Somehow she had never thought of her people without their herds of sheep and horses. The sisters gathered the plants they had come for and walked back soberly. Hesbah felt better than she had felt in years. She and María were like sisters and shared their families' troubles, but they knew that neither could do much to help the other. Somehow this younger sister seemed very wise, someone she could come to for advice. A flood of affection swept over her as she took her sister's hand and gently squeezed it.

47

A WEEK PASSED. KEE AND ALL OF THE BOYS LEFT for Fort Defiance to draw rations. They took four blankets with them and hoped to trade with the new man at the trading post for four horses. The trader knew the Navajos wanted horses more than anything else in his stock and had hired men to bring in a hundred head from the Rio Grande.

As usual, the Navajos who had come to draw rations and to trade were in no hurry to complete their business. They sat about and talked about their crops and their sheep. Kee joined a group of the men at the horse corral to look over the animals and to select the ones he would like to have. One of the men from the east side of Chuska Peak was telling the others of the death of a trader. "Yellow Hair was staying in an old rock hogan," he said. "He had fixed the roof and had his sacks and boxes inside. I took a blanket my wife gave me to trade for a pot and some other things she wanted, and he gave me a drink of whiskey. When I told him what I had come for, he did not understand what I was saying. I picked up the pot and he put the bottle in it and pushed me out of the door. I told him I wanted some other things but he pointed his gun at me and I left. I took another drink and went to my home. My wife was very angry with me. I was angry too, but I did not go back. The next day I heard the trader's hogan had burned, and I went with my brother to see if anything was left. The roof was caved in and smoke came from the logs. His wagon was burned so it could not be used anymore. The wood door was burned and we looked inside, but we could see nothing but burned wood and ashes, so we returned home.

"The soldiers came the next day to my hogan," the man continued. "They said they found Yellow Hair's body in the house. They asked if we had seen anyone with his horses. We told the soldiers we knew nothing. They said a Navajo man had told them I was at the trader's. I told them I had been there the day before the fire to get a pot for my wife, and I showed them the pot. They asked me if anyone else had been around when I was there, and I told them I was alone and had seen no one. They acted as though I was telling a lie, but they let me go and said

235

they would come back later. They said they would look until they found the Navajo who had burned the trader's hogan."

The following morning Kee and the boys drew their rations and then went to the trading post. The trader examined the blankets, then told one of the Navajos that worked for him to bring four horses out of the corral. Kee looked at the horses, then asked the trader if he could have a mare he had watched the day before instead of one of the horses. The trader agreed, and his helper made the exchange. Kee was satisfied and so was the trader. The blankets Kee had brought were well-made and well worth the price of a horse.

Kee mounted the mare, and the five boys got on the other horses and started for home. It was good to be on a horse again. Kee started singing one of the old riding songs that he had almost forgotten. The whole world seemed different with a horse trotting along between his knees.

At Gray Hat's camp, he told his father to choose the horse he wanted. Gray Hat looked them over carefully. He liked the mare, but a headman could not ride a mare when he rode about visiting his people. He decided upon the largest of the horses and led it away. Kee said he would keep the mare. Hesbah's husband chose his horse, and the one that was left was given to María's son, as it had been her blanket that had been given in trade.

As they sat around eating rabbit stew and corn bread that evening, Kee told the family all the news he had heard at the fort. He told them of the trader that had burned to death. "The soldiers seem to think that one of our people burned his house and stole his horses," said Kee. "They are asking all the Navajos if they saw anyone around the house." Shebah and Keedah listened, but said nothing.

Kee went on to say that he and the boys had ridden by their field in Red Lake Valley and that the corn was about a foot high. "There are many weeds in the field," he said.

236

"I think some of us should move down and hoe in the field. I will move my family to the valley tomorrow."

"I will move also," said Nazbah. "There are enough people here to take care of this small field. Now that Gray Hat has a horse, he should visit his people and speak for them at the fort."

The two families moved, and when they were gone, Shebah and Keedah spent more time working in the field and helping with the other family chores. Shebah had started weaving, but she made slow progress. Her thoughts wandered to the dead man. What would happen if the soldiers found out she had killed the trader? Would they just shoot her, or would they harm the rest of the family? If they found out, it would bring disgrace on the family. The only solution seemed to be for her to leave, but she could not bear to go. She could not take her son to live among strangers. His place was with the family. Shebah became more and more depressed as she brooded over what might happen. Hesbah tried to find out what was troubling her sister, but Shebah would only answer that she was not feeling well.

One day Hesbah's husband brought word that soldiers were coming up the trail. When she heard this news, Shebah made up her mind what she would do. She asked Hesbah to go with her to gather some plants and as they walked along, she questioned her about her feelings toward Keedah. Hesbah said, "We all love the boy. He is like a brother to my girls. I have never told you that I once had a son. He froze his feet when we were running from the soldiers, and we left him behind to die. He would have been about the same age as your son. Perhaps that is why my heart goes out to Keedah."

"If anything happens to me, I want you to take him as your son," said Shebah.

"Never say or think such a thing!" exclaimed Hesbah. "It is bad luck to talk that way."

Shebah was satisfied. She knew she was leaving Keedah